Rosewater and Soda Bread

Also by Marsha Mehran

Pomegranate Soup

Rosewater and Soda Bread

Marsha Mehran

FOURTH ESTATE • *London, New York, Sydney* and *Auckland*

Fourth Estate
An imprint of HarperCollins*Publishers*

First published in the USA in 2008 by Random House, Inc.

First published in Australia in 2008
by HarperCollins*Publishers* Pty Limited
ABN 36 009 913 517
www.harpercollins.com.au

HarperCollins*Publishers*
25 Ryde Road, Pymble, Sydney NSW 2073, Australia
31 View Road, Glenfield, Auckland 10, New Zealand
1–A, Hamilton House, Connaught Place, New Delhi – 110 001, India
77–85 Fulham Palace Road, London W6 8JB, United Kingdom
2 Bloor Street East, 20th floor, Toronto, Ontario M4W 1A8, Canada
10 East 53rd Street, New York NY 10022, USA

National Library of Australia Cataloguing-in-Publication data:

Mehran, Marsha, 1977–
  Rosewater and soda bread / Marsha Mehran.
  ISBN: 978 0 7322 8759 7 (pbk.)
823.92

Cover design by Natalie Winter
Cover images: bowl by Walter B. McKenzie/Getty Images; silhouettes and rose petals
by Shutterstock.com; ornamentation by Persian Designs/The Pepin Press
Author photograph by Jordan Matter
Typeset in 11/16pt ACaslon Regular by Kirby Jones
Printed and bound in Australia by Griffin Press
70gsm Bulky Book Ivory used by HarperCollins*Publishers* is a natural, recyclable
product made from wood grown in sustainable forests. The manufacturing processes
conform to the environmental regulations in the country of origin, Finland.

5 4 3 2 1   08 09 10 11

To Jennifer Heslin, an angel
when I least expected it, and for Sammy,
my huckleberry friend

My whole being is a dark chant
which will carry you
perpetuating you
to the dawn of eternal growths and blossoming
in this chant I sighed you sighed
in this chant
I grafted you to the tree to the water to the fire . . .

Ah
this is my lot
this is my lot
my lot is
a sky that is taken away at the drop of a curtain
my lot is going down a flight of unused stairs
a regain something amid decay and nostalgia
my lot is a sad promenade in the garden of memories
and dying in the grief of a voice that tells me
I love
your hands.

I will plant my hands in the garden
I will grow I know I know I know
and swallows will lay eggs
in the hollow of my ink-stained hands.

And it is in this way
that someone dies
and someone lives on . . .

I know a sad little fairy
who lives in an ocean
and ever so softly
plays her heart into a magic flute
a sad little fairy
who dies with one kiss each night
and is reborn with one kiss each dawn.

—FORUGH FARROKHZAD
"ANOTHER BIRTH"

Rosewater and Soda Bread

Chapter One

Much Ado About a Friar

MRS. DERVLA QUIGLEY, perpetual widow of James Ignatius Quigley, was the self-proclaimed arbiter of all that was decent and holy in the coastal village of Ballinacroagh.

By no sheer accident was her place of inhabitance situated over the Reek Relics shop, a musty amalgamation of crucifixes, laminated prayer cards, bottled holy water, and any paraphernalia pertaining to Saint Patrick. The dark apartment she shared with her spinster sister afforded Dervla a steady view of Main Mall, a crooked, cobbled main street that, despite all her efforts, had been greatly altered in the last year and a half.

There was a time, Dervla bitterly recalled, when a respectable citizen could sit by her bedroom window and not be battered by the smells of strange lands; a day when the only problem confronting decent folk was whether they should take an umbrella on the way out or brave unprotected the cold, pricking rain that plagued the western plains of Ireland eleven out of twelve months.

But then, that was before those three in that café came along.

Casting her rheumy eyes out onto Main Mall, Dervla settled her gaze on the squat stone building across the street. Its bright red door and purple shutters were closed, but it was nearly half past six in the morning, and as Dervla knew quite well by now, they would soon be opened for another day of business.

Another day of enduring the licentious smells of strange spices, the heady vapor of dishes that drew regular crowds of gluttons to the café's windows and had prompted *The Connaught Telegraph* to declare it "County Mayo's Best Kept Secret," a title that still eluded Dervla's caustic sensibilities.

"Divine" and "delicious" were how some had praised the food served behind that crimson door, but she was rather more inclined toward the sobering adjectives "debased" and "detrimental" to describe the goings-on of the Babylon Café.

During weekly meetings of Ballinacroagh's Bible study group, held conveniently downstairs in the religious relics shop, Dervla Quigley was quick to remind her fellow members of the dangers of the Eastern-flavored eatery: "Let's not forget who was behind Thomas McGuire's tragic accident," she would hiss, turning a portentous eye on the assembly of cobwebbed spinsters and whiskery matrons. "Drove the poor man to near ruin," Dervla would say, referring to the colossal heart attack that had struck Thomas dead for a whole minute in the café.

As the proud proprietor of Ballinacroagh's three smoky pubs, a title that also qualified him as its most successful businessman,

Thomas McGuire had kept a tight rein on the village's thin, and often precarious, economy. A workhorse of boundless stamina, he was rarely seen indulging in the drunken frivolities that passed as craic, or entertainment, in the small country town.

But for the heated caresses of his rotund wife, Cecilia, who enjoyed a nymphomania of epic proportions, Thomas had been a man devoted to the humorless world of stocktaking, profit margins, and the legalized peddling of Ireland's favorite imbibed brew—thick, luscious stout. There were few who could have guessed, then, the fanciful desires that lurked in the bar owner's congested heart.

Not even Dervla Quigley, Ballinacroagh's most scrupulous rumormonger, had gathered that Thomas would have given up ownership of his three pubs, two spirit shops, and the Wilton Inn on Main Mall, for the chance to open his very own neon-faceted, disco-themed nightclub.

Thomas McGuire's discotheque dream came to light one stormy afternoon, the weekend of the 1986 Patrician Day Dance.

The July festival, commemorating Saint Patrick's spirited Lenten fast, also marked the fourth month since the Babylon Café had opened its bright red door for business. Stealing the awakened appetites of the Wilton Inn's regular lunch crowd was reason enough for Thomas to unleash his mounting fury, but the fact that the café stood on the grounds where he had planned to open his long-awaited mirror-balled nightclub, Polyester Paddy's, sparked what could only be regarded as a moment of certified insanity: he broke into the Babylon Café. There, inside its warm and quiet kitchen, he met his fate.

Bubbling away on the kitchen range, a vast green Aga stove that had lived through four wars (civil or otherwise) and a revolutionary uprising of patriots alike, was a pot of shimmering pomegranate soup. From its open lid escaped a perfume so erotic and tantalizing that, like the bewitching Salome, it revealed false prophets with every veiled motion. The sweet, languid smell of cooking pomegranates clasped itself around Thomas McGuire's hardened heart and did not let go until it had smothered not only his stale breath but the decades of tyranny the drinks baron had imposed on Ballinacroagh's unwitting inhabitants.

Though Thomas survived the heart attack, saved at the last minute by the café's owners, he never returned to the run of his alcohol empire. The greater part of the publican's days was now spent sitting in a lumpy chair; he resurfaced in public during Christmas and Easter Masses, a pale and withered doppelgänger of his former self.

Yes, thought Dervla, things had definitely changed since those three foreign women moved into town.

Just then the red door across the street swung open. Dervla quickly disappeared behind her pastel chintz curtains, only to reemerge peeping a moment later. The oldest of the three, the one who made all the food, had just stepped out onto the damp sidewalk.

Dervla watched, following the dark-haired woman as she knelt to stop the café door open. The heavy door would shut easily were it not for the help of a stopper, which the woman was now securing at its corner. The doorstopper was none other than a crenellated iron, the same sort Dervla's mother had used to wrinkle out her father's Sunday poplin, heating it up on the turf stove that dominated their front parlor.

Those were the days, recalled the old gossip, when a woman knew her place in the world. No time idling in front of a pot of mash for her mother, no fiddling about with recipes and fancy trimmings, that's for sure. She had more sensible chores to bother about. Sewing on buttons and picking fieldstones, now *that* was a woman's true lot in life.

The woman, Marjan Something-or-Other, stood for a moment observing the iron stopper, then turned to face the Mall. Yawning, she took her time shrugging back her shoulders, shaking them loose with a smile. Her apron, a half-skirt bursting with pink and red roses, was tied loosely around her waist. She undid the bow at the back and retied it tighter, reaching in its deep front pocket for an elastic band. This she used to harness the mass of brown curls that would otherwise have fallen around her face.

Had it not been the modern year of 1987, thought Dervla, she would have sworn she had traveled back forty years in time, to when Estelle Delmonico had stood outside that very shop. Estelle would flash her thick hair and curvy bits on the street six mornings of the week, without a thought to decency or Jim Quigley's roving eye.

That Italian witch had certainly caused a hullabaloo the year she moved into town, she and that mustachioed husband of hers. Opening up a bakery smack in the middle of Main Mall, peddling coffees and puffy pastries like it was some tinker's wedding they were catering at. Not a loaf of brown bread or a potato farl to be seen in the entire shop. Imagine such a thing, now!

Dervla shook her head slowly, her tight gray perm anchoring any sudden toss. Her beady eyes followed the Marjan woman as she made her way to the café's window shutters. Standing on the tips of her toes, she unlatched the bolts at either side of the wooden panels. Recently painted a deep plum color, the shutters folded back across the glass like a gentle accordion. As they did, a large bay window, framed by hanging baskets of wispy honeysuckle and Persian jasmine, revealed itself to the morning sun. The flowers in the baskets matched the dewy blossoms planted in two deep barrels directly below the ledge.

With a sideways tilt of her stooped back, a sloping spine that began in a pouchy, mole-infested neck, and her pointed chin angled just right, Dervla was able to look straight through, all the way to the back of the café's dining room. There, on an elegant mahogany display counter, surrounded by teapots of various shapes and sizes, sat the showpiece of the Babylon Café, the machine she'd heard touted as "the greatest invention since the lightbulb."

Bloody blasphemous, if you asked her, especially considering it had been Father Fergal Mahoney who had made that insidious claim, right in the middle of Saint Barnabas's noontime Mass. That blasted contraption was the reason so many once-devoted parishioners rushed through their Sunday psalms nowadays, flying down Main Mall to that crimson door of hell with communion wafers still dissolving in their parched mouths. "Shameful to the point of senseless," muttered Dervla. There ought to be a law against such behavior.

Suddenly, a soft light flickered inside the restaurant. Dervla watched as the Marjan woman switched on the last of the café's five muted lamps, tapped the large belly of the gleaming machine with a silver spoon (a heathen ritual, no doubt), and positioned the diamond needle of an aging Victrola over an LP record. Cradling a short glass of tea in her palms, she walked back outside just as the sun broke through the cloudy sky.

MARJAN AMINPOUR SLOWLY sipped at her hot tea and studied the changing horizon. Mornings in Ireland were so different from those of her Persian childhood, she thought, not for the first time. Were she still in the land of her birth, Marjan mused, daybreak would be marked by the crisp sounds of a *sofreh*, the embroidered cloth upon which all meals were enjoyed, flapping over a richly carpeted floor. Once spread, the *sofreh* would be covered by jars of homemade preserves—rose petal, quince-lime, and sour cherry—as well as pots of orange blossom honey and creamy butter. The jams and honey would sit alongside freshly baked rounds of *sangak* bread, golden and redolent with crunchy sesame seeds. Piled and teetering like a tower, the *sangak* was a perfect accompaniment to the platters of garden mint, sweet basil, and feta cheese placed on the *sofreh*, bought fresh from the local bazaar.

And of course, Marjan thought with a smile, no breakfast *sofreh* was complete without the presence of a steaming samovar, the golden water boiler without which fragrant cups of bergamot tea could not be enjoyed. No meal could survive without a stop of that draft.

Marjan sighed as she took another sip of her bergamot tea. She might not be in Iran now, but she could happily boast a pantry full of jam jars. Jam jars aplenty, to be precise, as well as a domed oven whose heated bricks turned dough into piping morsels of bread—not to mention a verdant back garden, where stalks of cilantro, mint, and feathery dill bloomed season after season. And while she didn't have the time for an elaborate Persian breakfast, she did own a trusty electrical samovar, not to mention a view that had, throughout the centuries, mesmerized saints and sinners alike.

Marjan gazed up the steep and cobbled Main Mall, past the bright yellow frontage of Corcoran's Bake Shop and the fat sausage displays of the Butcher's Block, toward the obelisk monument at the opening of the town square. There, perched on his stone pedestal, with crooked staff in one hand and dead snakes splayed at his sandaled feet, was Patrick, patron saint of Eire. The old bishop looked rather triumphant in his regal robes, thought Marjan, free of the demons that had once haunted him. It had taken him a long time to get rid of them, but get rid of them he had.

From where she stood, Marjan could even see the rising summit of Croagh Patrick, County Mayo's most illustrious mountain. Conical in shape and steeped in its usual misty blanket of green, "the Reek" was a popular destination for devout climbers, contrite pilgrims who hiked its shrouded peak in hopes of spiritual release.

In quiet moments, before her sisters had woken and when the only sound on the street was that of Conor Jennings's Guinness truck, Marjan liked to take her morning tea with a view of the mountain. That old mound of penitence never ceased to amaze her, the modesty of its simple triangular shape filling her with peace and security.

Even the ancient Celts had felt the magic. Long before Saint Patrick had set foot on the mountain, druidic souls had ventured to its summit for worship. On days like today, thought Marjan, when the equinox was rounding its autumnal corner and the berries of surrounding hedgerows were turning from scarlet to deepest amethyst, their pagan exaltations must have been doubly poignant. Crops had been gathered, the old year was coming to an end, and winter was looming, dark and dangerous. Courage and faith had carried those early warriors through the bitterest of seasons. It was a great reminder of what could be done with a bit of luck, Marjan told herself.

Courage and faith—and a bit of Irish luck—had brought them to this little western town. It was still hard to believe that a year and a half had passed since she and her sisters had packed their bags and moved over from London. A year and a half! Marjan shook her head in awe. It seemed like only yesterday when she'd hung the wooden sign above the café door and begun serving platters of fried elephant ears and baklava to hungry villagers. She could still recall the anxiety with which she had prepared her first batch of *dolmeh*, the nerves that had threatened to get the better of her as she pushed the fragrant parcels into the hot oven. How she had prayed for strength on that spring day! Having planted her hopes deep inside for so long, she had *willed* them to burst forth, feeding her vision of a café filled with warmth, laughter, and light. And somehow things had worked out. Somehow they had found a home, here in this quiet corner of the world, this Ballinacroagh.

Amazing, thought Marjan with a smile, how some things turned out. There was much to be thankful for, that was for sure.

Nodding, she lifted the tea glass to her lips, drinking in the last of its orangey goodness. Taking one final look at the ancient mountain, she turned to go back into the café.

At the door she paused, lifting her fist to the small wooden shamrock nailed above the handle. The clover's heart-shaped leaves were powerful shields against the evil eye, protecting all who paid it homage. It was a potent good luck charm that couldn't hurt from some superstitious knocking, thought Marjan.

If nothing else, she told herself with a smile, her "heathen ways" would give Dervla Quigley something to nibble on for hours to come.

❋

"WHERE WERE YOU?" Bahar said as Marjan walked into the kitchen with her empty glass. "I had to put the dried limes in myself," she added, halfheartedly stirring a pot of herb stew with a wooden spoon.

Marjan gasped. "Did you just put them in?" She hurried to the Aga and grabbed the spoon from her sister. Four *limoumani* were bobbing happily amongst the stewing fenugreek. She deftly fished the limes out, placing them on a small terra-cotta saucer.

Bahar held up her hands. "Take it easy. It's only a few limes," she said, backing away from the green stove. Through the kitchen door she could see Fiona Athey and Evie Watson settling at their usual window-side seats. "Besides, aren't you supposed to add the *limoumani* with the meat?"

"The meat has to soften with the herbs before you can introduce the sour. Otherwise, it's too overpowering," explained Marjan, waving her pinched thumb and forefinger in the air as though she were conducting a symphony. "You have to let the fenugreek take hold of the broth, you see," she added.

Bahar sighed. "I don't know how you remember all those details. Just hand me a knife and lead me to the chopping block. Anything else is too hard," she said, tying an apron, one with maroon pheasants marching across the hem and pockets, around her neck and tiny waist. The apron was one of nearly a dozen their landlady and friend, Estelle Delmonico, had sewn for them that year.

"Looks like Fiona's ready for her jasmine tea. I think we should just give her a permit to use the samovar whenever she wants. She's in love with that thing!"

Marjan let out a laugh. "I know. I'm half-thinking of getting her one this Christmas. Mustafa's sells them now."

"Don't you dare!" said Bahar, stuffing a frayed order pad into her apron pocket. "She'll keep it in the salon, for sure. Then we'll never see her." She threw Marjan a creaky smile and swung past the kitchen doors.

Marjan returned to the pot and gave the thick herb stew another stir. The long, thin leaves of the fenugreek swam gracefully against the sides of her spoon, entwining themselves with the lighter cilantro, parsley, and chives.

According to the Persian seer Avicenna, whose *Canon of Medicine* Marjan often consulted, fenugreek is the first stop to curing winter chills. Combined with the hearty kidney beans and succulent meat of the herb stew, it made for an excellent *garm*, or hot, meal. Whenever she could, Marjan liked to adhere to the ancient Zoroastrian tradition of cooking, matching the needs and bounties of the season (as well as the individual eater) to ingredients.

"Ooooh! *Gormeh sabzi!* Can I take some to school?" Layla trundled down the stairs, skipping the last three steps with gymnastic flourish. She landed soundly on the woven runner that spanned the kitchen floor, her patchy knapsack bouncing off her back like a parachute in midflight.

Marjan placed the lid back on the stockpot and turned to her youngest sister. "It won't be ready for another two hours. You'll have to take some of yesterday's saffron chicken instead." She wiped her hands on a gingham tea towel and opened the cupboard door.

"Leftovers. God. Not again," Layla groaned, pulling absently on her stockings. As was often the case, her school uniform was not the tidiest of numbers: a spidery rip ran down the ankle of one brown stocking, and her Doc Martens were scuffed on all sides. In accordance with school yard fashion, her striped blue shirt was not tucked in; it stuck out from the back of her dark regulation skirt, wrinkled and uneven.

Layla's long black hair, Marjan was happy to note, was

immaculate as ever. It gleamed within the folds of an intricate French braid, perfectly framing her creamy, oval face.

"I don't know how I'm going to survive this year," Layla complained. "At least when Emer was around I could trade lunches—she always had a bit of colcannon with her sandwiches."

"You and your mashed potatoes," Marjan remarked, lifting down a large mason jar of chickpea flour.

"Mmmm, I could eat colcannon every day," said Layla, rubbing her stomach. She helped herself to a piece of *lavash* bread fresh from the brick oven. "Now it's just me and Regina. And all she eats is prawn crisp rolls."

Marjan grimaced. "That can't be too healthy," she said. She shook the enamel colander in her hand, sifting the flour into a large bowl. Thank heavens for Mustafa's. Were it not for the Algerian specialty shop in Dublin, she'd have to ship the chickpea flour in from London. With the state of An Post, that could take months, whole seasons even, to get to Ballinacroagh.

"It's not healthy. I don't know how Regina stays so skinny," Layla said, in between chews. "Must be all the farmwork she does after school."

"Speaking of after school," Bahar interjected, swinging in from the dining room, "can you please tell me once more why you need to personally pick Malachy up from the train station tomorrow? You can't wait ten minutes before seeing your boyfriend again?"

"Here we go," moaned Layla. "Miss Worrywart." She plopped down at the round table in the corner and unzipped her knapsack.

Bahar continued, ignoring the barb, "You know you can't drive the van without Marjan sitting next to you. I'm going to be left to fend for myself. At teatime no less," she added testily.

"The weekends are my only time with Malachy, and I want to make the most of them. Besides, he hasn't seen me with my L plates yet," Layla replied absently, referring to her learner driver's status. "I want to surprise him."

She ruffled through the knapsack, retrieving a small leather-bound volume of Shakespeare's *Much Ado About Nothing*, her favorite play. She opened the musty little book and breathed in its pulpy scent.

"You don't see *me* complaining when you disappear every other afternoon."

"My free time is none of your business," retorted Bahar. She tore off Fiona and Evie's order and pinned it to a silver carousel in the middle of the wooden island.

"Where do you go exactly on your breaks, anyway? Got some *lover* you're not telling us about?" Layla winked at her sister, teasing her with a smile.

Bahar stared hard at her younger sister. She opened her mouth but closed it just as quickly again on second thought. With teeth clenched, she turned to the island and began to prepare a plate of rose petal jam and breads for the two hairdressers' breakfast, her shoulders stiff with silent fury.

Layla exchanged looks with Marjan.

"Hey, I didn't mean that, Bahar," she began, softly. Bahar continued her buttering in silence. Layla bit her lip. "Bahar. Come on. We're only going to be gone a few minutes."

Bahar paused. She swiveled slowly on her heels, her left eyebrow arched high. "What, no necking on Clew Bay Beach?" Her lips twitched devilishly. "I expected more from you, Layla Aminpour!"

"Oh!" Layla grabbed the gingham towel and threw it across the kitchen at Bahar. "Cheeky!"

Marjan, who had been anticipating another row between her sisters, was happy to return to the harmony of her chickpea dough.

THE ANGELUS RANG on time as always, the bells in Saint Barnabas's tower pealing the six o'clock hour. Evening, and time for rest.

Marjan wiped the island with a tea towel and placed a jug of golden chrysanthemums squarely in its center. She could hear the Victrola playing Billie Holiday in the front dining room, interspersed with the television upstairs. Layla must have been done with her homework. At least Marjan hoped that was the case.

She gave the kitchen one last look and sighed. It was still a mess. The piles of dishes left from teatime were waiting for a wash, and the brick oven had to be brushed of its ashes one more time. The countertops sparkled from her rosewater spray—a cleaning solution that smelled absolutely glorious—but the wooden floor planks were still grimy from the lunch and tea rush. Her shoes made sticky sounds as she crossed to the round table.

She had to resist taking the mop to the floor herself. Cleanup always belonged to Bahar, after all. It was her duty to see that there were plenty of dishes clean for every turnover throughout the day, and to make sure the floor and counters were spotless by the ringing of the six o'clock prayer bell. That was the arrangement. Without it, the café would soon turn into one chaotic mess. Bahar knew this.

In fact, she usually liked nothing better than a good scrubbing—and pruned hands to prove it—at the end of a long working day. For as long as Marjan could remember, her sister had been a stickler for getting things spick-and-span, even obsessive in her quest. She never had to be asked twice to take a sponge to a crumby counter.

At least, that was how Bahar used to react to mess.

It was a rare sight to see the kitchen clean by this time of evening nowadays. Their tidy system had been in flux ever since Bahar began taking her afternoon breaks. Often, Marjan found herself doing double duty during tea, fixing the orders Layla brought in to her while rushing to the sink to replenish their dwindling pile of clean dishes, all the while keeping an eye on the brick oven, which delivered constant rounds of bread and kebabs of chicken, mint lamb, and onion. It was getting to be very exhausting. When she had pointed this out to Bahar, her sister's response had been tepid, offhanded even.

"I don't expect you to understand," Bahar had said with a quick shrug. "You've got the café and cooking and everything—this is what you've always wanted. But I'll go crazy if I spend every single moment cooped up inside. I need my time as well."

And so the advent of her afternoon breaks, taken every other weekday.

What she did on her time away, Marjan never asked. And Bahar wasn't terribly forthcoming about it. The only indication that she had accomplished something of substance was the glow on her face when she returned an hour before closing.

It was strange to see her usually mercurial sister so calm, thought Marjan. It was enough to incite some worry.

She knew she should be thankful to have Bahar in such a light mood for the rest of the night, but she couldn't help but ruminate, with some trepidation, on the cause behind her sister's recent demeanor. It wasn't the first time Bahar had been so secretive about a part of her life, after all.

Nine years ago she had changed from a normal enough teenager to a raging revolutionary in a matter of days. Wrapped in a chador, she had taken to the streets of Tehran, joining a pack of women who were protesting the reign of the Shah and his decades of tyranny. To some it may have seemed peculiar, this sudden change that had come over Bahar when she was only sixteen, but Marjan knew it was in accordance with her pendulum-like personality. Bahar had always had an unpredictable mixture of *garm* (hot) and *sard* (cold) coursing through her veins. Its wellspring could be found in the seasons of life itself, the day of the equinox and Bahar's birthday as well, March 21. That was when new and old converged, creating an unpredictable nature in anyone born on that date.

Still, even Marjan had been shocked when Bahar announced her engagement to a man twice her age.

Marjan took a deep breath, determined not to let her worry get the best of her. Eager to focus on something other than her sister's mysterious behavior, she grabbed a cup of bergamot tea and sat down at the round table to go over the menu for the next day.

It was one of the moments she most looked forward to, designing her schedule of treats. Planning and listing always cleared her mind of any stresses that had piled on her shoulders during the course of her working day. Cooking required a certain degree of compartmentalization, but it also involved a lot of variables, chaotic moments that were unscripted. With her lists, Marjan could be a lot more simple. Yet still adventurous.

Especially for this season: autumn called for a touch of nuance from every chef.

Marjan bit the end of her pen in thought. She'd stick to the *gormeh sabzi* she had made today: the two batches she had made were gone by one o'clock. But another *garm* dish was needed still, something warming, something like stuffed eggplants with turmeric-encrusted lamb. A poor man's saffron to some, turmeric. But for Marjan, it had much more use than just its ability to give rice a yellowy hue. The spice, when cooked with dark meats, tended to unseen inflammations in the body, which, if left unheeded, could mark the beginnings of disease.

Gormeh sabzi, stuffed eggplants, and turmeric-encrusted lamb. Yes, she nodded, that would work out just grand.

And she'd have to make some more chickpea cookies as well. She would need a few rounds for the Bonfire the next evening.

As for a soup, she was thinking of a nice noodle with meat and rice dumplings—like the ones their mother used to make before the first frost descended over Tehran. It had been Marjan's job to press the sides of the dumplings with a fork, securing them before they were plopped into the steamy, perfumed broth. What a joy it was to see them defy the heat, staying intact until they were in her hungry little mouth!

Marjan smiled softly to herself and scribbled away, sipping at her tea occasionally. She was down to her pastry list when Bahar swung through the kitchen doors, carrying a large mustard-colored teapot.

"Have you closed?" Marjan asked, without looking up.

Bahar shook her head. "There's one more person left," she said, a funny look on her face.

"At this hour?"

Bahar placed the pot in the sink and turned to her. "It's some English guy. He says he wants to see you."

"Me?"

"He said he wants to compliment the chef. I don't know what he's talking about. He only had a pot of tea and a cheese plate."

Marjan followed Bahar out the kitchen doors and into the dining room. The man was standing by the time she reached his table, the smaller one near the paisley-draped window.

He held out his hand. "Ms. Aminpour?"

"Hello. How can I help you?" she asked, returning his handshake. "Was your lunch all right?" She glanced quickly at the remnants of the cheese plate, happy to see all the herbs and feta polished clean from the oval dish. He had been drinking a pot of lemon oolong tea, the perfume of which still lingered.

"It was just grand. I didn't think there could be better summer savory outside Iran, but I see I was wrong."

Marjan blinked and took another look at the stranger. Behind her, she could hear Bahar pause in her clearing of tables.

He was at least half a foot taller than she was, well over six feet. The window behind him framed his broad shoulders and straight blond hair, which grew just past his neck, meeting the collar of his tawny corduroy jacket. He had a strong jaw and a narrow nose, Marjan noticed, an easy smile playing on full lips.

"You've been to Iran?"

"Hasn't everyone?" he said, a smile flashing across his face. "Actually, the last time I was there was in seventy-eight, right before the hostage crisis."

"We had left by then as well."

The man's green eyes flickered with interest. "We?"

"My sisters and I," Marjan said, surprised at the information she was letting loose even before knowing this stranger's name. She turned to indicate Bahar behind her, but she had already disappeared into the kitchen. Marjan turned back to the stranger. "I'm sorry, what was your name?"

The Englishman reddened. "Oh, I do apologize. Julian Winthrop Muir. How do you do?" He shook her hand again. It was then that Marjan realized he had never let it go. He had a strong grip, she thought, noticing the golden hairs along his broad wrist.

"Marjan Aminpour," she said, letting go of his hand.

"I know who you are," said Julian. "I've read all about it in *The Connaught Telegraph*. 'Mystic Marjan's Recipe of Magic. Mayo's Best Kept Secret.'" He swept his palm in the air between them, as though conjuring the heading as he spoke it. "'Ireland's Number One Exotic Destination.'"

Marjan blushed. "I think the *Connaught* was a bit biased. The editor eats here every Saturday."

"And why wouldn't he? Persian food's the thing, isn't it? 'Two days between layers of baklava, in the quiet seclusion where souls sweeten.' "

Marjan was surprised. "You know Rumi?"

"Did my thesis on the Sufi poets back at Oxford," Julian replied, shaking his head. "Decades ago now it seems."

"So you are a poet?"

"Not in the least, I'm afraid. Though I make my way by writing. Novels, mostly." He ran his hand through his hair, pushing it away from his face.

Marjan gave him another quick glance before moving toward his table. She began to stack the empty plates and tea glass on the platter, aware of his following gaze. "What have you written?" she asked, suddenly feeling strangely nervous. "Maybe I've read some of your work."

"Oh, I doubt that. My stuff gets the critics but not readers, unfortunately." He paused. "That's why I've come back. To get away from all the nonsense."

"So you've been to Mayo before?"

"Family was from here. Down Louisburgh way. I'm staying at the Wilton Inn at the moment. Just checked in today, in fact." Julian smiled again. "But I most certainly will be having my meals here from now on."

Marjan hoisted the platter on her arms. "Oh, I don't know, I hear the carvery does a mighty roast plate. Peppercorn gravy, turnip mash, and all," she said, her lips curving.

"But it doesn't hold its own to that cherry rice I saw being served. A meal that's taken its time to formulate. 'Let the kettle boil slowly . . .' "

" 'For stew boiled in haste is of no use to anyone.' " Marjan smiled again, recalling the proverb immediately.

Julian nodded. "Exactly. Makes you wonder what would have happened if Marco Polo and the Silk Road had made it all the way to Ireland."

"Potatoes would certainly have taken a hit," replied Marjan, tickled by the thought.

"Might have even stopped the famine. Imagine that now: the Irish could have been clear of the English earlier but for that. Change the whole course of the nation with just a bowl of sweet cherry rice."

Marjan laughed. "Somehow I can't imagine Paddy's offering *chelow* with their Guinness."

"Well, you never—" started Julian. He paused and turned around: a loud crash had just come from the street behind him.

They both glanced out the window, in time to catch Evie Watson storm out of the hair salon with a pair of sharp-looking scissors.

"You gobshite!" she yelled, stomping up the cobbled sidewalk on the heels of Peter Donnelly, her beau and all-round sparring mate. "You bastard! Stop, you hear me! Stop right there, Peter Donnelly!"

For once, the young hooligan chose to listen to his girlfriend. He braked directly in front of the Reek Relics shop and turned to face Evie. From behind her store door, Antonia Nolan could be seen watching the battle while chewing on a Picnic chocolate bar, delighted by the display.

"Now, Evie," Peter started.

The junior stylist stamped her foot. "Don't feckin' Evie me! I've given you the best year yet, and this is the return I get? You little bollocks! I could kill you!" The scissors sliced the air between them.

Peter sighed. "All I said was that a man in my position needs to be looking to the future." He held up his hands to protect the burdens of his sex. "It's called progress. Consolidation."

"Consolidate my feckin' arse! You're a chancer, you are, Peter Donnelly. Just looking for a cheap shag, that's it all right!" Evie took a step forward with the scissors snapping furiously.

Just when it looked as if she was about to mow through Peter's wavy brown hair, the latter came back with what in retrospect was not his wittiest rejoinder: "By 'shag' I don't suppose you're offering a haircut, now. Eh, babes?"

Evie screamed. Her reedlike body seemed to reverberate with the pitchy sound, a parenthesis of exploding fury. Opting for a weapon greater than the toothed scissors, she plunged deep into her bib pocket and pulled out a bottle of pink solution.

Aware of his fate but unable to stop it, Peter could only cover his eyes as his head was set awash with the entire contents of a bottle of Panto Perm XLRate, the most powerful permanent solution this side of Eastern Europe. The junior stylist then turned and ran back inside Athey's Shear Delight, wailing all the way.

Julian broke the tension: " 'Love is reckless, not reason,' " he said, quoting one of Rumi's better known verses.

Marjan stared at a dripping Peter Donnelly, who despite his soaked exterior had retained his swaggering air. No reason about that at all, she told herself; love *was* reckless, there was no other word for it.

❈

THE AFTERNOON TRAIN was to arrive at Westport station at forty-seven minutes past four. A noontime train by all standards, it had departed Dublin on schedule, but by the time it had crossed the river Shannon, it was running an hour and ten minutes late.

"Not bad for a Friday," Layla remarked when the ticketmaster informed them of the delay. "Remember during Easter break? What were we, five hours late?"

Marjan shook her head. "More like two, but the smell of those eggs made it seem like much longer," she said.

They had made the mistake of sitting across from a local sheep farmer on his day out. Clearly taken with the holiday spirit, he had bundled a crock jar of pickled eggs in his heavy houndstooth jacket. Every half hour would see him pull another sour specimen from the vinegary depths, popping it into his gummy mouth with the utmost relish—though not before offering it to both Layla and Marjan, a gentlemanly gesture to his credit, if not to their senses.

"I couldn't wash that stink from my hair," Layla recalled with a shudder as the two of them found seats in the cozy waiting room. "I didn't even smell like me for a whole week." Layla's natural perfume, an approximation of which could be reached from mixing rosewater and powdered cinnamon, had indeed been thrown off-kilter by the pickled hard-boiled eggs. Not since birth had she been without her personal scent, and Marjan recalled how panicked her sister had been that whole week to retrieve it.

"Thank God the van hasn't broken down since then." Marjan glanced out the small windows facing the front of the station. The lime green van stood at an awkward angle, the orange peace sign on its side warped by the window's mullioned panes. "I think we need to work on your parking skills next."

Layla gave a start beside her. "What do you mean?"

"Well, Clew Bay Beach isn't the best place to practice paralleling," Marjan commented in half jest. "At least not if you're serious about passing." She turned to her sister. A stark paleness was washing over Layla's cheeks. She looked as though she had just swallowed one of those ghastly eggs.

"Don't worry, *joon-e man*. Parking's the hardest part of driving. You'll pass it with flying colors," Marjan assured her. "Is that what you've been worrying about?"

"Yes. No." Layla blinked. "It's not that," she said, swallowing. She quickly surveyed the waiting room. "Marjan? Can I talk to you for a minute?"

Marjan sat up. "Of course. What is it?"

"Not here," Layla replied, tipping her head slightly to the right. Directly diagonal, sitting starch still next to a potbellied stove that crackled with turf, were Antonia Nolan and her middle-aged daughter, June. Regulars of Ballinacroagh's Bible study group, the two were caught in rapturous spying. "Let's go outside. We have time."

A canopy of ivy and delicate clematis shivered as they stepped onto the single platform. Settling into one of the wooden benches, painted red to match the large carriage wheels leaning decoratively against the awning beams, the sisters were greeted by a fresh westerly breeze. The smell of burning peat and muddled boysenberry from a nearby bush reminded Marjan of the Bonfire awaiting them that evening.

Layla cleared her throat. She fiddled with her blue school jumper and bent over to retie her Doc Martens. Then, after several fumbled attempts at her knapsack straps, she unbuckled its side pocket.

The leather-bound copy of *Much Ado About Nothing* fell onto her lap. She carried the book with her everywhere these days, thought Marjan. The play's parchment-like pages rustled softly as Layla flipped through them.

"Layla, what is this about?" Marjan said, feeling suddenly anxious.

"Just wait, I want to explain it right," Layla whispered, backing up when she reached a specific point in Act I, Scene II, of the romantic play. A small scrap, torn off from a newspaper, was stuck between the two pages. It was an advertisement for a pharmacy in West London.

"From the *Sunday World*. Tore it out of the back section," Layla explained, handing the newspaper scrap over to Marjan.

Marjan read the print, done in medieval lettering:

FAT FRIAR'S PHARMACY

FOR ALL YOUR WANTON NEEDS

INTERNATIONAL SELECTION
OF BIRTH CONTROL PRODUCTS FOR
THE MODERN COUPLE

CANTERBURY ROAD, CROYDON

LET THE FRIAR STOKE YOUR FIRES

"It's near Gloria's apartment," Layla said, blushing profusely. "In Croydon."

Marjan looked up from the piece of paper. "Gloria?" Her closest companion when they had lived in London, Gloria Delmonico had been a great comfort to Marjan in those dark months and years after they left Iran. It was Gloria who had calmed them down and helped pack all their belongings the night they heard again from Bahar's husband, out of the blue. It was her dear friend who had sent the three of them to Ireland with blessings, on to her dear aunt Estelle.

"Yeah, well, see, ummm . . . well, I know how she still sends you the odd package. I just thought— We, Malachy and me, thought that, uh, you could ask her to, to . . ." Layla paused uncomfortably and squirmed, looking down at the book in her hands.

Marjan had more than an inkling of where the conversation was going. "You want Gloria to send over some birth control. Condoms." She found herself blushing as well.

Layla nodded, sighing with relief.

"For you and Malachy?" Marjan gently prodded. Layla gave another quick nod, her eyes still on the Shakespearean masterpiece.

"They're not really sold in Ireland. Well, at least not so much in the West."

Marjan studied the advertisement again. "Let the Friar Stoke Your Fires." It would have been amusing in any other situation. She racked her brain for the right words of response.

"Are you sure you're ready?" she said hesitantly, peering into Layla's bent face. "What about just taking your time with, uh, kissing and the rest of it?" The station door creaked open just then, and out walked Antonia Nolan and her daughter. The two women stood under the awning for a moment.

"We've been doing all that. For two years nearly," Layla replied. "What do you think happens every time we park on the Beach?"

Marjan's eyes widened with realization. Parking. "Ah," she said, pausing. "Have you done—I mean, did you two, you and Malachy, have you done anything yet?"

Layla looked up, her almond-shaped eyes dancing impishly. "You mean *sex*?"

Marjan was taken aback. She had never heard that word come out of her youngest sister's mouth.

"We haven't," Layla said with a shrug. "We've come close, though."

"What do you mean close?" Marjan whispered, watching June and Antonia as they waddled slowly toward them. She placed her hand on Layla's arm. "Did Malachy try to force you into something? You don't have to do anything you don't want to. You know that, don't you?"

"But I do want to," Layla insisted. "I'm the one who's asking, Marjan. Malachy said he'd wait."

"But you're so young!"

"I'm sixteen! Bahar was married by my age."

"And that wasn't the best of decisions, was it?" Marjan asked pointedly. She folded the newspaper scrap in half, tucking it into the pocket of her belted jacket just as the two gossips squeezed into a nearby bench.

"This is a very important matter, Layla."

"I know. That's why I came to you," Layla said, a touch of desperation in her voice.

"And I'm glad you did. But that doesn't mean I have to approve of what you are doing. Or going to do, for that matter." Marjan gave her a stern look. "You understand?"

It did not look like Layla did. Or wanted to, which amounted to the same result. Tossing the play into her knapsack, she leaned back in the bench, crossing her arms with a large pout. "You just don't want me to grow up. That's what it is. You want me to be the baby forever, so you can keep making all the decisions."

"That's not true." Marjan felt hurt. "I'm only trying to do what's best for you." The train bell began to ring, followed by the whistle of an engine chugging its way into the station.

Marjan turned to the sound, sadness suddenly trickling through her. Was Layla right? Was she trying to keep her from growing up?

"You know, this is just like *Much Ado About Nothing*," Layla said, reaching back for her knapsack. "You want me to be just like Hero, all virginal and wimpy. You want to be just like Beatrice, not caring about dating or anything."

"I don't know what you're talking about, Layla."

"Yes, you do. You don't have a guy, and you think I shouldn't either." Layla opened the play once again. "Have you ever fallen in love, Marjan? Was that Ali guy you talk about even real? Or did you just make him up 'cause you're too embarrassed to admit the truth?"

"That's enough, Layla," Marjan replied curtly, standing up. The train was pulling in, carrying the squeals and cacophony of its iron wheels. "You're stepping over the line now," she said, feeling her face heat up. She felt just as shocked to hear her sister mention Ali's name as she had been to hear her say the word *sex*. She couldn't believe Layla had remembered about her first love, the boy she had left behind in Tehran so many years ago. They had only spoken about him once, after all.

Marjan brought her hand up to her hot cheek. She could feel it throbbing with embarrassment. The train's carriage doors slowly opened, passengers streaming out in all their rumpled glory. Behind her, Layla remained fuming in her seat, her arms crossed over her chest.

"So that's it, is it?" she huffed. "You're not going to do it? You're not going to write to Gloria for me?"

❋

ESTELLE DELMONICO'S THOUGHTS were on her doctor's advice as she stared out her rain-spattered bedroom window.

"I must insist on a change of scenery," Dr. Parshaw had said, his chocolate eyes fluttering in that mesmerizing way that always reminded her of her late and beloved husband, Luigi.

"This Irish damp is only going to accelerate your osteoarthritis. I know you have a niece in London, which admittedly is not much better for weather, but there is a rather reputable therapy program in Kensington that might be just the ticket. I hear their treatments are based on Ayurvedic principles."

Upon which Estelle explained, as extensively as she could, that she had already tried the ancient art of corresponding humors, with little positive result. It was among a list of alternative therapies she had attempted in the prior decade, including color therapy, Reiki, and an embarrassing session of colonic irrigation. Ayurvedic principles were not going to banish her arthritis, she had told her doctor, but a regime of sewing in the afternoons after a brisk morning walk would certainly ease the pain in her joints.

And what walks! What wonderful strolls. Not only was she cultivating a set of spectacular hamstrings from her morning exercise—an important vanity for a woman of any age—but her walks about the clover fields had prompted surprising discoveries in her adopted country. She had come to find the gemlike pockets of Mayo, the silent boglands and the shimmering waterfalls that made it the mystic's home.

Estelle had never known Ireland to hold such a multitude of diverse and magical places, for although she had been living under the gaze of its most celebrated elder, that mountain named after Patricio, her years tending the counter in Papa's Pastries had left her with little time for gallivanting.

As far as she could see, the only upside to the needles of arthritic pain had been this traipsing of late; the disease had forced her to finally get out from her small patch of cottage comfort and get some fresh air into her joints.

This morning's sojourn notwithstanding, of course; that adventure had been an entirely different kettle of cod, as the Irishman liked to quote.

What should have been a warming stroll around the western shore of Clew Bay had turned into a feat of Sisyphean determination—the better part of the morning given to transporting the injured mermaid from the inlet to the backseat of her rickety Honda.

Then there was that whole hour spent hauling her from the car, up the cottage's gravelly drive, and into the four-poster bed.

By the time Estelle had undressed the mermaid, changing her into a pair of Luigi's stripy cotton pajamas, and washed and chopped all the vegetables for her life-affirming minestrone soup, she had been too tired to blink, let alone tune in to one of her favorite weekend activities: roaming the vast and comic world of Irish radio stations.

Estelle returned her gaze to the window. Not even a good reel could lighten her mood now. Not after finding the poor darling mermaid.

A drop of water, a vestige from an earlier shower, trickled down the windowpane. It joined earlier drops, pooling in one corner of the frame like a sacrificial cup faced toward heaven.

To Estelle it seemed as though the rainwater mirrored her own tears, the crying that had not stopped since she had found the girl, naked and half dead.

The whole earth was crying for the shame.

Chapter 2

Godot Must Wait

"SO THAT'S IT? You're not going to do it? You're not going to write to Gloria for me?"

Layla's question ran through Marjan's mind as she stepped out of the café later that evening. She hadn't had much time to think of anything else, really. The shock of hearing her sister talking so candidly about such grown-up matters was compounded by her own mixed feelings, the confusion that had been brought to the surface by Layla's effortless confidence. It wasn't an easy decision—certainly not one she had prepared herself for making.

You'll just have to be patient, she had told a pouting Layla. I promise I'll be fair in my answer.

At least, she hoped she would be fair. The truth was she had no idea what to do about her youngest sister's request; she felt a thoroughly incompetent judge of it all. Her own romances were certainly not much to go by; her past dating experiences were limited, a fact she was sometimes embarrassed to admit, even to herself.

Not that she hadn't had her chances. There had been no shortage of lovely lads coming through the doors of Aioli, the restaurant where she had worked alongside Gloria Delmonico in London. With her accent and Italianate looks, she could pass as Gloria's cousin, a ploy that had often bought them a pint or two at the local tavern. But whereas her friend's bravado enabled her to flirt and frolic with many an Englishman, Marjan had always shied away from any serious commitment. It was a reticence born not from prudery but from too much experience, too many memories.

Keeping the two trays of chickpea cookies balanced in her arms, Marjan tilted back her head and looked up. The sun was quickly sinking behind Croagh Patrick, filling the autumn air with a rose-tinged mark. Bonfire Night was set to spark with twilight precisely twenty-three minutes from now.

Sunsets, whether voluptuous and pulsing or thin with the whisper of winter rain, held a special place in her heart. It was under another western sky, in an East over a decade ago, that Ali, her beloved Ali, had proclaimed his love for her. That was the night he had given her a beautiful brass jewelry box, a simple little chest etched with desert roses, with the promise that it would be the first of many keepsakes. It was a promise he had not kept, one he had no way of keeping, she realized, now that she looked back on it.

Back then, back when they had been seventeen and in the midst of the free-loving seventies, it had seemed as though they would have an eternity to plan and play out their dreams. Funny, thought Marjan, how she and Ali had only held hands when they started dating, their passions manifesting solely in long and languorous kisses.

While their school friends had taken full advantage of Tehran's heady modernism, a moment of amnesia for the traditionally staid capital, she and Ali had chosen to keep their bond fairly chaste. It would take a separation and the coming of the Revolution to bring them together in a deeper union.

When she allowed herself to think of those days, in moments when neither of her sisters was present, Marjan always marveled at the circumstances of their first night together. Unlike the white satin romance they had planned on that school trip to Istanbul, when he had bought her the brass box, their first encounter had been a hushed affair, played out tenuously on a springy cot in the darkened offices of *The Voice*, the revolutionary newspaper she and Ali helped print underground. The word *irony* did not have an equivalent in Farsi, but Marjan had long since come to regard that night as ironic.

It was ironic, after all, that she and Ali had come together only after she had joined his cause and started wearing a *roosarie*, a traditional head scarf. Ironic that through their words of rupture and revolt, constructed piecemeal on an old printing press, they had joined their bodies for those brief moments of bliss. Pure, uncomplicated happiness.

It was as if the secrecy of their revolutionary venture had allowed them a separate space of their own, a room with walls that only they could enter. Was it only within boundaries that people were allowed the freedom to be themselves, to be fully naked in both soul and body? Marjan sometimes wondered. It was, after all, the Iranian way, separating one's public and private worlds, allowing no stranger beyond your closed door. All those walled gardens and veils, those captive singing nightingales.

Was it better to give all of yourself and open up your wounds, your darker moments, to another person? Or were you richer for being conservative, for keeping your emotions to yourself? Maybe it was necessary to have a bit of mystery in life, Marjan told herself, to keep some things hidden from others. Perhaps there were secrets that you could share only with yourself. Or was this an argument for justifying the ever-gilded cage, the Republic that Ali had fought and, perhaps, died for? She just did not know. It was a puzzle that would probably never be solved. One of those questions that would eternally confound the human heart.

Maybe it was better to concentrate on the chickpea cookies she was toting for the Bonfire, thought Marjan, turning down Main Mall.

WITH THE COOKIE TRAYS held securely in her arms, Marjan quickly crossed over to a packed Fadden's Field. Even before she stepped onto the grassy knoll adjacent to Danny Fadden's Mini-Mart, she could feel the ground quiver with the excitement to come. This would be the first year Ballinacroagh would be celebrating the end of the harvest season in such a grand manner.

There had been an attempt at organizing a celebratory event last year, but that had gone the way of the proverbial smoke.

Bonfire Night 1986 had been a massive letdown thanks to a gale that had blown in from the nearby Atlantic. The night was to be forever referred to as Fadden's Big Fizzle, after the pile of birchwood that steamed out within a minute of being lit.

"Marjan! I'm so glad you're here!" Fiona Athey dodged a trio of nuns, two of whom Marjan recognized as Sisters Agatha and Bea, to get to her. The robust hairdresser was wearing an orange UCLA sweatshirt and her favorite pair of olive green fishing pants, handy for all their secret pockets and folds. Not a fan of feminine accessories, Fiona seemed slightly perturbed by the large plastic earrings hanging from her earlobes. Marjan recognized their shape—husks of yellow corn—as her friend approached.

"You wouldn't believe the mess I'm in, even if I told you." Fiona breathed heavily, taking one of the trays. "Have a look over there, Marjan, and tell me what you see, now."

Marjan followed her friend's gaze, past the already crowded refreshments tent, to the middle of Fadden's Field. Planted amongst the dark heather, in two semicircles that repeated themselves for three rows, were the white lawn chairs used for all of the town's meetings. The seats faced an open area marked by round fieldstones. The delineated ground resembled a giant pie or wheel, with its spokes leading to a pyre of spindly kindling.

Marjan blinked, unable to believe what she was seeing.

Tucked firmly atop the pyre, with its legs spread at a forty-degree angle, was a twelve-foot man made entirely of straw and dried nettle. Or what was left of a man. Marjan could clearly see a large hole gaping from his grassy pelvis.

"The Cat's goat," Fiona remarked drily. "Took a chunk off before I could get my hands on it." Balancing the tray on one palm, she pointed to a row of elms on the far edge of the field.

Roped to the smallest tree was a long-haired billy goat. Ballinacroagh's resident boozer and philosopher of no less than nine doctorates, the Cat had recently celebrated what he had claimed as his centenary on earth in his favorite manner, namely getting sloshed on a bottle of strawberry schnapps while grooming his new pet goat, Godot, in the town square.

Godot's sour-faced owner was currently crouched on his haunches next to him, feeding him from a pint of amber drink of which he also partook.

Marjan remained speechless, utterly shocked.

"And after all the work that went into connecting those limbs. Burning man, indeed," Fiona muttered, leading Marjan to the refreshments tent, where it seemed half the village was also gathered.

The stripy orange and white tent, one of the four used during the summer's annual Patrician Day Dance, was pitched in the field's northwestern corner. A pine table ran along its back width, showcasing Conor's crabapple cider, costing a punt a pint. Silver vats of steaming corncobs, buttered and sprinkled with paprika by Maura Geraghty, the Wilton Inn's formidable chef, were offered as savory sides.

Marjan approached a table piled with goodies. Along with wreaths of entwined hawthorn, gingham-lidded jars of rhubarb-apple jam and marmalade, and loaves upon loaves of Mrs. Boylan's brown bread were miniature burning men being auctioned for the cause. Marjan read the cardboard sign next to the mini-effigies: BET ON YOUR OWN BURN! SUPPORT OUR TOWN HALL THEATER REVIVAL!

"Fiona, you continue to amaze me," she said. "When did you and Father Mahoney have time to put this together?"

"Had the fifth-years at Saint Joe's help during their lunch hours. Didn't Layla tell you?" Fiona straightened a garland of alder and berries that had fallen.

Marjan shook her head. "Layla's got a lot on her mind these days," she replied. Scanning the sea of heads for her youngest sister, she finally spotted Layla and her boyfriend, Malachy, canoodling behind a bale of hay. The two hadn't left each other's sides since meeting up at the train station.

"I know how that is. Emer's been at that Californian school two months now and all I got was this jumper here. Not even a letter to go with it. Teenagers!" Fiona exclaimed.

"How's Emer doing with her studies?" Marjan reached for a tray of cookies, lifting the tea towels off the sweet, buttery nuggets. The cider being poured by Margaret McGuire wonderfully complemented the cookies' cardamom scent.

Fiona popped a cookie into her mouth. "From the little I can make of it, she's taking Los Angeles by storm. Been assigned already to stage-manage the first-years' production."

"What an honor!"

Fiona beamed with pleasure. "Imagine! A daughter of mine in the theater! Never thought I'd see the day!" The hairdresser stared off into space, briefly reminiscing on the years she had spent gracing the Irish stage.

"Testing, testing! One, two, buckle my shoe . . . er, there was an old maid from Tuvalu—" A terrifying shriek pierced the air. Godot the goat replied with a plaintive bleat, while the gathered crowd grabbed their ears in similar discomfort.

Father Fergal Mahoney was standing next to the gelded straw man, his hands clutching a microphone, which was connected to a nearby portable amplifier. A sixty-fifth birthday present from Ballinacroagh's premier welcome wagon and organizing body, the Ladies of the Patrician Day Dance Committee, the amplifier was one of Father Mahoney's most treasured possessions. He hardly gave a sermon nowadays without the accompaniment of his Ari 3000.

"Gather around, everyone. Don't be shy. That's it." Father Mahoney beckoned the crowd toward the semicircle of chairs. "This lad here won't bite," he said, patting one of the bushel legs. "But I'd keep away from that goat, if I were you!"

The crowd tittered and turned their attentions to Godot and his owner. As a likely response, the Cat narrowed his already puckered eyes and let out a loud and voluminous belch.

Father Mahoney shrugged emphatically. "Fine cider you've got there, Conor. I think the Cat's approval speaks for us all."

From under the tent, Conor Jennings could be seen raising a pint of the appley alcohol, pleased as punch. He turned to Marjan and gave her a big thumbs-up. It had been Marjan who had suggested he use cardamom and nutmeg instead of cloves in his home brewing experiment, a combination that had yielded an effervescent champagnelike drink that was nothing if not divine. Bonfire Night, the Guinness man had informed her only last week, was to be the debut of his lovingly coaxed crabapple brew.

"I'm only going to say a few words tonight," the priest continued. "The real show is what's going to happen when we light your man here. As some of you may have gathered, we're not only here to raise much-needed funds for a new stage in the Town Hall. Sure, it's the main reason, we're not to forget that and all. That platform we call a theater is a mighty disgrace, a sheer abomination of the altar of the gods— Ahem!"

Father Mahoney paused, reddening. "The spirits of verse, per se, those eloquent angels who look after the theater bards." He wiped his brow. "Call it what you will, I think our community deserves a better ground for covering the greatest, the mightiest talents of our western land: our poets and playwrights. Synge and Yeats deserve a better fare, you'd all agree with me, I think."

Father Mahoney stopped again, his pink, expectant face gazing out on his congregation. What he hoped had been a rousing cry for the Arts was greeted only by the sounds of cider slurping and another indignant bleat from Godot: a protest perhaps for not having his own namesake's creator, the great Samuel Beckett, acknowledged as one of Eire's venerable authors.

A professional comedian in a past life, Father Mahoney was terribly close to breaking out his Prince Charles impersonation for an easy laugh. Instead, he soldiered on. "As for the other reason we're all commingling here this day, it's to the credit of Fiona Athey and the Ladies of the Patrician Day Dance Committee. Not only do they work hard all year to bring us the best of entertainment's value for our July holiday but now they are committed to celebrating our greatest Celtic days as well—the important calendar moments our own ancestors, blessed they were, chose to commemorate."

As Father Mahoney went on to explain the significance of the harvest effigy, which offered its light to stave off the demons of winter months, Marjan moved through the crowd until she reached Layla and Malachy. The two hardly had noticed the hubbub swirling around them, so intoxicated were they by their own inflamed hormones. A considerate and shy boy when they started dating, Malachy McGuire had matured into a confident, and at times cheeky, young man. At the moment he had his face buried in Layla's neck, his arms holding her tight around the waist. He was getting quite the liberal university education, thought Marjan. Not that her sister needed much prompting. For her part, Layla was off in a dreamworld, her lips opened, her eyes closed in unabashed ecstasy.

A few passersby cast bemused smiles at the young, smooching couple, adding to the dark looks darting from a group of elderly women. Marjan considered turning away, leaving them to it, but on second thought remained where she was. An image of an overweight monk, the Fat Friar from the *Sunday World* advertisement, popped into her head. She let out a loud cough. The pair of them looked up with a start, Layla giggling coquettishly, Malachy wearing a wide grin, his arms still wrapped around his girlfriend. Marjan smiled back, handing each of them a glistening corncob wrapped in wax paper. "Have you seen Estelle anywhere? Weren't you two supposed to pick her up?"

Layla brought her hand to her opened mouth. "Oh, I completely forgot! She called right after you left. Said she couldn't make it tonight. Her arthritis is acting up again. Said she'll call you tomorrow." Layla twisted open the top of the papered cob with a guilty look. "It slipped my mind. Sorry, Marjan."

"Did you want me to check up on her?" Malachy assembled his shoulders into a manly stance. "I can borrow my aunt's car and go up there now, if you want." No longer at home in his childhood house, the young man spent his weekends down from Trinity College at his aunt Margaret McGuire's.

"That's okay, Malachy. The roads are still slippery from the shower earlier. I'll give her a call later," Marjan replied, her eyebrows knitting with worry. Estelle did not usually let her arthritis stop her from attending a party; this latest bout must have been especially debilitating. When it acted up, which was quite regularly nowadays, the older lady's arthritis could leave her just a shadow of her usual chirpy self.

A gentle ripple of applause filled the air, followed by a quick scrambling for seats. One of the first to settle near the front of the pyre was Bahar, who had been thoroughly captivated by Father Mahoney's pithy speech. Oohs and aahs resounded across the field as Fiona Athey stepped up to the straw man with a lighted match. She paused dramatically before the crowd, waiting for Father Mahoney's nod.

As the flames took hold of the dried grass, Godot the goat gave another bleat from his elmy hideout, mourning his burnt supper, no doubt.

❁

FIVE MILES AWAY, in a hillside cottage, an old lady was wincing in pain. As Estelle wrung the bloody washcloth into the bedpan, she could feel another wave stab the ligaments in her already aching fingers and wrists. She took in a deep breath and counted to ten, uttering a quick prayer to Saint Jude for mercy. If any ailment deserved its own saint, she told herself, then arthritis was certainly top of the list. The pain was nothing new; the changing season always triggered its darkest head. But in the last two hours her fingers had swollen to twice their size, and that was surely a record. It had taken her a whole five minutes to run a clean cloth under hot water and apply it again to the girl's sores.

The mermaid lay perfectly still as Estelle laid the warm compress between her legs. She didn't even let out a cry as a disk of greenish pus seeped from a cut, darkening the white gauze.

Estelle cringed and averted her eyes. It was an infection all right. There was not as much blood as when she had first found her, lying facedown in the sand—an improvement, she supposed—but this infection could mean a turn for the worse. And then, there was the fever to contend with as well. Estelle sighed, returning the soggy washcloth to the pan. She placed it on the bedside table and made her way around the perimeter of the large bed, tucking in the duvet as she went along.

Although she let out a low and breathy moan a few times, the mermaid did not open her eyes. It was as though she was no longer living, yet not passed through that shimmering threshold, the afterlife.

Estelle was glad she had called Dr. Parshaw, even if she had only gotten the nurse at the hospital this late in the day. Once he got her message, he would be right over, she was sure of it. The good doctor would know just what to do about the mermaid's loss. She knew she could trust him.

Estelle had chosen to call the girl a mermaid mostly out of romantic sentiment. It was a fancy prompted not by scales or a fish tail but rather by the girl's extraordinary hands.

At first glance, the young woman's fingers looked normal enough, delicate and pale like the rest of her body. But a second look revealed that they were something marvelous to behold. Linking her four fingers and thumb, right above where the natural base of each digit dipped into the palm, was a sheath of skin as delicate as organza pastry and so pale that, when fanned open, it resembled the fin of an ocean temptress.

The rest of the girl's body was typical of her age, which Estelle guessed to be in her early twenties—so she knew her mermaid fantasy would be remedied once her patient woke from her fevered sleep. *If* she woke from her fevered sleep, Estelle corrected herself, pacing around and around the bedroom rug in a ring of growing panic. If God would grant just this.

❉

THE RAIN HELD BACK until the flames had reached the burning man's head. Within minutes it had reduced the harvest icon to a pile of smoldering ash, purple plumes swirling toward the starry night's sky. Marjan helped Fiona collect the fold-up chairs as the town's two-man police guard, Sean Grogan and his deputy, Kevin Slattery, stood by the dampened pyre, sequestering wayward sparks with all the protocol of a major stakeout. By the time Marjan and Fiona joined the rest of the revelers in Paddy McGuire's Pub, the place was packed for the rousing music *seisiún*.

"Will you have a pint, Marjan?" Fiona asked, as they pushed through the smoky, cheerful pub.

"Some cider, if there's any left. Thanks!" Marjan had to yell over the bustle of the front room. From the back parlor thunderous clapping followed the beat of a bodhran drum, that goaded cry of battle dawns. "I'm just going to make a phone call!" She pointed toward the back of the pub as Fiona sidled up to the long oak bar.

Weaving her way through the crowd, Marjan passed by a plank table tucked under a low alcove. Known to regulars as the Confessional, the spot was a favorite of amorous couples, chosen mainly for its darkened crannies and velvet-curtained nooks. She caught a glimpse of Malachy sitting with Peter and Michael Donnelly in one corner. Wedged in with the lads was Layla, her lips glued to a pint of stout, drinking greedily from its creamy top.

Wonderful, thought Marjan, as a trio of tweed-capped farmers blocked her view. That was all she needed: a hormonal teenager with curious taste buds. It was a good thing Bahar had gone home early; the sight of Layla sipping Guinness would not have gone over well with their more conservative sibling.

Marjan took another look around the busy pub. Quite a few families had gathered under its cozy rooftop tonight. Children of all ages were among the patrons; newborns and toddlers cradled in corners and benches while their parents drank and gossiped about the brilliant but all too brief Bonfire. There was even a carpeted area reserved for young ones to crawl, next to a corner table where a gang of school-age kiddies had set up a house of cards.

It was a time-honored tradition in Ireland, bringing the whole gang out to the local pub for some craic and grub. The bar was an extension of the family parlor, after all, a big living room where loneliness and the constant rain could be cast away for a few precious hours.

Still, Layla should know better than to take advantage of that singular strain of hospitality, thought Marjan, reminding herself to make a stop by the Confessional on her way back.

She slipped past the crowded back parlor and descended a flight of sloping wooden stairs. The Covies, with Conor Jennings on the tin whistle, had just launched into a spirited rendition of U2's "With or Without You," a big hit of the summer charts. At the bottom was a narrow hallway that housed the ladies' loo. One of the many additions to the pub since Margaret McGuire had taken over its management, the restroom had initially caused quite a rumpus with Paddy's male contingent. Generations of drinkers had taken their bathroom breaks in the outhouse beside the beer garden, it was fervently argued, and any woman who thought herself equipped for the stout should be expected to likewise abide. Well aware that the criticisms were fueled by envy over the powder room's soft toilet paper and lavender-scented potpourri, Margaret ignored the comments and went ahead with her renovations.

Marjan slipped a ten-cent coin into the wall pay phone opposite the restroom door. She dialed from memory, easy since she called the number at least once a day.

Estelle finally answered on the fifth ring. "*Si?*" the Italian widow whispered.

"Estelle? It's Marjan. How are you?" Marjan cradled the receiver closer to her ear as the tin whistle revved through a series of dizzying triplets directly above her.

"*Si?* Eh, hello?"

"Estelle, can you hear me? Is everything okay?" Marjan raised her voice, not realizing she had also been whispering.

"Hello, Marjan. Uh, sorry I could not come tonight."

"I was worried it had to do with your arthritis. Is it acting up again? Do you want me to come up and get you? You could stay with the three of us tonight."

"No, darling, that is okay. I have your lentil soup from yesterday. That warmed me very nice. Oh, so good," the widow said with a sigh.

"But is it warm enough up there for you? I can send Malachy up to chop some firewood."

"No, no . . . you go now and have a good time. I can hear the music. I come to you next week again."

"Let me come up tomorrow. I can bring some *gormeh sabzi*, all right?"

"Ah, no, that is all— Oh, okay, yes. Tomorrow, tomorrow. Okay, bye-bye. Bye, Marjan."

And she hung up.

Marjan stood staring at the receiver in her hand for a moment. Estelle's voice had sounded awfully strange. Distant, as though it was being sifted through layers of mountain fog.

Marjan was glad she had made such a large batch of *gormeh sabzi* that day. The stew would give Estelle some of her strength back.

Marjan replaced the phone in the cradle and turned toward the staircase.

"I was hoping to find you here."

The Englishman she had met yesterday, Julian Winthrop Muir, stood at the foot of the stairs. He had to duck to avoid the low oak frame.

"Hello," said Marjan, catching her breath.

"It seems I missed the pyrotechnics. How was the Bonfire?" he asked, amusement dancing across his face.

"Better than expected. You can never tell with all the rain."

"Ah yes, the West with all its rain," Julian remarked. " 'To Connaught or to Hell,' as Cromwell liked to say. Now there was one Englishman not welcomed in these parts."

He moved aside, letting a group of middle-aged women pass by. Already on their third gin and tonics, they had no trouble giving him the twice-over. They muffled their giggles and shuffled into the ladies' loo, though not before throwing him some suggestive grins.

"Looks like you're doing all right," said Marjan with a smile. "Being welcomed, I mean."

"Oh, I wouldn't be too certain, now. You never know what the locals think of you straight out," Julian said pointedly. "A lot goes on behind closed doors in Ireland."

Marjan agreed. "Same as in Iran," she said.

"Oh?" Julian looked at her with genuine curiosity. "How do you mean?"

"Well," Marjan said, "we like our privacy in Iran, as well."

He nodded. "You mean your veils. I'm afraid I can't get used to that image. Only old women and the very religious wore your black chadors when I last visited. Now it's something else, indeed."

"It's not something I can get used to seeing either. On television, I mean." She paused. "But that isn't what I meant by privacy. It's part of it, perhaps, but only a small bit."

Julian leaned against the wall, his arms folded across his broad chest. "Go on. This is fascinating."

Marjan cleared her throat, surprised by the tingle of attraction in her belly. "It has something to do with our history, I think," she began. "Something about being conquered so often."

"You mean by the Arabs?"

"Them, and there was the Mongolian invasion. And later on the British and the Americans, in their own way." She looked up, blushing. "Sorry."

"Not at all. I'm only part British, so I'm only half-insulted," he said, jokingly. "But you might have a point about the comparison. A complicated topic."

Marjan nodded. "Yes, complicated. It's funny, I was thinking about this exact thing earlier this evening," she said, as much to herself as to the man standing next to her. She turned to the stairs, still in deep thought.

Julian came up from behind. "Mind if I follow you up?"

Marjan shook her head and smiled softly back at him. She climbed the stairs, her hand gripping the banister. She wondered if he was staring at her backside and found herself blushing at the thought.

At the top of the stairs, they both paused, dodging the jostle of the pub crowd. The band had finished with their butchering of Bono's solo and its members were taking a drinks break.

Julian turned his green eyes on her. "Can I get you a pint?"

Marjan stared at him, feeling the jolt in her stomach once again. "Umm . . ."

He flashed her a smile, nodding. "Go on. I have some great stories to tell. Spent an entire five weeks with the whirling dervishes of Kush once, if you can believe that."

"Sounds wonderful. But . . ." She could see Fiona waving to her from the bar.

Julian followed her gaze. "But you have your pint waiting, I see."

Marjan ducked her head shyly. "Thank you, all the same."

"My pleasure," he replied. He turned to go, then looked at her once again. "I'll take a rain check, as the Yanks say. Not bad odds, from where I'm standing." He nodded at the misty darkness outside the pub window before disappearing into the crowd.

Marjan took a deep breath. The whirling dervishes of Kush— she had heard him right, hadn't she?

At that moment she couldn't be too sure: she felt as though she were whirling herself, her heart turning and turning as rapturously as those mystical dervish men.

❄

"YOU'RE GOING TO LOSE your looks if you keep going the way you do. Besides, it is *illegal*, Layla." Bahar's voice was as stern as her march across the kitchen tiles.

"Oh! How can you be such an old lady at twenty-five?"

"It's not about being an old lady. It's about being right!"

Marjan sifted through a bowl of walnuts and dried apricots as she observed her sisters from the corner of her eye. They had been at each other ever since the café had opened for Saturday breakfast.

"When I am right, I am right. That's all there is to it," said Bahar, opening the refrigerator door.

"You mean *righteous*. God, who made you queen of Ireland all of a sudden?" Layla was preparing a roasted eggplant and hummus roll at the wooden island. She held the stuffing awkwardly down with the blade of a knife as she tried to roll the bread tight.

"I'm telling you, it's not right. And the guards there as well. Are there no laws in this country that people actually obey?" Bahar poured cherry water into two tall glasses and placed them on a small brass tray.

Marjan left the island and walked over to the swinging doors. Hungover faces, many familiar to her from the pub the night before, filled the cozy café.

Bahar paused to address her on the way out: "You see these?" She pointed to the glasses of cherry water. "Cures for those two in there. Drunk still, from that bar. That bar our little sister was in until all hours last night. Humph!"

She disappeared into the dining room and plunked the two glasses in front of the Donnelly twins, Peter and Michael. The young men gratefully slurped back the refreshing drink, a sweet and sour mixture that cured hot flashes as well as nights of excessive tippling of the black and tans.

Marjan returned to the sink. "I'm not getting involved. I told you how I felt about you drinking last night," she said to Layla. "I want to leave it at that."

Layla pouted. "It was just a little sip."

"Still, you are underage. And it isn't that healthy for you either."

Layla looked indignant. "But you drank. I saw you at the bar with Fiona."

"I'm older, Layla. And this is not about what I do at the bar." Marjan rolled her tired shoulders and turned back to the island. "Just take it easy with Bahar, all right? All this arguing is making me lose my concentration."

She stared at the bowl of walnuts and apricots for a moment, trying to remember the next step in her stuffing recipe.

Was it chop first then fry, or fry then chop? It was simple enough. So why couldn't she remember it? Her mind was all over the place today, fractioned. Scattered, even.

Layla raised her hands in protest. "She just won't stop. How did she find out anyway? She wasn't even at the pub."

Marjan hadn't seen Bahar at the bar either, but she wasn't too surprised to hear that her sister had uncovered Layla's Guinness venture. Bahar had access to an intuition that could come only from her sensitive nature.

"I don't know how she knows, but I do know that she hasn't had one of her headaches in a very long time. And you are not helping keep it that way." She gave her younger sister a knowing glance. "All right?"

Layla shrugged, nodding reluctantly. She placed her hummus roll on a small plate and sat down to her snack. Halfway through her roll, a devilish smile stole across her face.

She put down her food and crossed her arms. "So, who's that guy you were talking to last night?"

Marjan did not answer right away. She moved to the stove as casually as possible, turning up the back burner. She let it crackle under a deep pan of butter before giving a small shrug. "Just a customer," she said, dumping the fruit and nuts into the sizzling butter.

"I've never served him before. He was nice," Layla said, throwing her sister a bemused smile.

Marjan shook her head, stirred the golden mixture. "What happened to Malachy being your one true love? Are you growing fickle in your old age, Miss Layla?"

Layla shrugged. "I have eyes, don't I? And they told me that guy was nice."

Marjan blushed, sending Layla into a peal of laughter.

"Okay, okay. But you haven't heard the end of this conversation." After a moment she spoke again: "Marjan?"

"Yes, *joon-e man*?"

"Have you thought more about, you know, that thing we talked about? At the train station?"

Marjan turned to face her little sister. "Fat Friar's?"

Layla nodded, her turn now to become shy.

Marjan sighed. "I have to be honest with you, Layla. I'm not sure if I feel comfortable with the whole thing."

"Why? You said you'd think about it."

"And I have. But I just haven't made up my mind yet. You have to respect that."

"But you said I should come to you with stuff like this." Layla's voice took on a slight whine.

"Like I said at the train station—just because you came to me doesn't mean I have to agree with what you ask. Like it or not, I am the eldest. Sometimes I have to make decisions that might not make you happy. All right?"

"You don't have to tell me that," Layla replied. She sank into her chair, her long legs flopping open before her. "I live with you, remember?"

Marjan let out another sigh and rubbed her neck. She placed the lid over the simmering nuts and fruit and walked over to Layla. "We need to set some time aside and talk about this properly," she said, placing a hand gently on her sister's shoulder. "We'll go through everything, why you think you're ready, what Malachy really thinks, and then . . ."

"And then?"

"And then, I'll decide whether to write to Gloria or send you away to a convent," she said, patting her sister's dark head.

"Ha, ha," Layla said, narrowing her eyes. She stuck out her

lower lip and stared at her roll, appearing suddenly to have lost all her appetite.

"A BOWL OF *ABGUSHT* for Father Mahoney, lamb kebab for Mrs. Boylan," Bahar said, backpedaling into the kitchen with the dregs of what had been a Persian chicken salad. She placed the empty bowl next to the chopping block and stuck the order to the carousel.

"And that Englishman's back," she said. "Takeout order for the morning."

Marjan looked up from the stove, her heart pounding.

"He asked for you again," Bahar added, her eyebrows raised.

Marjan wiped her hands on her apron and walked to the double doors. She could see Julian Winthrop Muir standing at the Donnelly twins' table, his fists in the pockets of his tawny jacket. All three were laughing at something he had just said.

Bahar sniffed as she set out two bowls on an empty tray. "Between you and Layla, I'm surprised this place is running at all." She scowled and took off her polka-dot apron.

Marjan wiped her hands on a tea towel and patted her ponytail. "Is it three o'clock already?"

"Nearly. I need a few more minutes today." Bahar slipped into her coat and turned to her older sister, who was still staring out the kitchen doors. "What are you doing?"

"Nothing," Marjan replied as casually as possible, giving a slight shrug. She returned to the stove and lifted the lid of the eggplant stew, adding a pinch of black pepper. She made an effort to keep her hand steady but didn't quite pull it off.

Bahar came around to the stove, making sure not to get too close to the burners. She tilted her head, a sign of an oncoming interrogation.

"Who is this guy anyway?"

"I don't know. A visitor, I think."

Bahar sniffed. "I heard he's some rich landlord's son, thinks really highly of himself and all."

Marjan stirred the eggplant stew, placed the lid back on the stockpot. "And where did you get this piece of news?"

"Fadden's. Danny said his family used to own most of the land around Ballinacroagh. He's probably looking to own it all again."

"Honestly, why do you always look at the dark side of things first?"

"What do you mean, 'dark side'?" Bahar said, looking thoroughly offended. "Why am I suddenly the bad guy?"

Marjan sighed. "I didn't mean it that way." Bahar stared at her. "Look, forget I said it. It's just that sometimes you have to give people a chance. They might surprise you with their goodness."

Bahar snorted. "I don't know what fairy tale you're coming from, but that's not how the real world works. You know that as well as I do, Marjan."

Point taken, thought Marjan. She fell silent as she watched her sister open the back door and step into the garden. It was not until she was fully over the threshold that Bahar opened her large plaid umbrella against the falling rain.

Superstitious as always, thought Marjan, shaking her head. She patted her tidy ponytail again. Reaching for the strings on her apron, she tightened them to give her waist nice definition. Her heart leapt again as she swung through the double doors. Passing Father Mahoney and Mrs. Boylan's table, she paused for the priest's assessment of the day's special ("I'll be having the barberry hen for my last supper, you can count on it!") before making her way to the Donnelly twins and Julian. The three men were still laughing but quieted down as soon as they saw her.

"Top of the mornin' to ya," Julian said, tweaking an imaginary cap at her. His blond hair was combed back, Marjan noticed, revealing his strong, clean-cut jaw. "Or should I say afternoon."

"Hello there," she replied with a smile. "Are you staying for tea?"

"Just stopping to place a breakfast order. The lads on site can't get enough of those marvelous pastries, the baklava you've got there." Julian indicated the glass cabinet, where platters of baklava, sugary fritters, and almond delights sat in honeyed rows.

He turned back, giving her an appreciative look. "Have to say, it's been quite a while since I've seen an apron worn so right."

"Oh . . ." Marjan looked down, smoothing the skirt of red toile against her jeans. "Thank you." She could feel her cheeks warming.

"I brought you something," Julian said, motioning her to a quieter corner near the door. He handed her a fat paperback he took from his jacket pocket. "My latest."

Marjan turned the book over to read the black-and-white cover: *Dominions of Clay: A Novel.* "By Julian Winthrop Muir III." She looked up, impressed. "That's quite an achievement."

"Well, I wouldn't go that far. According to my publisher, you'd be the third person to attempt to get past the first chapter—that is, if you do read it."

"Of course I'll read it. I'm sure it's great." Marjan glanced behind her. She could see Siobhan Kelly from the shoe shop leaning dangerously over her seat for a spy. Julian seemed to take no notice of the curious faces in the dining room.

"I thoroughly enjoyed our conversation last night."

Marjan smiled at the memory. "Yes, it was nice." Why was her heart suddenly pounding so hard?

"Perhaps we could do it again? This evening, at Paddy's?"

Marjan looked to her right. The Donnelly twins winked at her, giving her their customary cheeky smiles.

She looked down at the paperback in her hand. The embossed name stood out to her: Julian Winthrop Muir III. He was asking her for a date.

She wasn't ready for this. Was she?

"Do you always leave men hanging, or is it just with me particularly?"

Marjan looked up again, met his gaze. "I'm sorry, it's just that—" She took a deep breath.

"You have previous engagements?"

Marjan nodded apologetically. "I'm just very busy for the next while."

"I understand. Well, sometime soon, then," Julian said. He started to lift his hand to touch her arm but dropped it to his side when she moved slightly to the right. "Another rain check."

"A rain check. Yes."

Julian chuckled. "I'll look forward to it." Bidding the twins good-bye, he tipped his imaginary cap at her and walked out of the café, closing the door behind him.

Marjan watched him hunker into his jacket and disappear up the drizzly street, along with most of the lunchtime diners, who had suddenly found the topic of their day's gossip.

Chapter 3

Dance of Many Veils

STANDING IN THE BRIGHT VESTRY of Saint Barnabas Roman Catholic Church, Father Fergal Mahoney took a few moments to study the airmail cartons piled precariously to the corniced ceiling. They had arrived earlier in the day, his trusty housekeeper Mrs. Boylan had notified him, just as he was about to celebrate what he liked to refer to as his *Matinee* Mass and Eucharist.

He had ordered the boxes from a reputable dealer in Akron, USA, whose seasonal catalog featured other marvels of human ingenuity, among them a talking sundial and a set of nunchucks that sprang plastic flowers when swung in a full circle.

The nunchucks were a waste of money, thought the priest. No practical use for them whatsoever. He would never stoop so low as to buy himself a pair. He had, though, been tempted by another item: an autographed section of track from the set of *The General*, that silent-era film starring the wunderkind of comedic timing, Buster Keaton. The train track was particularly poignant as it was featured in the climax of the film, when the hero has to save his beloved from a deadly oncoming steam engine.

Buster Keaton was a hero unparalleled, in Father Mahoney's opinion, who had perfected the marriage of absurdity and pacifism on-screen like no one else. No matter what tragedies befell him in his cinematic escapades, be they man-made or natural disasters, he always kept his cool, preferring to neither laugh nor cry at destiny's whims. Such stoicism had earned Buster Keaton the title the Great Stone Face; a nickname the priest felt did not encompass the tender empathy Keaton showed for the weaknesses in his adversaries, or the kindness in his dark, drooping eyes.

In the end, Father Mahoney had decided against the autographed piece of train track, opting instead for what he found on page 26 of the color catalog, a product that promised him freedom, if only temporarily, from his daily collar:

As a special introductory bonus to its pirate radio kit, Penzance Productions was throwing in two cassette tapes of sample clips from some of radio's most piquant programmers, including those legends of the disc jockey arena Casey Kasem and Wolfman Jack, as well as an hour tutorial called "The Art of Segues" by no other than Dick Clark himself.

Father Mahoney felt utterly powerless against such a bargain; he placed his order that very day.

Reaching into the vestry's scroll desk, the priest grabbed a butter knife perched on a crumby tea plate. He turned back to the boxes before him, boxes of infinite possibilities, and tore voraciously through the first silvery cross, the masking tape coming deliciously undone. An excited guffaw escaped his lips as he gave a little hop.

Fergal Mahoney, of one-parish Ballinacroagh, former warm-up man of comedic revues large and small, was ready to launch on the waves. The Irish airwaves. Ahoy and away!

❋

"YOU'RE NOT TO BLAME A BIT, now, Joan. I never thought that Evie Watson was much to look at, to be honest," Antonia Nolan opined, reaching for another digestive biscuit, which crumbled duly upon entry into her mouth. "Far too like a foundling, like something they pulled out of the bottom of a well, if you ask me."

Saturday afternoons, as always, found Ballinacroagh's Bible study group huddled in the dusty environs of the Reek Relics shop. Milky tea and plain digestives served to fortify the ladies, along with a regular diet of gossip and prayers.

Currently the topic was one of Joan Donnelly's twin sons, the elder by three minutes, and his affair with the junior hairstylist at Athey's Shear Delight.

Joan sniffed in contempt. "Far be it from me to give my opinion on a co-worker," she started, pausing dramatically when she saw teacups poised in the circle around her. "I'm only at the salon half days now, but I still have my professionalism to keep."

Dervla Quigley pursed her lips. "You're among friends, Joan. Don't hold back on your feelings. Purge if you need to, so." She nodded at her sister, Marie, who remained as she usually did, silent and concentrating on her uneaten digestive biscuit.

"Purgin' won't be necessary," said Joan. "But a mother knows what a mother knows—that snippet won't be right for my Peter, that's what. From the moment they got together I was unhappy about it all."

"Sure, I hear her people are from the North," commented June Nolan.

"She could hail from Timbuktu, for all that matters. She can't look after my Peter like he deserves." Joan sipped at her white tea and continued. "He's got to think of Michael as well. The poor lad's been off to the wayside ever since those two got together."

"At least you can say he sowed his oats. It's time for the proper way of things, from this moment on," said Dervla, no doubt thinking of her late husband Jim's tendency to sow voraciously and well into his sixtieth year.

"I'll say this about Evie: she may be a bag of bones, but at least she's not some street Arab like you know who." Joan shook her head in relief. "Thanks be to God that little floozy didn't get her claws into either one of my boys."

Antonia agreed. "Sure, it's not five minutes that Thomas's boy is down from Dublin she doesn't have him to the Beach, doing God knows what."

June commiserated. "Cheap, that's what. No faith to guide her."

"That's what happens when you're brought up a heathen." Dervla uncrossed and crossed her legs, placing a hand over the Bible on her lap. "You'd think those three had a scent for our men, all the way from wherever it is they came from."

"Iran," Marie Brennan whispered from her corner.

"The wild-beasted desert, that's what," her dominating sister interjected.

The clink of teaspoons gave way to a momentary pause. The gathered women drank their tea in deep thought. Another round of digestives was in order before June spoke up.

"I hear that Marjan's now making the rounds," she huffed. "Got her eye on the Muir clan, from what Siobhan tells me." June arranged her knobby cardigan around her large center with an indignant air. "As if a man like Julian Winthrop Muir would give the time of day to the likes of her. Imagine!"

"My Peter says he's moving into the Hall with his men Monday at daybreak. Going to patch the big house up to all its former glory. Think of it now, a proper family in these parts again."

Dervla looked over her cup with disdain. "You can keep your big house empty, for all the sin it brings. Those Muirs have a lot to be shameful for, starting with that Julian there. Julian *Winthrop* Muir."

Her sister looked at her quizzically.

"Don't look at me with those big eyes of yours, Marie. As if you don't recall that summer clearly."

Assumpta Corcoran leaned in, followed by the rest of the women. "What summer was that, then?"

"The year of my Jim's passing, God rest his precious soul. July 1965."

Antonia squinted her eyes, traveling back. "Nineteen sixty-five . . . July." She sat up. "Oh, now, *that* Muir boy."

"That's right, *that* Muir boy. Sort and the same. The whole clan of them staying in Jarleth House up on the Bay. He and his Dublin kin did a right number on that poor laddeen from Clare."

Antonia nodded now, remembering. She turned to the other women. "Strung the boy up on a tree. Left him naked and hanging from his limbs the entire night. Near caught his death, that young one. What was his name?"

"O'Cleirigh. Dara. Island Gerry's boy."

"That's right. O'Cleirigh. The boy didn't say boo for a whole year after the torture."

"The shame," said Dervla, shaking her head. "And not one of the guards doing mite about it. Makes a person want to take the law into their own two hands, it does. Vigilents law, that's what they call it in America. Isn't that right, Marie?"

Her sister nodded. "Vigilante," she corrected, softly. "Vigilante law."

"That's what I said. Vigilantes. Taking matters into their own hands. It's what needs to be done at times, ladies."

The women of the Bible study murmured their agreement and reached for more digestives.

❋

A KNOCK CAME FAINTLY through the bedroom wall, causing Estelle to spring up in her chair. She scanned the room in alarm, her eyes passing from the bed to the door and back, adjusting to the limited light.

When the sound came again, she quickly covered the girl's bare legs with the down-filled duvet and moved around the foot of the bed. By the time she reached the bedroom door, Marjan was already in the hallway.

"Estelle! Oh, thank God. I've been knocking on the front door for a while. Are you all right?"

Marjan stooped to place the heavy basket of food she had brought on the ground. She blinked to readjust her eyes to the dark passageway, which when lit showcased a gallery of framed sepia and cream photographs.

"Oh, darling. I forgot you were coming," Estelle whispered, closing the bedroom door softly behind her. She moved down the hallway, tiptoeing nearly.

Marjan followed. Even in the diminished light, she could tell her friend looked drained of every last ounce.

"I brought the *gormeh sabzi* I promised," she said. "And some chickpea cookies. I made an extra batch."

She was about to tell Estelle about the pistachio halvah she had also packed when the old widow's peculiar behavior stopped her.

Bringing her index and middle fingers up to her pursed lips, Estelle blew a silent shush and shook her head. She then waved her left hand back and forth as if swatting a stubborn mayfly.

Before Marjan had a chance to speak again, Estelle pushed her gently into the nearby kitchen.

The room's periwinkle blue cabinets and daffodil-colored walls compounded the cheerful effect of the interminable sunshine streaming in from a large south-facing window. The light revealed purple shadows under Estelle's eyes, casting shadowy wrinkles not usually seen on her vibrant Mediterranean face.

Estelle lowered her fingers from her lips, but not before Marjan caught a glimpse of the state of her hands: sandpaper red, they were stiffened into large, immobile claws.

"I knew you weren't feeling well," Marjan said, guilt flooding over her. "I should have come up to see you last night."

Estelle tsked. "I am fine, darling. It is not me that is sick." She might have sounded more convincing had she not begun to sway on her heels, her bandy knees wobbling dangerously.

"You need to sit down," Marjan said, pulling a kitchen chair beneath the widow. The old lady sank into it immediately, sighing with relief.

"I wish you had told me how you were feeling sooner." Marjan grabbed the tin kettle off the stove and filled it up in the sink. She positioned it back on the front burner, the gas licking its sides until it burnt out a bright orange-blue flame. "You promised me you'd call whenever you felt this weak," she said, turning to her friend.

"You look tired too, darling."

Marjan waved away Estelle's concern. "Not at all. The café's been really busy lately. That's all." She opened a cupboard and took down a large ceramic mug. "You're the one who has to take it easy. All right?"

Estelle was so tired that her eyes seemed to forget their ability to blink.

"Estelle?"

The widow shook her head abruptly. "Oh, sorry, darling. I think I just fell asleep with my eyes open." She smiled weakly.

"Let's forget about the tea," Marjan said. "I want you to get into bed and I'll bring you a cup of hot milk. Come on now." She prodded Estelle's arm.

"No, no. I have to tell you something. Something about what is in my bed," Estelle insisted. "Sit, sit." She patted the wooden hearth chair next to her.

Marjan bit her lip and settled reluctantly into the seat. She turned to the widow, who without further ado began her story. The story of the mermaid on the shores of Clew Bay.

❀

"IN THE INLET?" Marjan asked, as Estelle concluded her tale.

Estelle shook her head solemnly. "Terrible, absolutely terrible. I could not believe it myself, but it's true."

Marjan looked down for a moment. It was too much to take in. "Do you think someone did something to her?"

"I think this at first. I was about to call the guards, but then I look more." She paused. "I look at her body, at her belly, and I saw more."

Marjan frowned, missing the meaning behind the widow's words. "So this girl you found, you think she was trying to kill herself by drowning? In the Bay?"

"A person can kill themselves in many ways. It is not always physical, you know. You can kill your heart, your hope, your future, if you don't believe that life is a gift."

Estelle paused, aware that her explanation was more enigmatic than she had intended. She peered into Marjan's puzzled face. "I don't know if she was trying to kill herself, darling," she said. "But I am very sure she was trying to kill her baby."

Chapter 4

Nipped in the Bud

BEING THE MIDDLE-BORN had its advantages, Bahar told herself. There was so much more scope for the personality, if you really stopped to think about it. Without the responsibility that came from being a trailblazing eldest, or the encumbrance of always playing the baby, a middle child could really find the freedom to discover her true self. And, if occasion called for it, to properly reinvent herself, as she, Bahar Aminpour, was getting ready to do in a few months' time.

Bahar stared at the bowl on the table before her. Twenty radishes, washed and piled one on top of the other, sat ready for her knife. As she always did when prepping vegetables, she took a moment to square her shoulders, draw a deep breath, and observe the task at hand. When she was ready, she reached over and plucked one of the pinkish bulbs. With a snip of her sharp paring knife, she set about making a quick incision into its magenta skin, her lips pursed with concentration.

Round and round the blade went, producing petals that opened one on top of the other, white against the red. Ribbons fell from the knife's edge, curling around her crossed legs. And so it went until all twenty were done, the radishes cleared of their perky heads, their bodies floating in a bowl of chilled water like a delicate bouquet. No longer ordinary root vegetables, they were now brilliant roses carved to blooming age.

The radish roses made pretty garnishes on the many cheese and herb plates that went out during the hungry hours of the afternoon. They were also tangible, not to mention edible, proof of one of Bahar's greatest talents to date: hands that were extraordinarily agile, and arms of immense strength.

She had first noticed the power of her hands and arms as a nurse, working at the Green Acres Home for the Newly Retired. Switching intravenous tubes with the speed of a master seamstress while holding down the likes of a two-hundred-and-fifty-pound grafter turned geriatric convalescent had earned her the respect of her colleagues; the coveted title of Most Valuable Matron was hers for two years straight. In constant demand throughout the nursing home, she was most wanted in the Alzheimer's Suite, where her ability to soothe patients with the mere lock of her elbows left the burliest of male nurses speechless.

The respect of her workmates had not transferred itself into any friendships, however—a fault that Bahar now considered entirely her own. Instead of mingling with the interns and happy-go-lucky nurses at Doc Watson's Pub, she had opted to roam the streets of London's antiques district alone, dreaming of the day when her own house would be filled with dainty Victorian décor.

She had turned herself into a recluse, hidden her heart from her workmates—even from her own sisters, if she had to be honest about it. She just hadn't been ready to share that organ, torn as it was, with anybody back then.

Bahar placed the paring knife in the empty bowl and wiped her hands on a tea towel. She paused for a moment, glancing at the kitchen doors, before reaching inside her apron pocket.

The edges of the small laminated card felt smooth and correct along her fingers, an effect that was quite soothing to her usually overwrought senses. She pulled the card out halfway and turned it so she could read its message in the dying afternoon light:

Our Lady of Knock, Queen of Ireland, you gave hope to your people in a time of distress and comforted them in sorrow . . .

The card came from the village of Knock, not thirty miles from where she sat, here in the kitchen of the Babylon Café. Bahar had not been there herself, though it was very much a destination in her immediate future, she was sure of it.

According to Father Mahoney, who had given her the prayer card, a pilgrimage to the Shrine was as necessary to the system as an annual climb up Croagh Patrick, both journeys a sign of commitment to the new life she was taking on.

It was at Knock, after all, where the Blessed Virgin had once appeared, wearing a brilliant rose crown.

"When the Blessed Virgin first graced the village," the priest had said, "it was the English who wanted to claim her, Queen Victoria herself sending in her fancy envoy. But it was to the Shrine that the Pope made his visit in the year 1979, not to the throne of England. It was on Knock that he bestowed his Golden Rose—on the Irish!"

Bahar returned her gaze to the message, feeling a shiver of pleasure run up her spine.

Ask and you shall receive, seek and you shall find . . .

She sighed. The delicate calligraphy was imprinted on her mind, words learned by a heart growing more constant with every passing hour. That muscle would soon be as strong as her slender but powerful arms.

Like she had done with the good old radishes, Bahar Aminpour would soon carve out her own rosy little spot.

The time was just about right, she told herself. Not yet, but soon enough.

❋

"ONE CHEESE AND HERB PLATE with *barbari* bread; two *abgusht*s and a plate of angelica fava beans. Mains: chicken kebabs for two, lamb and cherry rice, and a yogurt and cucumber dip, no bread, to go. That's for Maeve Cleary. She's on another diet."

Layla swung backward into the kitchen with a tray of empty plates. She left them on the sink counter and turned to Bahar.

"What's that you're reading?" She walked over to the kitchen table. "A note from your lover?"

Bahar scowled. She slipped the laminated card back into her apron pocket and pulled her hand out just as fast.

"Give me your pen," she said, thrusting out her empty palm. "Why?"

"I'll take over the orders. You can stay here with those instruments of torture." She pointed to the three stockpots simmering on the green stove.

Layla shook her head. "No way. Deal was I do the front of house, you do the food. For once."

"That was before Marjan was gone for three hours. Where is she anyway? You'd think she'd have the courtesy to call."

Bahar moved toward her younger sister with a determined gleam in her eye. She reached for the pen behind Layla's ear, but not before Layla pulled it out.

"I don't know where she is, but I'm doing the orders," Layla said, waving the pen above her head.

At five foot two, Bahar had little hope of reaching it without jumping, risking her dignity in the process.

She clapped her hands in frustration. "As your elder, I demand you give me that pen! Now, Layla!"

"Uh-uh. Malachy goes back tomorrow—it's the only time I get to see him all day. I won't be stuck in this kitchen just because you're afraid of a little stove."

"Don't tell me your boyfriend's out there again. Doesn't he—"

The wall phone shrilled. Both sisters reached for it, Bahar securing the cherry red receiver with a smug smile. Her smile soon turned, a deep frown hollowing out her brow. "What do you mean you're staying? What happened?"

Layla nudged her ear into the other side of the receiver, and both listened as Marjan told them of her plans to stay the rest of the afternoon at Estelle's. By the time Bahar hung the phone back up in its cradle, her frown was a triangle strung from her temples.

She stared at the floor for a moment. "I don't like the way her voice sounded," she finally said. "She's hiding something."

Layla shrugged. "That's just you being paranoid. Mrs. D's hands are acting up again. That's why she wasn't at the Bonfire last night. She shouldn't be up alone in the cottage anyway."

She handed the pen to her sister. "I'll look after the poor *abgusht*. Tell Malachy to come back and keep me company."

Bahar took the pen and stuck it in her apron pocket. She was about to voice her opposition when her fingers brushed against the laminated card.

All at once her shoulders relaxed, her worry lifting like an eddy of dust; the card's message of love was as instantaneous as a shush, as peaceful as Gabriel's breath on a long-fevered brow.

"THE DAMAGE IS MODERATE, but I won't know more until we get her into the examination." Dr. Parshaw peeled the latex gloves off his steady hands and shook his head. "There is a considerable infection that needs immediate care, that is certain. It is lucky her aim was not so precise."

As both her personal physician and chief internist at Mayo General Hospital, Dr. Hewey Parshaw was the only professional Estelle could trust for medical advice. He had arrived minutes after Estelle showed Marjan into the bedroom, where the girl lay sleeping under the down duvet.

"So you think she is with a baby?"

"Your instincts were right, Mrs. Delmonico. She is in her second trimester nearly. My estimate is eleven weeks. However," he said, turning his serious eyes on them, "the inner lacerations do indicate an attempt at termination."

All three fell silent, taking in the gravity of the situation. Beads of sweat rose on the young woman's face. Estelle reached over and wiped them gently with a cold cloth.

The young woman's eyes twitched under her closed lids, her ragged breathing breaking the silence.

"What is the longest you have been able to keep her awake?"

Estelle shook her head. "Not much. Her eyes open three, four times, but closed again. And painful noises, nothing else. No talking at all." Her face crumpled up. "Oh, I hope I did not do the wrong thing by not calling you yesterday."

From across the room, Marjan could see tears springing up in the kind widow's eyes.

"You have done the honorable thing by bringing her to your home," Dr. Parshaw assured her in a voice of smooth velveteen. "If you hadn't found her, the worst imaginable circumstance could have been a reality today."

"That's right," Marjan said, giving the doctor a grateful smile. "And the guards would not have been any help either. By the time you got home yesterday, they had already closed up for the Bonfire."

"What we need to concentrate on now is the future," said Dr. Parshaw. "We must get an ambulance up here as soon as possible. The chance of this becoming septic is there, I'm afraid."

Estelle blew her nose on the silk handkerchief she always kept tucked in the sleeve of her blouse. "I will go make the call."

"I've got the van," suggested Marjan. "It'll be quicker that way."

As Estelle packed a few essentials in a small overnight bag, Marjan and Dr. Parshaw set about creating a makeshift gurney. They spread the duvet on the floor next to the bed, doubling it up to make for an easier carry. Dr. Parshaw then knelt to gently scoop the girl from under her shoulders and legs.

Her reddish brown hair hung limply as the doctor lowered her onto the duvet, her thin, angular face a frightening shade of green. Like an opal stone, thought Marjan, without the benefit of its rosy veins.

"To the right, please," Dr. Parshaw directed Marjan as she backed out of the cottage door.

They took their time descending the gravelly path, the corners of the duvet clenched in their hands. The girl made no indication that she knew she was being moved and remained deep in fevered sleep. Although not nearly as heavy as her long and lanky frame would suggest, she would surely have been a weight for one short old woman. Marjan simply couldn't imagine how Estelle had ever managed to climb this drive with the girl hanging off her shoulders. Where had she gotten the strength?

"I know a shortcut to the hospital," Marjan said after the girl was safely laid on the van's carpeted floor. "We'll have to go through Ballinacroagh." Dr. Parshaw slid into the back with his new patient, and she closed the double doors.

"Okay. We go." Estelle locked her front door and began to slide down the gravel walkway. Marjan rushed up and took the basket of chickpea cookies and *gormeh sabzi*, as well as the overnight bag packed with a spare toothbrush and Luigi's pajama tops.

"I don't know where you find your strength," Marjan said in awe.

"Pfft! This is nothing!" Estelle exclaimed. "You should have seen me when I was young. Who do you think carry that kitchen island into the bakery, eh? My Luigi call me his Herculeana Neapolitana," she said proudly.

She turned to the rosebush flourishing at the end of the drive. With a loving smile, the old widow threw its flushed petals a kiss, bidding her husband's resting place a temporary good-bye.

THAT NIGHT, Marjan dreamt of Mehregan.

The original day of thanksgiving, the holiday is celebrated during the autumn equinox in Iran.

A fabulous excuse for a dinner party, something that Persians the world over have a penchant for, Mehregan is also a challenge to the forces of darkness, which if left unheeded will encroach on even the brightest of flames.

Bonfires and sparklers glitter in the evening skies on this night, and in homes across the country, everyone is reminded of their blessings by the smell of roasting *ajil*, a mixture of dried fruit, salty pumpkin seeds, and roasted nuts. Handfuls are showered on the poor and needy on Mehregan, with a prayer that the coming year will find them fed and showered with the love of friends and family.

In Iran, it was Marjan's favorite holiday. She even preferred it to the bigger and brasher New Year's celebrations in March, anticipating the festivities months in advance. The preparations would begin as early as July, when she and the family gardener, Baba Pirooz, gathered fruit from the plum, apricot, and pear trees behind their house. Along with the queen pomegranate bush, the fruit trees ran the length of the half-acre garden.

Four trees deep and rustling with green and burgundy canopies, the fattened orchard always reminded Marjan of the bejeweled bushes in the story of Aladdin, the boy with the magic lamp. It was sometimes hard to believe that their home was in the middle of a teeming city and not closer to the Alborz mountains, which looked down on Tehran from loftier heights.

After the fruit had been plucked and washed, it would be laid out to dry in the sun. Over the years, Marjan had paid close attention to her mother's drying technique, noting how the fruit was sliced in perfect halves and dipped in a light sugar water to help speed up the wrinkling. Once dried, it would be stored in terra-cotta canisters so vast that they could easily have hidden both young Marjan and Bahar. And indeed, when empty the canisters had served this purpose during their hide-and-seek games.

Only twice while growing up did the Aminpour sisters not celebrate Mehregan: in 1971, after their mother had died giving birth to Layla, and then again in October 1978, when the three sisters had been sequestered in Pakistan, taking refuge from a revolution and a man with a face full of terrible pockmarks.

Hossein Jaferi's face propelled Marjan out of sleep.

She sat up in bed, blinking quickly. It took a few deep breaths before she could orient herself, remind her mind and body that she was safe in her bed. The crackling bonfires of Mehregan must have somehow morphed into the shadowy image of Bahar's estranged husband during the course of her dream, the sweet, woodsy smell of kindling flitting away to another, more primal scent.

It wasn't often that her dreams turned to darkness.

She swallowed hard and looked to her left. Bahar was still wrapped in her customary two duvets. A quilted eye mask covered most of her small face, rising to the rhythm of her soft snoring.

Saturday tea must have been especially busy, thought Marjan, enough that it had tired even Bahar's neurotic tendencies.

Normally her sister would have remained awake and waiting at the kitchen table until Marjan was home safe and in one piece. Bahar would never have fallen asleep had she known what—or rather who—Estelle had found beneath the dunes of Clew Bay Beach.

Drawing her legs up to her chest, Marjan laid her chin on her knees and let her mind roam the day's strange events. She still had a hard time believing what she had seen at Estelle's. It all seemed like a fantastical dream, something from one of Layla's Shakespearean plays.

Who was she, this girl with the strange hands and pale skin? Where had she come from? And why had she chosen to do what she had done in the Bay?

There were a lot of questions and, it seemed, only one person who could answer them.

Dr. Parshaw's examination had at least shed some light on the situation. After an hour's wait in Mayo General, the doctor had appeared with his verdict: "There is slight tearing of the lower cervix," he explained, his face ashen from lack of sleep, "but no damage to the uterus itself. She is going to keep the baby—for the moment. Of course, things may change entirely once she is discharged."

The meaning behind his words was clear: although to do so was not legal in the Irish Republic, the girl could terminate her pregnancy elsewhere in Europe.

Marjan asked her name.

"She was awake for most of the diagnosis but refused to answer any of my questions," Dr. Parshaw replied. "I'm afraid I do not know any more than you both about her origins."

He paused, choosing his words carefully. "Most likely she is in shock. Trauma of these kinds, even if self-inflicted, has the effect of leaving some numb. There will be more time for questions later."

"Yes, yes." Estelle nodded, following the doctor's words attentively.

"I have not told any of the staff about the circumstances that brought her here. Just that she was suffering from an infection and would rather not talk about it. I am keeping most of her records in my office."

"Thank you, Doctor," Marjan said. "I know that's asking a lot." She put her arm around Estelle, who had begun to sniffle again.

"I am not sure if what I am doing falls under the Hippocratic oath or not, but I do not believe in handing her over to the guards," continued Dr. Parshaw gently. "The infection should be cleared up in the next fortnight. There were some serious cuts to her cervix. Had Mrs. Delmonico not found her when she did, she might have lost her baby."

Estelle dabbed at her eyes with her handkerchief and nodded. "You are a good man, Doctor."

"There is nothing good or bad about what I do, Mrs. Delmonico. It is merely my job."

"Yes, but you know, good or bad, her body is fighting her heart. It knows she tried to erase pain, so it is still fighting. You must please tell her she is not alone. Please tell her there are people here to help," insisted Estelle.

Marjan could see that the topic had struck a deep chord with her friend. Barren during what should have been her fertile years, Estelle Delmonico was never able to have her own children. Something in this mysterious girl, it seemed, had triggered her latent regrets.

It had set off Marjan's own memories, too. There was no denying it, she had been here once before, they all had; the young woman's inner wounds were too similar to another set of inflictions, the marks of a baton that had caused Bahar so much pain. But unlike here, in the quietude of Mayo General Hospital, with its staff of whispering nurses, Bahar had not been properly treated for the assault that had left her so battered. Instead, she had cooled her wounds with a paste of grated potato and mint leaves, a recipe from their grandmother Firoozeh. She had treated herself and kept her secret for four months, never calling Marjan for help.

A shudder ran through Marjan. She glanced once more at Bahar, thankful that she was still asleep.

Maybe she should wait a while before telling her sisters about the girl. She had weighed the thought on her drive down from Estelle's but had still not decided whether it would be right to tell them about the girl and her attempted abortion. The more she thought about it, the more it seemed like a bad idea.

It would only cause panic, she told herself, especially since no one knew who the girl was, or even where she had come from. There would be no point in worrying them as well, at least not until she knew more about the situation.

Yes, she told herself, she would wait—for answers and a new day. Marjan took a deep breath and rubbed her arms. She couldn't seem to stop the shivers running up her spine.

Slipping quietly out of the bed, she tiptoed across the small room to the door. She knew one surefire way of dashing the nightmare: a big cup of warm milk and honey, with just a pinch of powdered cinnamon.

Maybe a piece of *barbari* bread as well, to dip into the frothy surface. Comfort, Baba Pirooz used to say, comes easily from such simple pleasures.

In the living room, Marjan found Layla sprawled where she usually slept, on the opened futon sofa before the television. Her youngest sibling was also in a deep sleep, a smile on her dreaming face.

From the latticed skylight, the moon was sending a series of hushed beams into the small parlor. The light was just strong enough to reveal the mottled cover of *Much Ado About Nothing* tucked in the girl's long and slender arms.

Chapter 5
Familial Seats

MARJAN HELD THE CASSEROLE DISH close to her chest as she climbed the stairs to the convalescent unit. She followed the arrows on the polished floor, making her way to the room as she had done the day before.

She spotted Dr. Hewey Parshaw as she turned a corner. He was talking to a plump nurse near the check-in station but nodded at her as she approached.

"Good afternoon, Miss Aminpour." He smiled, sniffing the air. "My, whatever you have hidden in that dish, it smells delicious. Makes me wish I were a patient, if only for this lunch hour."

Marjan smiled. "It's *bagali polo*. Dill and lima bean rice," she said, holding out the casserole.

Dr. Parshaw sniffed again. "Mmm . . . takes me back to my mother's kitchen in Pakistan. What years they were!"

"How long have you been away?"

"Nearly five years. Too long, too long for any son."

"I'm sorry to hear that," Marjan replied. She had wondered about the doctor's story. Estelle had told her a little about his background, how he had escaped a civil war for Germany and then residencies in hospitals around the Emerald Isle. He looked much older than she had expected after hearing Estelle's description.

Loneliness had a way of aging people, Marjan thought. "I know how hard it is to leave everything behind," she said gently.

Dr. Parshaw nodded sadly. "Indeed. I sometime wonder if it is all worth it. Not sharing this prosperity with my loved ones." He looked at her. "But you are lucky. You have your sisters, Mrs. Delmonico was telling me."

Marjan nodded. "I am very lucky. I don't think I could have survived the move from Iran without them."

"Indeed."

"Do you have any family in Ireland?"

Dr. Parshaw shook his head. "None, I'm afraid. Some cousins in Frankfurt, that is all." He paused, attempting a cheerful tone. "But I have hope of bringing them here, and in the end, that is everything. Hope."

"I agree," said Marjan. Courage and faith, she reminded herself. She lifted the casserole dish. "Can I leave some of the rice for you? It might help with the memories."

"Well . . ." Dr. Parshaw paused, sniffing the buttery dill again. "Normally I would not intrude on a patient's dinner, but I am willing to make an exception this time."

Marjan smiled. "Good. I'll put aside a dish every day if you like. It's the least I can do," she said, when the doctor tried to protest, "for all the help you gave yesterday."

"Well, then . . . there's nothing to say in argument. Much obliged."

Marjan glanced toward the room opposite the check-in station. She lowered her voice. "How is she doing? Estelle said she's been awake for most of the day."

Dr. Parshaw's expression became sober. "The antibiotics are taking effect. One must be careful with any treatment, but especially in the condition she is in."

"So there is still a baby? Definitely?"

"For now, this is certain. It is, of course, important to monitor her recovery."

Marjan sighed with relief, surprising herself. "Does she know? About her condition, I mean?"

He paused and looked around, making sure he was out of the nurse's earshot. "I have informed her of her pregnancy," he said, in a low voice. "I explained to her that she will need to rest and heal. She has yet to make any comments."

"Estelle said she was keeping quiet."

"Yes, and we still have no name. I have taken the liberty of naming her for the records. Otherwise, the rest of the staff, and I daresay the guards, would have to be notified," he said. "From now on she will be known as Bella Rosa. That was Mrs. Delmonico's suggestion."

Marjan's eyes widened. "Can that be done?"

"I don't know, Miss Aminpour. Sometimes it just must be done."

Marjan nodded, understanding the doctor completely. "Thank you, Dr. Parshaw."

He tapped the casserole dish with his pen. "Perhaps your delicious rice will loosen her tongue, yes?"

"I hope so." Marjan thanked him again and made her way to the door.

She walked in to find the old woman talking animatedly to the silent patient.

"And this, this is very special," Estelle said, pointing to a photo album on her lap. "Beautiful day." She scooted to the edge of her chair, opening the album page further.

"Luigi wanted to bake a special cake for my birthday. But I didn't even want a piece of biscotti. Not even a *macchiato*, I was so depressed."

Estelle sighed, looking at the photo thoughtfully. "You know, fifty years is a very important time for a woman. The hips get big overnight, the skin looks tired, and if you are unlucky with marry, the husband looks like a bad piece of eggplant you want to compost, not eat. I had good husband, but I was still getting old.

"So, okay, I was a little sad that day. Very missing Napoli. And I wake up in morning and I see Marcello Mastroianni. Believe me, I almost scream. I think my Luigi has turned into Marcello Mastroianni while I was a-sleeping!" Estelle waved her hands above her head.

She turned her head dreamily, as though reliving that moment in bed.

"Then, I look again and see that it *is* Luigi, but he dressed like so handsome, and he is sitting on top of a Vespa. A white new motor. I always want a Vespa, but you know we left Napoli after the War, and how can you find such a thing here in Ireland, eh?

"Okay, so now I wake and I have the best present. A present made by my Luigi's own hands. Would you believe he had made a Vespa for me? All from his famous meringue recipe! A meringue Vespa! What a baker, eh?" Estelle laughed. "We did not leave the bedroom that whole day!"

She blushed. "Ah, but I don't think you want to hear about that," she said. That was when she noticed Marjan.

"And look who is here!" Estelle exclaimed, getting up from her seat. "It is Marjan. You remember Marjan, yes? She make that nice stew for you. The one you like so much!"

The girl made no show of having heard Estelle. She sat with her back propped against the three pillows, staring out the window to the cold clover valley below. The nurses had given her hair a good wash the night before; it fell around her shoulders in gleaming waves of auburn.

Estelle persevered. "A few more bowls and you will be strong enough to walk around my garden, yes? That is what Dr. Parshaw said. Only a few more days for you to be strong again."

She patted the girl's covered legs. "We will have to make you good and fat, yes?"

The girl took in a shallow, raggedy breath. She continued to stare out the frosted window, her profile thin with sadness.

Her hands, Marjan noted, were curled in tight fists on her lap, her interesting fingers hidden from sight.

A mermaid, Estelle had called her.

Maybe she was.

With the blanket pulled up all the way to her chest, and the silence that still pervaded her every breath, she could definitely have been mistaken for a Victorian heroine; the Lily Maid, thought Marjan, on her way out of Camelot's reign.

Tennyson's poem had been a favorite of Marjan's when she was younger; she had learned it in high school in Tehran, during a particularly spirited semester of English literature.

Still, it took a minute for her to remember the story's fateful outcome: the Lady of Shalott had not made it alive out of the fabled kingdom; she had left on her death barge, floating down a dark river.

***

THE VAN SIDLED UP to the backyard, chug-chugging along the wide gray cobblestones. It took a whole minute for it to reverse and downshift before finally nosing in with a precarious dive.

Marjan let go of the breath she had been holding as she watched the awkward maneuver. If Layla could pass this test, she told herself, she would soon be ready for her full license.

Cobbled back when donkey carts were the mode of privileged transport, the alleyway that ran behind the café was a dodgy steer at the best of times. Narrow enough for one vehicle to pass, it required careful navigation, especially for the green hippie van.

Marjan always made a concession to the space by parking the Volkswagen at an angle. As Corcoran's Bake Shop boasted no back garden, and had no need for parking space thanks to its owner's preference for wheelbarrow delivery, the arrangement was a sound one for both parties. Benny Corcoran never minded having to share his alley space, encouraged it even, as the sharing allowed him proximity to his primary source of inspiration, Layla Aminpour's rosewater and cinnamon scent.

Ever since the Babylon Café's opening, that first day when Benny had crossed paths with Layla on his way from Fadden's Mini-Mart, the baker had been on a steady chrysalis-like course of transformation. Not only had he tripled his hot cross bun production and experimented with a black yeast and soda water ferment that pumped his sugar loaves to near Blarney Stone proportions, but he had dedicated himself to the rigors of an exercise regime that found him running up and down Croagh Patrick's stony path once a week, showers notwithstanding.

Metamorphosis would have been an exaggeration had it been anyone but Benny Corcoran; the once puffy baker had turned his body and libido into a sinewy machine of redheaded virility—a development that did not bode well for his wife Assumpta's version of the marriage sacrament.

Marjan opened the back door as Layla approached the gate. "Assumpta's going to be over in ten minutes about the way you parked there. You're blocking half the vent," she said, pointing over the fence to a tin contraption sticking out of the bake shop's wall. Shaped like a small chef's coronet, the vent let out daily puffs of flour into the drizzly morning air. The van's side panel was blocking the passageway.

"Benny said it was fine. He's finished baking for the day," Layla replied, latching the gate behind her. She giggled. "He was doing his pull-ups again," she said.

"I guess he has to practice his patience some way," Marjan said, returning her sister's smile. "Baking requires a whole set of virtues, patience top of the list."

"You bake a great *lavash* bread," Layla pointed out.

Marjan smiled. "But I'd rather be making *chelow*, if it came down to it." They both stepped inside the kitchen. "It's somehow less complicated to pull off."

Layla shrugged off her knapsack. "Well, your *barbari* bread was so good I even got Regina to taste some today."

"What did she think of it?" Marjan said, returning to the island. She poured hot water into a small glass of saffron strands. The water turned an instant liquid light.

"She said it was nice, but she much preferred cream crackers. I tried to explain it wasn't the same thing, but there's no point, really. She still thinks we eat curry, even though I've told her a dozen times we're *Iranian*, not Indian."

Layla picked one of the aprons hanging from a wrought-iron hook on the kitchen wall and tied it around her waist. "I can't wait until Emer gets back."

Marjan looked up, surprised. "Emer's coming back? For good?"

Layla shook her head. "Just for the Christmas holidays. Father Mahoney's already got her thinking up set designs for the nativity show. He stopped by school today. Auditions are next month," Layla said, a mischievous twinkle in her eye. "I'm thinking of trying out for Mary. What do you think Bahar would say to that?"

"Say to what?" Their middle sister pushed her way into the kitchen, using her behind to swing open the double doors.

She needed little help with the brass tray of empty dishes she carried in her strong arms. She slid them effortlessly onto the counter and whipped off her yellow checked apron. Underneath she was wearing a shin-length gray skirt with double pleats and pockets.

"Mary, Mother of Jesus. You know, the Virgin." Layla flicked her eyebrows up and down in a teasing manner.

Bahar stared at her younger sister for a moment. "What about her?" Her voice was laced with tension.

"Well, Father Mahoney's writing his own version of the nativity—"

"Oh"—Bahar waved her hand dismissively—"the Christmas show he's auditioning." She stopped short, her face reddening.

Layla squinted her eyes. "How did you know? He only announced it at school today."

Bahar shrugged quickly and turned her back to Layla. "Mrs. Boylan. She told me about it at the Mart." She stretched to reach her coat from the stand near the pantry. "What about it?"

Layla smiled, reaching over to a bowl of plums. "I'm thinking of auditioning." She kept her eyes on Bahar, waiting for her inevitable reaction.

"For Mary."

Layla nodded. She popped one in her mouth, chewing it with irreverent gusto.

Bahar sighed, her lips pursed tight. Then she nodded, moving her head up and down slowly. "Good. I think that's a very good idea. I'm proud of you, Layla. Good for you."

Layla nearly swallowed the plum whole from shock.

Both she and Marjan watched in silence as Bahar slipped into her coat and opened the outside door.

"I'll be back in an hour." She paused and turned around. "There's three construction workers at table one who want to know about the hookah. I told them it's only for show, but they want to smoke it anyway. You deal with them, Marjan."

She nodded at Layla once more. "Good for you," she said before trotting down the garden path to the wooden gate. She disappeared down the cobblestone alleyway beyond.

Layla turned to Marjan, her eyes wide. "What just happened?"

Marjan looked out the window and shook her head. "I have no idea," she said, feeling her worry creep up.

❋

THE LATCHES ON THE SHUTTERS slid into place as dusk surrendered to night. The smell of turf laced the cool twilight, filling Marjan's lungs with its smoky sweetness. All across Ballinacroagh, fireplaces roared with blocks of dried bogland, the bricks of turf that were preferred over logs of any kind.

It was a pity the flat upstairs did not have a fireplace. It would have been a delicious treat to sit near a crackling fire after a long, hard day. Put her feet up with a cup of tea, tuck into a great gothic novel, something by those gorgeous Brontë sisters maybe.

Or perhaps continue on with *Dominions of Clay*. She hadn't had time to read much of Julian Winthrop Muir's novel, though she had cracked it open to read the first paragraph the day he'd given her a copy. The language was as rich and beautiful as she imagined it would be, though she had not yet grasped the story's intentions. According to the jacket flap, it told the story of one day in the life of an architect, a man who had built his entire life on shoddy foundations. It sounded intriguing, thought Marjan. Very intellectual.

Yes, a fireplace and a great fat paperback would indeed be lovely. She stooped to remove the iron doorstop. The footsteps behind had her rising almost immediately.

"This is beautiful country, isn't it? You forget, being away as long as I have."

Julian stood next to her, observing the view down Main Mall.

"Oh. Yes, it is beautiful," Marjan said, her heart leaping into her throat. He had a way of catching her unaware, she had noticed. She wasn't entirely sure she didn't like it.

"Busy day?" he asked, moving around to face her.

Marjan nodded, swallowing. "Packed for lunch and tea. I haven't had time to catch my breath." She looked at the iron doorstop, suddenly too self-conscious to lean down to move it.

"No better time to catch it, then. Especially with this wonderful turf-filled air around us." He smiled, inhaling deeply. "A turf fire supersedes a log one any day, don't you think?"

"Yes," said Marjan, taken aback by his comment. "Yes, I do." He seemed to read her mind as well.

"Elemental. Do you know what I mean?"

"The fire?"

"Exactly," Julian replied. "The fire. A piece of turf comes from the ground, mulched sediment thousands of years old, then gets

fed into the air to settle once more. That's what I call a full cycle."
He crossed his arms and took a few moments to observe the
darkening sky, giving Marjan ripe opportunity to look at him.

He had changed slightly since the last time she had seen him,
she realized. He seemed more relaxed, somehow less constrained
by the London he had left behind.

Even his clothes had taken a Mayo turn: instead of his usual
blazer, he was wearing a weathered jacket and an old cable
sweater, work boots and a pair of roughened jeans. It was the first
time she had seen him so casual, so rugged and handsome. He
looked good in denim, she thought, feeling that tingle again.

Easy, girl, she chided herself silently, a little shocked by her
thoughts. She hadn't felt anything remotely similar in a very long
time. She cleared her throat. "How's the Wilton Inn working
out? Are you enjoying your stay there?"

"It'll do for the moment. It's not my final destination." Julian
pointed to the elms bordering Fadden's Field. "My family's estate
is beyond the woods there," he said. "Muir Hall. It's been around
for over two hundred years. I'm renovating it, actually."

"Oh, I didn't realize," replied Marjan, then remembered
the gossip Bahar had overheard. "Is the field part of the
property?"

"It used to be. Now it belongs to the county." Julian paused,
staring thoughtfully at the field. Then he looked at her again.

The dark green hunting jacket he was wearing matched his
eyes, Marjan noticed, as her heart started in on its now familiar
jig. Ali had green eyes too, though his were lighter, with inner
golden flecks.

"I was down for lunchtime yesterday, but your sister, is it? She said you were out on business."

"It's been a crazy few days," admitted Marjan. If only he knew how crazy.

Julian shook his head. "I'm amazed at the work you take on," he said. "All by yourself."

"What do you mean?"

"The restaurant, for one. It's a serious venture, a great business success. And we're not talking about in the middle of Soho London. Here, in the lonesome West of Ireland." He looked at her with admiration. "Not many can claim that kind of victory."

"Well, I didn't do it alone. I have my sisters. And some great friends who made it possible. Without them, none of this could have happened."

She looked up at the little stone building with its purple shutters with fondness.

"Friends and relatives aside, I know you are still the one that makes it all happen inside that bit of a kitchen. You could bottle up that magic of yours and make a fortune, Miss Aminpour." Julian ran his hands over the wooden shutters, stopping midway. "May I call you Marjan?"

"Of course." Marjan paused. "Julian."

"Well, Marjan. I know it's not drizzling in any sense of the word, but I was hoping to take that rain check after all. How about a pint next door?"

Marjan stared at the pub's glowing windows. Paddy McGuire's was filling up with its usual crowd of weekday locals.

It was the first evening she had had free all week, in a couple of weeks, actually, she thought. Her nights were usually spent in prepping for the next morning's menu, or going over the café's books, which, if not extensive, still challenged her elementary mathematics skills. The idea of sitting down to a ledger suddenly seemed very unappealing.

Julian was looking at her expectantly.

Bahar was not impressed when her older sister stuck her head in the kitchen a minute later. "Back by ten," Marjan said, whipping off her apron. "Lock the front door, will you?" Before Bahar could voice an opinion, Marjan found herself seated in the Confessional, a carafe of the pub's house red between her and Julian.

He held up the carafe. "Now this is something you don't see every day in a pub," he said, pouring her a glass of the rose-colored wine.

"It's a new addition," said Marjan, taking the glass in both hands.

"Something tells me you had a hand in that suggestion."

Marjan laughed. "Maybe. But Margaret—she runs the pub—is really good with new ideas." She tipped her head toward the bar, where a buxom woman with gingery curls was laughing uproariously with a few punters.

Julian persisted. "I think you're underestimating your powers over this little hamlet of ours. I've seen you rushing about in that van of yours, spreading those peace signs all over the place."

Marjan gave an indulgent nod. "It's not the most glamorous car, I know. But it's been really handy when I've needed it." She raised the glass to her nose, inhaling cherry, vanilla, and blackberry tones. Delicious.

"It's a grand piece of machinery. Especially those peace signs. Quite apropos to the responsibility you've taken on."

Marjan turned to him with a curious look. "Responsibility? What do you mean?"

"Well, it's not every day a backwater gets a taste of the world's greatest culture. The seat of all learning."

"I wouldn't exactly call it a backwater," Marjan said. "But thank you for the compliment."

"Don't mistake me—I think this is one of the loveliest spots on the planet, right here, this town, the Bay. I come from a long line of Mayo men, after all."

"But you've never lived here yourself?"

"Boarding school and Oxford, London all the way. But I always knew I'd come back to Mayo," Julian said, a fondness in his voice.

"So you're renovating your family home?"

"Yes, that's right. Restoring the ancestral seat to its former glory—that sort of thing. I've hired a firm from Dublin to oversee the finer details. Don't want some local Mick taking a sledgehammer to its precious walls." He turned to her intently. "I would love to show the old place to you sometime."

Marjan paused, took a sip from her wine. "I'd like that," she said softly. She glanced up. Fiona Athey had just come in with Father Mahoney.

Her friend raised her eyebrows and nodded provocatively at Julian, a large grin spreading across her face. Marjan's eyes widened, embarrassment rushing over her.

She'd be hearing about this tomorrow, she could bet on it.

She turned her attention back to Julian. "So, why Iran?"

"Why?"

"Yes. I mean, how did you get interested in traveling there in the first place?"

"I fell in love with a Persian girl. At Oxford." Julian settled back in the booth. The tasseled curtain brushed over his hair, ruffling it attractively.

"Ah. A Persian girl." Marjan nodded.

Julian chuckled. "That's all there is to know, isn't there? Fall in love with a Persian girl, and you'll never be the same?" His lips twitched with amusement.

"I didn't mean that," Marjan started. "I just meant—"

"I know, I know . . ." He reached over and touched her hand. A ripple of pleasure ran up Marjan's arm. "I just wanted to see your reaction."

"Oh." Marjan blushed. She sipped some more wine to steady herself. "What was her name? The Persian girl from Oxford?"

Julian looked off into the distance. "Mina Khalestoun. I met her in the registration line that first day." He turned his gaze back on her. "We were choosing our alternatives, and I thought it might be nice to rehash some of the old guard: Blake, Wordsworth, the Romantics. A good chance to get a bit of a kip after a weekend at the local, the Lamb and Flag."

He smiled at the memory. "Here I was contemplating a pile of dusty old codgers, ready to plunge into what promised to be one numbing ride of a term, when I saw her. She was signing up for a poetry class as well, but hers was a tutorial on the Sufi tradition. I had no near notion what that was, but I was going to find out. Signed right under her, and that's where it all began.

"We had a glorious two years together, and then she left. Packed up and went with her family to California. Heartbroken doesn't begin to pin it. Her family never liked me, but it was nothing to do with who I was, I think. It was where I was from. I wasn't an Iranian. And they wanted their daughter to marry an Iranian. Tell me, are all Persian girls like that?" Julian planted his green eyes on Marjan, catching her off-guard.

She blushed again. "I don't think so," she said, looking down at her glass. She could feel his intense gaze on her, and it took her a few seconds to look up again.

Julian stared at her for a moment longer before continuing. "I pined for two more years, and after my thesis, I took to the road. Backpacked. Followed Marco Polo's trail, the Silk Road, from China through Samarkand, hitched all the way to the Black Sea. But it was in Iran I stayed the longest. Strange way of getting over a broken heart, you might say. Going to the place where your beloved was born. But I wasn't thinking too clearly back then."

Julian paused to drink from his wine. "Best experience of my life, it was. Nothing like the desert to make a man out of you."

Marjan shook her head in awe. "I am not sure I could ever do anything like that."

"Oh, I'm sure you could. You've seen a bit of the world. Am I right?"

More than he could have known, thought Marjan, briefly recalling the arid mounds of the Dasht-e Lut. The desert of the East, where she and her sisters had escaped the first time

Hossein Jaferi had coming looking for them. "I suppose, but it was more out of bad timing than for adventure's sake," she said, shaking the dark vision away. "Even in Iran, I never visited Hafez's grave. And our father was from Shiraz, as well."

"Ah, Shiraz! What a town! The rose gardens, the nightingales. Paradise. You know, I got hold of some wine while I was there. I'll never forget that bouquet." Julian cleared his throat. " 'Rose petals let us scatter and fill the cup with red wine, the firmaments let us shatter and come with a new design.' "

He lifted his glass in a toast to Hafez's ode to the fermented grape.

Marjan met his toast with her own glass.

The evening flew by in the same hazy, soft manner. It seemed as though they were in their own world, and it must have been so because no one had approached them, not Fiona, not Michael and Peter Donnelly playing darts in the back parlor. Their only interruption came around nine o'clock, when the Cat wobbled in with an equally teetering Godot.

A persona non grata before Margaret McGuire had taken charge of her brother Thomas's affairs, the Cat was now as ever-present as the iron-rich stout that kept Paddy's a known destination. Swimming in his scotch and water with one ice, the old drunkard would spend entire days in the bar, tossing out Schopenhauer and Jungian theories with his customary mixture of native Bulgarian, English, and pig Latin.

And that was before the bottle of Dewar's had had its effect.

Most of the punters at Paddy's found it a mystery why Margaret allowed such a spectacle the most prized stool in the house, near the roaring, sweet turf fire, but the proprietress had her reasons: it was the Cat who had saved her nephew Tom Junior from true oblivion. Were it not for the philosopher's hospitality that strange summer before last, Tom Junior would never have been able to escape his father's domineering shadow and find his inner serenity. Tom Junior's letters to his aunt, written from the Northern California ashram he was living in, attested to the Cat's sincerity.

But catering to his burps and foggy philosophies was one thing; having to accommodate a hiccuping and clearly intoxicated billy goat was something entirely different—pushing the bounds of hospitality, the "*Céad Míle Fáilte*," or "100,000 Welcomes," written above the pub's front arch.

After ordering the alcoholic duo off the premises with little effect, Margaret had been forced to pull the goat by his beard and the Cat by the tail of his tweed overcoat, a sight that had provided punters with a good few limericks and one very dirty pun.

The Cat wouldn't have wanted it any other way.

Chapter 6

A Craic in the Wall

DERVLA QUIGLEY LEFT her thumb poised on the dark rosary bead as she reached over to part her chintz bedroom curtains. The two inches of space was all she needed to confirm her deepest suspicions: there it was again, the midday muck, the pitiless horde, the bustle of that café named for all things sinister: *Babylon*. To think, naming a place of dining after some heathen palace, some Oriental den of diversions. No one born and bred in Ballinacroagh would think to do it, that's for certain.

She squinted through the partition again, sniffing in contempt. Midday muck it was, though those foreign women were calling it lunch—not dinner like decent folk, mind you, but *lunch*. Every day from noon to the time of tea, at half past three, then swinging until the evening Angelus took its beat.

Sure, the Wilton Inn's carvery had no chance. Not with those three knocking their hips up and down the dining aisles.

Next thing you knew there'd be a string of the like: stinking spots, places run by hippies and degenerates, places where they would serve those plant things, that scourge called Mary Wanna in their teas and cakes.

She had heard a radio program about it the other day. A place in Europe proper called Amsterdam, where that very thing went on under the guards' watch. The shame, the absolute horror was beyond her reason. If only Thomas McGuire were here to stop it, thought Dervla. He'd never have put up with such a display if he were still running the street.

Sooner or later the big man would have found a way of closing the place for good, got his brother-in-law Padraig Carey down at the council to find them a loophole, some sort of bylaw to prevent leasing to foreigners. What good was it having a politician marry into the family if he couldn't pull a few strings? Then again, the gossip conjectured, had it not been for Thomas breaking into the place two summers ago, they'd never have this problem.

The eejit. He should have come to her before taking his hand to the place. Had Thomas let on his intentions beforehand, she could have sent him a word or two of caution. She could have told him it wasn't the slam of his fist that would do the café in but the force of a stronger punch. It was the Word that brought down empires; good old-fashioned gossip that sent highfalutin floozies to their judgment, not a banged-up kitchen and a half-arsed heart attack.

Her tongue, lashed with the right fortitude, could move mountains and Babylons, if it so desired. Sure, Dervla reminded herself, hadn't it been her very words that had sent Headmaster

Finton packing some fifteen years back? The man was found crawling the convent's ridgepole, in clear view of her window at night. Finton later claimed to have lost his keys to Saint Joseph's, but that was a likely tale if she ever heard one. No doubt he had been having a gander at those poor, helpless nuns in their slips and garters, not a habit among them. The dirty thing, the terrible liar.

Dervla clucked her tongue at the memory. And what about that jeweler down in Louisburgh, that swarthy, round one with the mustache? Hadn't she seen him tuck a ring box into Bachelor Jennings's post slot one spring dawn? Wasn't she the first to blow the whistle on that dirty affair? The jeweler, a married man of thirty years and with eight children grown, had later claimed it was the drink that made him propose the Claddagh to another fellow. As if that was going to fly with the decent folks of Ballinacroagh. The last she heard he had been peddling his baubles in some seaside kiosk in Cork.

Good riddance to them all.

"Wetted the tea, so. It'll be ready when you come out of the toilet."

Dervla turned toward the squeak over her shoulder. Her sister was slouched in the doorway with a plate of digestives cradled in her hands. Dervla curled her lips in disgust. Why did Marie always have to look as though she were on her way to some sacrificial altar? she thought. Of all the sisters to be granted, God had given her one without a spine.

The old gossip huffed up from the bed. "Thanks be to God," she said. "Take the seat before I go." She waddled toward the bedroom door. "Make sure you note the father's whereabouts. I haven't seen him come in or out of that place for four days—could be looking at sheer mutiny on our hands and we wouldn't know it."

"Maybe he's taken to his bed," Marie suggested. "The change in weather could have sent the bug his way," she said, settling onto the edge of the bed with the cookie plate.

"Don't be daft, Marie! Sure, didn't you see him at Mass this morning? Taken to his bed!" Dervla threw her sister a disappointed glance before turning in to the narrow hallway.

As attested by the worn carpet, the path from bedroom to toilet was one well traveled, a route she took at least every hour. Incontinence was the condition's official name, and in her opinion, it deserved its very own rosary. To think—Dervla grimaced—of all those years she went through her working hours on the farm without a break, not a thought to having another cup of tea or baking Jim Quigley's bread, only to be saddled with this godforsaken affliction so late in the day.

No doubt the bastard was having a laugh at her expense in his final resting place.

"Dervla! It's Antonia Nolan, so. She's coming up the side door!" Marie leaned away from the window, her face flushed with excitement. "She says not to move a muscle."

Dervla grunted. "Wasn't a muscle I was thinking of moving, but all right. Get the door, will you?"

Marie hurried to the apartment door, where a moment later Antonia appeared, out of breath and full of hot air.

"Lord save us! What's got into you?" Dervla muttered.

Antonia huffed and puffed for another few seconds before spilling her news. "Anne-Marie O'Connell. At hospital. Abomination! Abomination!" She paused to drink from the glass of water Marie handed her before relaying the rest of the story. When she was finished, she plopped down on the telephone seat near the door and crossed herself. "She'd been fed and clothed by those two. And that darky doctor as well!"

Marie blanched, looked to her sister. "Maybe it's only the flu, so. She could be from one of the islands," she began. "They say it's reaching Clare and the Aran, the flu sickness is."

Dervla stayed silent for a moment, rubbing her chin with her knuckles in thought. She nodded. "It's a sickness, all right. And it's catching. Like hellfire, so it is."

She moved to the telephone seat, lifted the receiver, and began dialing. Yes, thought Dervla, there was a reason why He had granted her the ability to see far and wide; a reason why she was— incontinence aside—able to keep watch over her beloved street.

The power of the Word was the greatest gift God had ever given to man, to one Dervla Quigley of Ballinacroagh, County Mayo, Ireland. It was up to her now to harness it to the cause.

❋

"WHAT'S THIS?" Bahar asked. She had her coat already buttoned and was in the process of tucking her ears into a furry gray beret.

Marjan stopped spooning the cucumber and mint salad and looked up. Bahar was holding a paperback book, flashing its black-and-white cover. "Where did you find that?"

"On the ground. Next to the coat tree. What is it?" She turned the book over, peering at the large embossed title.

Marjan took the paperback from her sister. "Nothing. Just a book," she said with a shrug. She stuffed it between the bread tin and a jar of cardamom pods and turned back to the salad with a frown. Her mind was getting so scattered. She had spent a whole hour last night looking for Julian's novel, even turning the tidy pantry inside out, without any luck. She was sure she had looked under the coat tree as well. Or had she? Placing the salad bowl on a platter, she topped it off with a piece of *barbari* bread and pushed it across the island. "Order up, Layla."

Layla looked up from her after-school meal, tomatoes stuffed with almond rice. "Is that for Fiona?"

"Yes, that's for Fiona," Marjan replied. "What are you waiting for?" Her tone was harsher than she intended. "I know it's a cold salad, but that doesn't mean you don't send it out when I ask you."

"I was just saying, 'cause—"

"Because? Why?"

Layla swallowed her bite. "Because, I just took a bowl out ten minutes ago. Don't you remember? Evie was having one too."

"Oh." Marjan looked at the bowl, then grabbed it and tossed its contents into the rubbish bin. Of course she had. Sluggish, that's what her mind was. She seemed to be forgetting everything the last few days. This morning she'd stood in the middle of the Butcher's Block staring at a pile of black pudding for an entire five minutes, wondering whether it would suit her red lentil soup or as a side to *bagali polo*, before realizing that none of her dishes contained that very Irish of delicacies.

She was even beginning to forget some of her recipes, and that had never happened. Marjan looked up from the island. Bahar was staring at her. "What?"

"So, where did you get the book?"

"Oh, uh, he, Julian wrote it."

"The Englishman. Full of himself, isn't he? Shouldn't he wait until you buy a copy of his masterpiece?" Bahar narrowed her eyes in disapproval.

Marjan grabbed a tea towel and wiped down the island. "Isn't it nicer that I got it as a gift?"

Bahar sniffed. "Beware of gifts, Marjan. They always come with a price." She paused, picking up her purse. "Besides, there's only one book worth reading in my opinion."

Layla piped up from her seat at the kitchen table. "And what book is that? *The Joy of Sex*?" She burst out laughing.

Bahar grabbed her umbrella and pointed it at Layla. "You need to get some soap for that mind of yours, missy." She turned the umbrella at Marjan. "And you," she said, "you need to stop encouraging her."

Marjan stopped wiping. "And what have I done wrong now?"

"Out with that English guy until whatever time it was the other night."

"I am a grown woman, Bahar. I can go out wherever and with whomever I like."

"You could at least have told me you were going to be so late, you know. I came down at nine, half past nine, then ten. You weren't home until nearly half past ten!"

"I don't want to talk about it. Don't you have your break to go on to?"

"You tell her, Marjan!" Layla stamped her feet excitedly.

"See? That's exactly what I'm talking about. Next thing we know she'll be doing drugs!"

"Oh!" Layla turned toward Bahar, a roll of lavash in her hand. "Take that back!" she yelled, brandishing the bread.

Bahar looked smug. "Hit a nerve, did I? What's with the guilty look? Doing something you shouldn't, eh?"

Marjan dumped the empty salad bowl into the sink, a loud clang breaking through the raised voices. "All right, that's enough! Both of you."

She took the canister of salad and shoved it impatiently back into one corner of the counter, unaware of the looks of surprise from her sisters. "I've had enough, do you understand?"

She picked up a ladle and turned to the soup pot, swiveling almost as quickly back to the cupboard. Yanking open a drawer, she plunged her hand into a pile of silverware and nicked her finger on something sharp. "Where are the spoons? Why aren't there any soupspoons?"

Layla scrambled from her seat, reached for the tray of utensils sitting on the counter. She handed Marjan a spoon and stepped back, surprised at her sister's harsh tone.

"What's wrong, Marjan?"

"What's wrong? What's wrong is we have a café to run, if you haven't noticed." She stared at the spoon in her hand, unsure of why she was holding it. Her shoulders were aching terribly, and a band of tension was beginning to tighten across her chest. What was she doing?

"Marjan . . ." Bahar started.

Marjan continued to pull open drawers. "Where's the colander? I put it under the sink. Where is it? Is it even washed?" She pointed to the forlorn pile of dirty dishes in a plastic pan.

"Marjan."

"See, this is what I mean. I'm losing my mind with all this mess, all this noise. Do you two understand me?"

She stopped, turned around. Her face softened instantly when she saw her sisters' concerned eyes. Sighing, she let her shoulders drop, placing the ladle and spoon she was holding in each fist on the island.

"I'm all right. Don't look so worried." She pushed the drawer shut with her hip. "You two just have to understand that while you indulge in your petty arguing, I have to think of a hundred different things at once." She spotted the colander on top of the refrigerator. "I would just appreciate some understanding," she said, reaching for the implement.

Layla bit her lip. "Sorry," she said contritely, moving to the order carousel.

"I'm sorry too," said Bahar. She started to take off her coat. "I'll stay."

Marjan held out her hand. "No. You go. Take your break. But just some quiet next time, okay?"

Bahar and Layla nodded, both still rather stunned. They couldn't remember the last time Marjan had reacted to their nitpicking in this manner, and they were not able to properly register it.

There was quiet indeed after Bahar left. Layla did not say a word for a whole five minutes.

And then, when she could no longer stand to see Marjan so sullen at the stove, she walked over and poked her eldest sister in the ribs.

"Anyway, I think we should go with my theory about Bahar," she said, nodding emphatically.

"And what theory is that?" Marjan said quietly.

"She's got a boyfriend, for sure," Layla said with her customary naughty grin. "Some Irish lover with a beer belly and orange hair coming out of his ears." She doubled over, laughing raucously at the thought.

Marjan allowed herself a small smile. "Oh, Layla," she said with a shake of her head.

Bahar was the last person she could think of who would keep a romance hidden away, she told herself. Not anymore, anyway; not after Hossein.

❋

"AND THAT IS HOW Luigi found the secret to his cannelloni menta cream. One part cream, two parts sugar, three tablespoons peppermint extracto, and one drop of me. He said my sweat tasted like nectar. Imagine if these Irish people knew about it! They would have never even looked at Papa's Pastries, eh?"

Estelle paused, nodding her head at the girl sitting in the hospital bed. She hadn't planned on revealing Luigi's secret ingredient, the sugary essence that made his pastries so dear, but had somehow gotten carried away with her story.

The flush of delight in the young woman's usually pale face told Estelle it had been a wise decision. Her cheeks, which had had a sunken look to them only yesterday, were now rounded and hosting gingery freckles.

She was looking much better than that first day, thought Estelle, when she had been lying with a fever in this big bed. Perhaps her love stories did more good than harm, she told herself.

"I think it is time for a bowl of good food, yes? Plum stew the best for you!" Estelle waved her hands again.

It may have been just a blink of the eyes, but it seemed to Estelle that the girl returned her nod.

Since coming to the hospital, they had made do with a series of pantomime moves for everyday speech; along with the language of blinks and nods, these had been sufficient if not desirable for someone with arthritic tendencies.

The power of speech should never be underestimated, the old widow told herself.

She uncovered a bowl of heated plum stew and set it on the tray in front of the girl. "Marjan brought this last night, when you were sleeping, yes? She says this is the best for strength. We will build your blood now, make it thick and strong, okay?"

The girl blinked again, encouraging Estelle to carry on with her tender nursing. She wasn't speaking, but that was okay. What was more important was that she did not try to hurt herself again. Estelle vowed she would do anything to stop that from happening.

Bending slowly to retrieve a large silver soupspoon from the side table, the widow couldn't help but cringe at the creaks in her weakened hips. Every inch of the descent was a painful reminder of what it is to be human, to be moving toward an inevitable fate.

Straightening with a grimace, she turned once again to her patient. "Yes, that is right. Open for strength," she said, ladling some of the stew into the spoon.

She nodded at the girl's opened mouth and smiled once again.

The fragrance of plumped-up prunes, their burst skins cradling the fortifying strands of *garm* spinach and softened saffron lamb, swirled between them.

She must make an effort to eat more from the list of hot foods Marjan had written for her, Estelle told herself. The darling had meticulously charted the best ingredients and dishes to take at such times, times when she felt not only the pain of her joints but the darkness that came from watching your body turn slowly to stone.

Yes, she must remember the power of balance, thought Estelle, lifting the spoon toward the girl.

Just as she was about to minister the heartening stew, it happened: a terrible force intervened. Her clumpy knuckles suddenly stiffened, opting for a last-minute retreat.

Estelle's hand froze; she dropped the spoon, the silver shattering the stew's purple surface, splattering it onto the clean hospital sheets.

"Santa Maria! *Dio mio!*"

Estelle gasped, squeezing her eyes shut. She leaned against the side of the bed and panted, her calcified hands remaining in the air, suspended by a Svengali of pain. Lightning sparked every single nerve and membrane.

"Please, God." The old widow breathed heavily. "Take my hands, please take this pain." She grimaced as needles stabbed her hands, arms, elbows, neck, and collarbones. Her spine was seizing up as well, the pain moving inch by inch toward her neck. "Please," huffed Estelle, "Santa Maria, I don't want to be a statue today."

Estelle wasn't expecting an immediate answer to her prayer, but an answer came anyway—from as close as the hospital bed.

The girl, the mermaid Estelle had rescued over a week ago, decided to return the favor today.

Leaning slowly over the bowl of piping plum stew, she reached for Estelle's clenched fists.

In a moment the widow would later remember for its intense warmth and little else, the girl fanned open her strange fingers, closed her eyes, and took a deep breath.

Chapter 7

The Female Eunuch

"LADIES ARE HERE for their tea. Two kebab *kuftideh*s, one fried chicken salad, one *gormeh sabzi*, and a bowl of *rosetachio* ice cream," Layla said, pinning the order to the carousel. "The last one's for Filomina Fanning. She says she heard a scoop of ice cream a day was good for the love life. Says she read it in a book called *The Perfumed Garden*. I've never read it, have you, Marjan?"

Marjan placed the lid back on the saffron rice and looked up, mulling the title for a few seconds. "No, I don't think I have," she said. Though she was sure such a book existed, even if she hadn't heard of it.

As the town's librarian, Filomina had resources that ran the gamut of the world of letters: whether it was a question on Laplandish garden trolls, or a treatise on Tahitian hygiene rituals of the late 1700s, Filomina could be relied on for facts.

She had been the first person Marjan had turned to when she needed a copy of Avicenna's masterpiece; Filomina had promptly ordered the *Canon of Medicine* from a fellow bibliophile at the University College of Dublin, with a wink to forget about late fees.

The only topic worth avoiding with the librarian was the latest sunbathing methods; Filomina was still reeling from the last time she'd tried to cultivate a tan and got severely burned by one of Thomas McGuire's faulty sun beds thirteen years earlier. She was one of many in town who had been glad to see the tyrant take to his thorny bed.

"*The Perfumed Garden*," Layla repeated. "Isn't that what you're growing out there?" She pointed to the blooming herbs outside the kitchen window.

Marjan followed her gaze. The hour's rain had left fresh sparkles on the stalks of dill and swathed the mint in a lovely veil.

She shook her head. "You know, I still can't believe they're growing so well, even in this weather. I'm half-thinking of planting a pomegranate bush next."

Layla set down the tub of vanilla ice cream she had taken from the freezer and jumped up. "Just like home! Oh, you have to, Marjan. Plant a pomegranate bush!" she said, clapping her hands.

Marjan laughed. "We'll see, now. It's one thing to plant herbs, but a pomegranate needs constant sun."

She lowered the heat on the simmering plum stew and turned to the brick oven. Using a large paddle, she stoked the smoldering logs inside its large belly. The heat was just right for the kebabs ordered by the Ladies of the Patrician Day Dance Committee.

Marjan turned to Layla once more. "Do you think about Iran often?"

Layla scooped three large, creamy balls into a turquoise bowl. "Sometimes. Not always, not as much as I used to in London." She drizzled rosewater over the ice cream, then reached for a large jar of shelled and crushed pistachio nuts sitting on a shelf over the counter. She held the jar against her hip and stared at the bowl. "I mean, I think about good things, mostly."

"Like what?" Marjan said. She was surprised to find herself whispering.

"I don't know, like my friends at school. Do you remember Christina from across the street? Her family was from Ohio?"

Marjan nodded. There had been many American families living in their neighborhood in northern Tehran during the 1970s. Most had been under contract with the new companies sprouting headquarters like yesterday's barley, bringing with them a confidence in fast-food emporiums and a distaste for everything that was subtle and Persian.

Unlike the British, who in previous decades had lived in dusty, make-do abodes while tending to the demands of their oil executives, the Americans had built themselves movie theaters and hot dog stands, replicating the good old Main Streets of their prairie homeland.

Marjan stoked the embers in the oven again. "Christina . . . she was a couple years older than you, if I remember," she said.

Layla sprinkled a handful of pistachios onto the bowl of ice cream. "She was eight, I was four. She taught me to play hopscotch," she said, grinning at the memory. Then her smile disappeared. "I remember Baba as well."

At the mention of their father, Marjan closed the oven door on the kebabs and turned to her sister. "What do you remember exactly?" She leaned against the counter and folded her arms.

"I remember his Brut cologne, and that he liked to play chess with you. I mean, I know what he looked like, we have that one picture. The one at the ruins of Persepolis?"

Marjan nodded, thinking of the exquisite palaces of Iran's Zoroastrian kings. "That was before you were born."

"I was in Maman's belly." Layla smiled wistfully.

A pang of loneliness shot through Marjan; Layla's memories were so potent, in spite, or perhaps because, of their diffused quality.

Layla placed the bowl of ice cream on a small round platter etched with filigreed patterns. "I remember Baba's face, but only the one in the photo. I mean, I can't remember what he looked like before he died. Is that normal?"

"Well, of course it is. You were a little girl then."

"I still think I should remember more about him. And about Maman, even if she died before I had a memory," Layla said.

Then, tossing her long black hair as though discarding the sad thoughts, she turned to Marjan. Her almond eyes were tilted up and shiny. "Filomina can't wait until the kebabs are done," she said, holding up the tray of ice cream. "Three scoops for a really good day."

Layla exited the kitchen, leaving her oldest sister to conjure her own childhood memories, the Polaroids of that brief and golden age.

✳

THAT AFTERNOON, minutes before the Babylon Café was to close for the day, Marjan allowed herself an indulgence. Shutting the door to the bathroom in the flat above the café, she settled onto the covered toilet seat and opened her box of memories.

The brass jewelry box, the same engraved keepsake Ali had bought her on that high school trip to the Grand Bazaar in Istanbul, was kept on the top shelf of the tiered medicine cabinet installed by Luigi Delmonico all those years back.

The bottom three shelves were Bahar's and Layla's to fill as they pleased, but it was understood by all three sisters that the top tier would be reserved for Marjan and her few precious belongings.

Marjan placed the jewelry box on her lap and opened its lid. She balanced the box on the edge of the bathtub, making sure not to shed any of the sand still embedded in its lining.

The sand, along with a patch of kilim carpet woven by a Baluchi tribe, was a souvenir of their time spent crossing the eastern deserts of Iran. It had taken the three of them only a week to reach the border with Pakistan, that autumn in 1978, but by the time they arrived at the Red Cross refugee camp in Quetta, it had seemed as though a lifetime had gone by.

The box's belly was soft, a pink satin with more than its share of secrets. Within its caresses were their baby gifts, among them the three gold identity bracelets, one for each of their infant wrists.

Bought on the days of their births, the bracelets were engraved with their names—Layla, Bahar, and Marjan—in swirling Farsi script.

Pity the bracelets were too small for any of them to wear now, thought Marjan.

She picked through the bits of jewelry, the stud earrings and ruby ring that had belonged to their mother, Shirin. There was something almost meditative about this ritual of hers, combing through the photos and small keepsakes, even if she touched on some painful memories. It was as if her fingers were actually tracing the milestones each piece represented.

Her hand closed on a smooth, round object, something resembling a marble egg. It was a miniature bar of lotus soap, still in its wrapper, bought on their last trip to the *hammam*. The public bathhouse had been a favorite spot of theirs, a place the three of them liked to go to on Thursdays, the day before the Iranian weekend.

Marjan held the soap to her nose. She took a deep breath, inhaling the downy scent of mornings spent washing and scrubbing with rosewater and lotus products. All at once she heard the laughter once again, the giggles of women making the bathing ritual a party more than anything else. The *hammam* they had attended those last years in Iran was situated near their apartment in central Tehran. Although not as palatial as the turquoise and golden-domed bathhouse of their childhood, it was still a grand building of hot pools and steamy balconies, a place of gossip and laughter.

The women of the neighborhood would gather there weekly to untangle their long hair with tortoiseshell combs and lotus powder, a silky conditioner that left locks gleaming like onyx uncovered. For pocket change, a *dalak* could be hired by the hour. These bathhouse attendants, matronly and humorous for all their years spent whispering local chatter, would scrub at tired limbs with loofahs and mitts of woven Caspian seaweed. Massages and palm readings accompanied platters of watermelon and hot jasmine tea, the afternoons whiled away with naps and dips in the perfumed aqueducts regulated according to their hot and cold properties.

There was always a bridal shower carousing their way through the *hammam*'s various tiled rooms. Equipped with bedroom banter and every hair removal product known to womankind, the ladies of these rowdy parties would pluck and prep the flushed bride for the next night's encounter.

When Marjan had heard of Bahar's intended marriage to Hossein Jaferi, on that awful day she had returned from the detention center at Gohid, one of the only hopeful images she had clung to was the thought of a happy bridal party.

She might not be able to change her sister's mind about marrying, Marjan remembered thinking, but she could prepare Bahar for her new life with a strengthening rosewater rinse. The tonic was sprinkled over the bride's head at the end of her ablutions, a cleansing ritual meant to wash away all doubts about her new life ahead.

Marjan returned the soap to the box. She closed its lid, tracing her thumb over the engraved desert roses.

She had never been able to throw her sister a party; as head of the neighborhood's most conservative family, Khanoum Jaferi abhorred such public displays of sensuality. Bahar's future mother-in-law had insisted on a more subdued bridal get-together, consisting of prayers to the Almighty and a long supper of *khaleh pacheh*, roasted sheep's head.

"Are you all right?" A knock came from the other side of the bathroom door. It was Bahar.

Marjan quickly placed the box back on the top tier of the medicine cabinet and opened the door. "Just finishing."

Bahar stepped aside to let her onto the landing. She looked at Marjan with concern. "What's wrong?"

"Nothing. Why?"

"Well, I don't know. After your outburst yesterday—"

"It wasn't an outburst." Marjan stepped down the stairs. "Honestly, Bahar, you're not the only one who gets overwhelmed by things in the kitchen. I am allowed to feel stress sometimes, you know."

Bahar followed her down. "But you never have before. What's wrong? Is it that Englishman? That Julian?"

Marjan threw her a withering look.

Bahar lifted a shoulder. "I'm just mentioning it. I've heard a few things, that's all."

"And what's the gossip today?" Marjan asked, undoing her apron. The kitchen was shining from its latest cleaning: Bahar had taken her worries out on the counters, it seemed. They smelled deliciously of rosewater cleanser.

"Oh, just that he's got his eye on the street. Probably getting ready to buy shops after doing up that old house."

"And why is that a bad thing? If we have the right to build a new life, so should he, don't you think?"

Bahar sniffed. "Maybe. Sounds fishy, that's all I'm saying."

Marjan shook her head. "What else have you heard on your daily walks?"

Bahar blinked. "What do you mean, daily walks? What walks?"

"Your walks to the shops. What other news have you gathered in that nest of yours?"

"Nothing. Why?"

Marjan turned to her sister. It suddenly crossed her mind to tell Bahar about the girl Estelle had rescued, about all that had been going on the last week at the hospital, but she quickly shook the thought off. Bahar would not be able to handle it. It would do neither of them any good to get into that story.

"Marjan."

Marjan looked up. "Yes?"

"You're daydreaming again."

"Was I?"

Bahar drew her lips into a thin line. "Better not be about that Englishman," she said, taking up the scrubbing brush next to the sink. "He's not worth it, if you want my opinion."

Marjan did not reply. There was no point in it: no man would ever be good enough for either of her sisters in Bahar's eyes.

❋

"HE'S MY NEPHEW, and I was standing right over him and his brother during his christening," Marjan heard Fiona Athey say as she pulled open the salon door, "but I have no qualms in saying he's being a right old bastard the way he's treating you."

Fiona turned at the tinkle of the door chime. She beckoned Marjan in with her hand. "Which reminds me, I've still to lend you that book I was meaning to."

Her junior stylist, Evie Watson, was crumpled up in one of the salon's pink leather armchairs, her eyes rimmed with tears. She was still holding a broom in one hand as she blew her swollen nose with the edge of her flowery smock.

"What book's that?" She sniffed, giving Marjan a pathetic smile.

Fiona switched on the row of theatrical vanity lights over the mirrors. "*The Female Eunuch.* It'll open up your eyes, Evie my dear," she said, slipping on her bib. "Men are as incomplete a sex as there ever was, and that Peter Donnelly is one likely candidate."

Fresh tears rolled down Evie's thin face, causing her to plunge further into the folds of her smock.

"What's happened, Evie?" Marjan asked softly, kneeling down to pat the young woman's hand. She noticed the Claddagh ring that Evie always wore on her right ring finger was turned around, the heart in the middle open to the world, an eligibility sign. "Did you and Peter have another fight?"

Evie nodded her head and blew her nose again.

Fiona tugged at a tissue carton, handing her the last Kleenex. "It's more than a fight, I'm afraid, Marjan. She's told him she'd rather snog a donkey than get back with him again. Mighty improvement, if you ask me."

At the reminder, Evie threw back her head and bawled, letting go of the broom in her hand. The broom handle swung toward the salon's mascot, a mannequin by the name of Fifi O'Shea, just missing her tissue-enhanced bosom.

"He said he was moving up in the world! Needs a woman with more meat on her bones!" Evie howled, pummeling her thighs with her bony little fists.

Marjan threw Fiona a bewildered look.

"For rearing children," Fiona explained. She patted her own generous curves. "That *amadan*," she said, shaking her head.

"Moving up? Where's he going?"

Evie blinked, her eyes red-rimmed. "He's starting a real estate course in Castlebar. Him and Michael. Fancies himself a landlord all of a sudden."

Fiona sniffed. "Landlocked is more like it."

"To think, Marjan," Evie said with remorse, "I gave up all your lovely sweets for the sake of my diets!"

Marjan stroked her hand sympathetically. "It's never too late. Stop by for tea later and I'll set you a proper pastry plate, okay?"

Evie sniffed her thanks and grabbed the broom again.

"Make one up for me while you're at it." Fiona patted the seat before her. "What'll it be this month, Marjan? Your usual trim?"

"I was thinking of something a little different," said Marjan, settling into the chair. She stared at her reflection. Her cloud of wavy hair was usually impervious to modern hairstyles. "Maybe some layers or bangs?"

Fiona tapped her chin with a wide-toothed comb. "Layers, huh?"

"Or maybe a color? Something warm for the autumn?"

"Hmmm . . . I don't know now. Not that kind of warmth he's going after," Fiona replied. "Not from what I hear, anyway." She winked at the mirror.

Marjan turned around. "Who?"

"You know who. I'd be careful, Marjan. That one looks like he's read a few books, if you know what I mean. Got a way with words, Julian Winthrop Muir."

Marjan's lips curved. "I told you, there's nothing going on. We're just friends."

"Wish I had a friend like that," Evie remarked, sweeping the floor around Fifi O'Shea.

Fiona grinned, jabbed her back with the comb. "Go on, open your gob. What's the latest there? Getting some loving or what?"

Marjan flipped through the magazine, well aware that both Evie and Fiona were waiting. When neither of them moved, she closed the magazine and glanced in the mirror. "It's nothing. Just a bit of talk."

Fiona snorted. "Nothing, huh? Didn't look like it from where I sat the other night. Did you at least get a good rubdown after all that talk?"

"Fiona!" Marjan could feel her blush.

"What?"

"Isn't that a bit on the crude side?"

"You want romance? Okay." She nodded. "Has he declared his devotions to you yet, madam?" She swept the comb in her hand into a deep bow.

Evie sidled up to the mirror, her face lit from excitement. The rush of fresh gossip had cleared her tears.

"Go on. Has he asked you out again?"

Marjan turned to face the two women. "He's come in a couple of times for lunch . . ." She trailed off.

"And?" Fiona tilted her head to one side.

"And, no. Nothing. He said he had a good time at the pub and that's all."

"His loss," replied Fiona, taking a clip from her bib collar. She pointed it to Evie. "See? Incomplete. Something missing, even from the ones who look like they should know better."

Evie commiserated with a small nod.

Marjan turned back to the mirror. "I'm glad he hasn't asked me again, actually," she said, staring at the magazine on her lap.

Fiona pinned the side of Marjan's head. "And why is that, exactly? You're entitled to a bit of craic like the rest of us."

"I'm just not ready yet. For dating, and everything." Although she had not told Fiona all the details of her time with Ali, the hairdresser was the one person in Ballinacroagh who knew of the first time Marjan had ever given her heart away. Only to have it shattered.

Fiona dragged the comb down her customer's crown. "I know. But who ever is ready? Listen, incomplete sex or not, men are still handy for a few things, if you follow my meaning."

"Maybe . . ." Marjan shrugged. "I just—I don't know much about him." She looked up. "He's been to Iran."

"There you go. Don't know anyone for miles who can claim that."

"Peter says he bought back the Hall for beggars' pay," offered Evie. "You could be a landlady if you play your cards right, Marjan."

Marjan glanced in the mirror. She could see Fiona and Evie grinning behind her. "You two! You think you're so funny!"

Fiona laughed. "What's funny is the way your ears turn a beet at the mention," she said, reaching for her scissors. She snipped a lock of Marjan's curly hair.

"I've got news that'll keep them rosy as ever—" Evie stopped short, grimaced. "Oh, maybe I shouldn't . . ."

Fiona stopped snipping. Both she and Marjan looked at the younger woman expectantly.

" 'Fess up. You've gone and started it already," Fiona said.

Evie bit her bottom lip. "Well, it's sort of about Layla."

Marjan turned in her seat. "What about Layla?"

Evie held up her hands. "Now you didn't hear it from me. If she asks, wasn't even I who saw him."

"Him?"

"Oh, for the love of— Just get on with it." Fiona blew out an impatient breath.

Evie raised her shoulders, tilted her head. "Well, the other day, on the Saturday, now, I was making my way into Castlebar, down the roundabout near Dunne's. You know the one that's always getting the scraps? Sure didn't Tom Ford's bull take a licking the other month, coming in from the side road and all—" Evie stopped. Fiona was tapping her feet impatiently. "Oh, right. Well, who do I see coming out of Alfred Bennett's Chemists but Malachy McGuire himself. There he was, rushin' out, head down, with a nice brown bag tucked under his arm. A *small* brown bag, if you get my drift."

Marjan turned to Fiona, confused.

"There's only one thing Bennett's tucks away in plain bags," Fiona explained. "Every young lad's worst nightmare."

"What nightmare?" Marjan stood up from the chair, locks of cut hair falling from her shoulder. "What are you talking about, Evie?"

"It's nothing, nothing to worry about, I'm sure. It could be any number of things," Evie said uncomfortably.

"Protection, Marjan. Malachy was buying protection," Fiona said.

Marjan brought her hand to her forehead. Protection. Oh, God, she had completely forgotten about Layla. She looked up. "When did you say this happened, Evie?"

"Last Saturday. Day after the fire."

Marjan sat back down, trying to register the information. "I can't believe it. She promised she wouldn't do anything."

Fiona patted her on the shoulder. "Ah sure, it's better safe than sorry. I don't want to even think of what my Emer's up to in that Los Angeles. Between the three of us now—and that includes you, Evie—I had her get a prescription from a doctor up North. Best have her prepared for the land of men, eh? Not likely they'd take the step. Malachy's a rare boy, that's what I say."

"But she's not ready, Fiona! I told her so. I told her to wait," Marjan replied in frustration.

Evie took up the broom again. "Sure, I've waited, Marjan, and look what happened. Tossed to the ditches by Peter Donnelly himself. Should have gone to the Beach like he wanted. Now he's off getting some Castlebar heifer up the pole, I bet."

"You two." Fiona shook her head and took up the scissors again. "Remind me to get two copies of *The Female Eunuch*, Evie." She snipped another layer of Marjan's dark hair with expert swiftness. "I'll make feminists of you lot yet."

Chapter 8

Walking the Plank

"HAVE YOU SEEN LAYLA?" The door slammed behind Marjan as she looked around the kitchen. Bahar was at the island, prepping eggplants for the next day's stew special, *khoresht bademjoon*.

"What's wrong? What happened?"

Marjan stepped onto the landing. She could hear the television upstairs. "Nothing. I just need her for something."

She placed her hand on the banister and was about to turn when a knock came on the back door.

Bahar stopped chopping again. "Marjan." She put down her knife and craned her neck to the stained-glass partition. "It's a man."

Marjan made her way back down and to the door. After a moment's glance, she recognized the face behind the colored glass: it was Padraig Carey, from the town council.

Layla bounded down the steps, stopping short when she saw her sisters. "Hey, isn't that the councilman? What does he want?"

"I don't know," said Marjan. "Maybe he's here about that license extension. I applied for it last month, remember?"

She reached for the door handle. "For goodness' sakes, Bahar. Don't look so frightened."

❄

PADRAIG CAREY LEANED over the wooden island, staring curiously at a jar of mixed *torshi*. "Looks like your vegetables need a bit longer in the pot," he remarked, tapping the glass with his finger.

"They're pickled. *Torshi*," Marjan explained. "Margaret's thinking of putting it on the pub menu, you know."

Padraig looked shocked. "She's getting to be very cosmopolitan, my wife."

"She's a very smart woman," replied Marjan. It was no secret that Padraig was often referred to as Margaret McGuire's Little Big Man. An apt description, considering the councilman's many shortcomings. She made her way to a stack of clear tea glasses. "Can I get you a cup of tea?"

Padraig raised his briefcase to his chest. "No, no—thanks all the same, Marjan. No, I'm here on some town business." He coughed, shifting from foot to foot as his eyes darted across the kitchen. He thought of throwing a perfunctory smile at the three women standing before him but decided against it. Best not send out the wrong signals, he told himself. Who knew how a smile could be translated. Especially by these dark-haired vixens. "Yes, town business it is," he repeated.

"I thought so," Marjan remarked. It was rare to see Padraig near the café. As far as she could remember, he had tried their lunch only once, on Margaret's fortieth birthday. "You've never come around the back before."

Padraig let out a strained laugh. "You've got a point there, Marjan. You've got a point there, all right."

He glanced at the counter, with its piles of pots and plates, washed and gleaming. It was the first time he had seen the café since the fire that had taken half its back wall two summers ago. The entire place was spotless, he marveled. It wasn't nearly the backward operation Thomas McGuire had claimed.

"Is it about the license? I think I filed all the proper papers."

Padraig patted his briefcase. "Filed away all right. No problem there." He turned to Marjan. "No, no, it's another sort of business I've come about." He cleared his throat. "Concerning Mrs. Delmonico."

Marjan looked apprehensively at her sisters. "Estelle?"

Padraig held out his palm. "Now, I wouldn't be here if it were not for the concern of a few folk. Personally, I see no point in stirring the breeze if there's no need for it." He pressed his lips grimly. The council post had its perks, he thought, but this was not one of them.

Marjan nodded for him to go on.

"If it were up to me, you realize, I'd say we'd best look straight ahead, put the past behind us."

"I understand," said Marjan.

"I'm not so daft not to know there's not a whole world out there, filled with all sorts of creeds and colors. Sure, there's been more than once I've hoped for a tan myself, to be honest. Going dead white to pale would be a mighty improvement." He broke into a grin at his own joke.

When Marjan did not respond, he coughed again, embarrassed, and pulled his short body up straighter. "But I have to ask all the same."

"Of course. What is the problem, exactly?"

"The problem, the problem is the problem of a lawbreaking exactly," Padraig said with a sober expression. He reached into his breast pocket, pulled out a small piece of scrap paper. "It's been brought to my attention that there's a patient up at Mayo General. A relative of Mrs. Delmonico's." He squinted at the piece of paper. "A niece, is it?"

"Is Gloria here?" Layla piped up from the landing.

Marjan held out her hand behind her, shutting Layla up. "Her niece? I don't think so." She paused. "I think Estelle would have told us if Gloria was in town," she said, turning to her sisters with a nod. Their only response was confused stares.

"Well, then, who is this Rosa Bella?" Padraig consulted the paper again. "Yes, that's right, is it? Rosa Bella. Sources tell me she's been taking a bed at the hospital the last week. A friend of yours, then?"

"Marjan, what's going on?" Bahar's face was ghostly.

Marjan shrugged, trying to keep her voice as composed as possible. "I don't know," she said, aware of her lie.

Her mind raced to her last visit to the hospital; one of the nurses had been very friendly with her, she remembered. Spent a few good minutes asking her about Iran and London.

She hadn't asked anything about the girl, though.

Padraig was waiting for an answer.

"I'm not sure I understand, Mr. Carey. Why are you asking all these questions?"

"Well, I'm not one to call out falsehoods, but to be fair, you have been seen coming in and out of Mayo General every day the last week. I've got an eyewitness that would vouch to your deliveries."

"Yes, I've been taking meals up to one of the patients. It's not against the law, is it? Feeding someone?"

"It's not against the law, no, but holding information from officials is. This is Ireland, after all," Padraig said pointedly. He paused for a moment before continuing. "Now, what can you tell me about this patient, this friend of yours?"

Marjan shook her head. "She's not a friend. I don't know anything about her, actually. Estelle—Mrs. Delmonico—and I, we just make an effort to visit the sick in our free time." She made an effort to smile broadly. "It does Estelle good to get out and meet people. The hospital is a good place for her. We take food and give it out to patients, that's all."

It was a stretch, but it seemed to appease the councilman. Perhaps it was because his thoughts began to move to the pot of saffron lamb shank softening on the Aga.

He took a long sniff and sighed. "Well, I'm glad to hear of it," he replied. "Wouldn't want Estelle to fall into any kind of mess."

He snapped his briefcase and nodded to Bahar and Layla. "Now if you tell me there's nothing to be concerned with, I'll leave it at that. Won't even bother Mrs. Delmonico or the hospital about it."

Marjan nodded. "Of course."

The councilman took a moment to formulate his question. "It's about this lass, now. This Ms. Rosa. The one you've been feeding, like." He paused, squaring his gaze on Marjan. She nodded again, meeting his gaze head-on. She hoped he hadn't noticed that she had been holding her breath for the last minute. Padraig continued. "Is she or isn't she at this moment, while still at Mayo General, is she or isn't she with child? A child she tried to do away with, mind you. Against the law, and with her own two hands." The councilman raised his eyebrows. "Otherwise known as abortion, Marjan. Abortion of a sacred child."

"SO WHAT YOU'RE saying is, you lied. You lied about a law that was broken." Bahar paced the space around the wooden island, wringing her forearms red.

"It wasn't broken. And I'm very aware that I lied. But I had no other choice, and you know it." Marjan sat at the kitchen table, suddenly exhausted.

"Who is she, Marjan?" Layla asked.

"I don't know. No one does. She just appeared."

"I can't believe you, I really can't." Bahar swiveled abruptly on her heels. "Who cares who she is? She was trying to kill her baby."

Layla frowned. "Go easy. You don't even know her."

"I don't need to know her to know it's a sin. *Haram*, Marjan," Bahar said, pinching the thumb and forefingers of both her hands to punctuate the word. "You remember what that means, don't you?"

Haram, forbidden.

Marjan shook her head. "That's not for us to say. And it wouldn't have done any good if the guards went up to the hospital. It wouldn't have changed anything."

"Of course it would. If someone breaks the law, they have to pay for it."

Layla threw Bahar a look of disgust before turning back to Marjan. "Can we visit her?"

"No—maybe later. Obviously people are talking in the hospital."

Bahar huffed, her hands on her hips. "Great, just great. How do you think I'm going to feel, walking down the street, going into shops, doing all those errands you've got me running on, with everyone chattering about this? Everyone will know you've lied!" Her voice was at its highest pitch.

"Since when do you care what everyone around here thinks?" Layla asked, with marked sarcasm.

"Wait, Layla." Marjan held up her hand as she got up from the table. She went over to Bahar, who had propped herself against the sink, her shoulders trembling from a mixture of fear and fury.

Marjan took her sister's cold hands in hers. She looked into her sister's heart-shaped face, her own expression softening. "Bahar."

"What?"

"Can you please look at me?"

Bahar shifted her gaze to Marjan. Her pupils were as large as her dark brown eyes. Marjan rubbed her sister's hands, pausing for a moment. "I need your promise, Bahar. Both of you."

"Promise? What promise?" Bahar's upper lip began to tremble.

"You have to promise me you're not going to tell anybody about this. No one is to know what she tried to do in the Bay. Do you understand?"

Bahar sniffed. "Too late. Everyone knows about it anyway."

"We don't know that for sure," Marjan said, with studied patience. "It won't do anybody any good if we acknowledge the gossip, now, will it?"

"Can't I tell Malachy?"

"Not even Malachy. All right?" Marjan gave Layla a knowing glance. She'd have to deal with Malachy and Layla later, she told herself. After she sorted Estelle out.

Her mind began to swim with everything that needed to be done.

Layla nodded. "I've got some clothes you could take up to her," she offered.

"That's a great idea." Marjan turned back to Bahar. "Bahar? Not a word, okay?"

Bahar stared straight ahead again.

"Bahar?"

"What? What do you want?"

"I want to know that you won't tell anyone. I want you to understand that I kept this from you because I thought it was the best thing to do."

Bahar turned her eyes back to Marjan's. They had a cold, steely glare. "I don't understand," she said. "I don't understand who this person is, why she's someone you and Estelle need to protect. I don't understand why I'm always the last one to know about anything."

She took her hands out of Marjan's. "And it's still a sin. Even if I don't talk about it."

She pushed past her sisters and out of the kitchen, the double doors flapping hollowly behind her.

❄

THE WHEELCHAIR WHEELS crunched easily up the gravel walk, arriving smoothly at the cottage door thanks to Dr. Parshaw's exertions. A minute later they were stationed next to Mrs. Delmonico's linen couch, near a side table holding a bowl of fruity bonbons.

Dr. Hewey Parshaw led Marjan and Estelle into the kitchen, where they resumed the talk they had started earlier in the hospital.

"I would have preferred another week, but it's not a possibility we can entertain, you understand."

He tried to keep his worry in check, knowing it would be of no help to the two women. The fact that they'd had to rush through the discharge procedures, bundling his patient into Mrs. Delmonico's little Honda—with furtive glances over their shoulders—had not helped maintain the calm he strove to achieve most times.

As it was, all three women looked as though they needed some medical attention. They were far too pale and agitated for his liking.

Estelle laid her chubby hand on his arm. "Thank you, Doctor," she said. "You have done enough. Now I take it from here."

Dr. Parshaw shook his head. "I should have known someone would surmise the cause of the infection. Her skin has all the markings of trauma." He leaned out the doorway to check on the young woman. She was still sitting in the wheelchair, looking down at her hands.

"I will have to show the guards those records if they ask. It is my duty, you understand." A look of unease came over him.

Estelle turned to Marjan. "So you think that will happen, Marjan? Will the police come to ask questions?"

"I can't be sure. Padraig Carey seemed to take it that it was only an infection." Marjan paused, biting her lip in consternation. "I did lie."

"There is lying and there is lying. You did what was right, darling. I only pray that this is not bad for you, Doctor. For your job," said Estelle.

"If it comes to pass, then I will deal with it. Though I must say, it would be a pity to leave Mayo. Homesickness aside, I have come to appreciate this Ireland. A fine place, despite some of its more archaic laws."

Dr. Parshaw left the Delmonico cottage after helping to settle his patient in Estelle's four-poster bed. Uncomfortable with the money Estelle had offered for his extra services, he had bartered with the women for a plate of barberry rice and cucumber yogurt dip instead.

"Just one more thing," he said on his way out. "Try to get her to say something. If she talks, we can get a better grasp on things. Then she can defend herself and her decision."

Marjan stood next to the bed as the widow rushed about pulling open drawers.

"I will take in all of Luigi's pantaloons, yes?" Estelle whipped out an enormous pair of striped pajama bottoms. She added them to a pile growing on her arm. "You are a quarter of his size, can you believe this?" She looked nervous, thought Marjan, not her usual exuberant self. "A man must be round, that is what I always say. Round and soft. Yes, yes."

The old widow threw the pile of pajamas on the edge of the bed. The young red-haired woman remained in her usual silence, staring out the nearest window, which in this instance looked on to Estelle's fine lavender and rosemary garden.

Marjan bit her lip, took a deep breath. This was as good a time as any to try talking, she decided. Dr. Parshaw was right: they needed something to hold on to in case Padraig Carey came knocking.

She moved around to the right side of the bed, choosing a spot halfway down the patchwork cover. The girl kept her eyes on the outside garden as Marjan sat down.

This would be the first time she would be speaking to her directly, Marjan realized. All the other days, when she had delivered food or helped Estelle with arrangements at the hospital, she had kept her distance, unsure of what, if anything, she could say that would make a difference.

The silence had never stopped Estelle from chattering away. But that was Estelle, thought Marjan. Kindness incarnate.

She turned to the young woman. At the moment she was wearing one of Layla's T-shirts, one with cartoon bears frolicking on a marshmallow cloud. This close up Marjan could see the freckles on that smooth, pale face, the girl's delicate nose and wide gray eyes filled with immeasurable pain.

She looked only a few years older than her youngest sister, thought Marjan, feeling maternal instincts rush over her. She looked down at the girl's hands. They were clenched at the duvet's end, the thin skin between her fingers almost indiscernible when they were closed so tight.

Syndactyly, Dr. Parshaw had called it. "Webbing of the digits. It is an abnormality that is quite rare, especially the kind she has. A linking of all the fingers is almost never seen, even among syndactylics."

"So she is not a mermaid?" Estelle had looked somewhat disappointed.

Dr. Parshaw's tired face had cracked into a smile. "No, not a mermaid, I'm afraid, Mrs. Delmonico. But you never know, eh?"

The hands suddenly disappeared under the duvet. A stark look came across that young face.

"Hello," Marjan started. Where was she going to begin? she wondered. "I'm Marjan. I'm Mrs. Delmonico's friend."

Those gray eyes took their time to travel up.

They concentrated on a point right behind Marjan's shoulder, glistening with a wet sheen.

"You know who Marjan is, yes?" Estelle stepped beside the bed. She had a pair of Luigi's striped pantaloons wrapped around her neck like a scarf.

Marjan nodded, continuing. "I know this is really hard for you to do, to talk, I mean. I want you to know that whatever you tell us, it'll stay right here."

Marjan paused, floundering for the next sentence. "You are not in any kind of trouble," she said finally.

"No trouble at all!" exclaimed Estelle, moving closer to the bed. "Eh, remember when I told you the story about the War? How me and my mama hid in an underground train station while there were bombs flying everywhere? Remember I said we were so quiet, like a mouse, catching our breath so those soldiers above our head did not hear our thoughts? Yes?"

She perched on a nearby armchair. "That was a time for silence. Sometimes it is right to keep quiet. Sometimes it is right to shout. Yes?"

The girl looked from Marjan to Estelle, then back to the coverlet's cross-stitched squares. Her long, pale lashes held back the welling in her eyes, but only just.

Marjan looked at Estelle in desperation. This was not going well.

Estelle took her cue. "Maybe you have a mama, a mama that is looking for her little girl. Maybe you tell us, and we can bring her to you?"

The tears began then, streaming steadily, hanging on the girl's small chin before plunging onto the cross-stitch.

"Oh . . ." Estelle flew up from the chair and put her soft arms around the girl's shoulders. "Shhh, *cara mia*, it is okay. It is going to be okay." She rocked the girl and shushed her crying as the soft sobs kept coming.

Marjan felt the heavy lump in her throat. It wasn't time for secrets after all.

"Marjan?" Estelle tilted her head to the dresser. "Can you please turn on the radio? A bit of music for everybody?"

Marjan nodded thankfully and made her way to the oak dresser. A blue transistor radio, with fabric-covered speakers, sat to one corner, staid and petlike. She twiddled with the power setting, the lump of sadness making its way down to her stomach.

She should have been more sensitive with her tone, she told herself. She should have taken her time and not rushed the girl.

"Forty-five point five AM. That is the nice Irish music," suggested Estelle, rubbing her hands up and down the young woman's arms. She had quieted her crying, but the girl's face was still bent with the weight of her troubles.

Marjan turned the dial, stopping just before the desired number. She thought her ears had tricked her, but no . . . they had been right.

Her eyes widened when she heard the familiar voice crackling through the static lines: "And that's it for our brief history of the Rat Pack. Sure, Sin City never sounded so grand.

"Right so, folks, the bell has rung for my first day on the mighty airwaves. A big thank-you to my lovely assistant, Mrs.

Boylan, who kept the sanity and craic aflow, not to mention lovely takeaway cups of bergamot tea from our very own Babylon Café. Couldn't have gotten through the three hours without some salubrious refreshment of the liquid sort.

"I'd also like to thank the good folks at Mid-West FM for their lend of an ear and a hand when it came to my proposition. We all know what a competitive world it is, this business of show, and I'm glad to say that there are a few pure hearts left out there to shine the way.

"So it's a *sláinte* from me until the next. You've been listening to Craic FM! And don't forget to tune in every teatime but Sundays for your regular dose!

"Here's a bit of Cyndi Lauper to take you into the noon hour—'Girls Just Wanna Have Fun' . . . This is Father Mahoney, and all is right with the world!"

Chapter 9

Cycles and Revolutions

"A GRAND MORNING TO YOU ALL! This is your deejay, Father Fergal Mahoney, coming to you live on Craic FM!

"Well, folks, I was laying out the tunes and craic for the day when I came across a bit of local trivia that might be of interest to some of our older listeners—and maybe those with a long memory as well: there seems to be a newcomer among our fold. That's right, folks, a certain prodigal son that's returned to claim the ancestral home, not far from the shores of our own village. It's been a good few years since we've seen life in those hallowed grounds, and I for one am welcoming a return to the good old days.

"Speaking of good old days: my lovely assistant, Mrs. Boylan, has just reminded me of the Samhain next fortnight Saturday— that's All Hallows' Eve for the more puritanically minded.

"Our very own councilman Padraig Carey has graciously offered the Town Hall for what I hope will be our last hurrah of a fund-raiser—a ceili, in the name of all the sprites and fairy creatures who will be roaming the land at midnight. The dance will be one of many get-togethers for this holiday season, and I'll be expecting all your earthly faces there.

"And on that note, to celebrate the start of the holidays, and to welcome the latest addition to our shores, I'm starting things off with one of my favorite love tunes, 1968's 'Son of a Preacher Man': take it away, Dusty!"

Father Mahoney felt his stomach flitter and flutter. He didn't think he could do it. Not really. But done it he had, and with just that bit of pizzazz.

It wasn't as hard as he'd thought it would be. All it had taken was one little money order in the mail, and six weeks later here it was: his very own radio studio, transmitting throughout the whole of the West of Ireland!

Was this feeling, he wondered, what artists called "tapping into the collective unconscious"? Now there was something to think about, all right. The priest leaned back in his chair and studied the bulky transceiver on the table before him. It had weighed a mighty kilo, he'd discovered while taking it out of its large carton, but it was a sciatic he was happy to pull for the joy it was going to bring him.

Of course, the priest reminded himself, it wouldn't be enough to play his extensive collection of Hall and Oates records and be done with it; he needed a platform of sorts, a metaphysical pulpit that would serve to expedite witticisms without the slightest hint of preachiness. It was all about seduction when it came right down to it; he needed a hook at the very get-go.

Having curtailed a heady and youthful career as a stand-up comedian before entering a Tipperary seminary in 1945, the jolly priest knew more than your average frocked professional about the importance of seducing one's audience. In the bustling world of entertainment, he would be vying for hearts and souls with a vast and varied selection of options, all of which were growing more fractured and peculiar as the years rolled toward the millennium.

Take Beta machines, for instance. Those cumbersome boxes were nothing compared with the elegance of a silent projector, beaming Keaton and Chaplin onto a giant screen. Still, "videos" were all the rage at the moment, as were the emporiums to rent the tapes.

Even nearby Castlebar had its own video rental store now, a likely reason why the film house was advertising two-for-one tickets to the latest Eddie Murphy blockbuster.

Now there was a comedian, thought Father Mahoney, that wily Eddie. He had hoped to catch the ever-cheeky chameleon's show on his trip to New York City last May but had ended up going to an interesting do in a place named Brooklyn; it was called a house party, if he remembered correctly. Not unlike the ceilis, the dances and roaring sing-alongs one could still find in homes on this side of the Atlantic.

Father Mahoney shook his head. He had been daydreaming again. Sure, if he didn't stop himself, he could go on forever, contemplating all the trappings of entertainment now available to the public at large: he hadn't even gotten started on the uncontrollable charms of those singing devices, those very Japanese of creations, the karaoke machines. He could devote an entire show to talking about those electronic Circes.

A gentle tapping on the large window in his makeshift studio ended the priest's mental meanderings. He looked up to find Mrs. Boylan's kindly face staring back at him.

His housekeeper was making gestures akin to those of an air traffic controller giving the go-ahead for another takeoff. The priest motioned for her to come around to the small side door at the vestry, where she appeared a few moments later.

"Sorry, Father, but I wasn't too sure if you were on air or not. Didn't want to barge in there so, while you were making your accounts."

"That's quite all right, Geraldine. Point to be taken—might have to construct myself a system of warning."

"Maybe we can get one of those spare confessional lamps, and whenever you are on air, you can just flick it on, so."

"Now, that's a grand idea," praised Father Mahoney. He looked at his housekeeper of fifteen years expectantly. "Was there something you wanted?"

Geraldine Boylan started. "Oh! Forget my own head if it wasn't stuck to my shoulders now. Marjan Aminpour's here to see you. She's just outside the door."

"Well, let her in here, then. And bring down some of those lovely scones you have perfected so. The boysenberry ones. Topped yourself this time, Geraldine."

Mrs. Boylan smiled with delight. She disappeared out the side door, letting Marjan in.

Timing couldn't have been more fortuitous, thought the priest. If there was one person to give him a good critique of his progress, it was the lovely cook of the Babylon Café.

❖

AFTER A SCRUMPTIOUS TEA BREAK of boysenberry scones and the bergamot tea from the packed leaves Marjan had brought, Father Mahoney found her primed for questioning.

"All right, be honest now. I can take a critique like the best of them. From one artist to another, what did you think of my new pet project? Do you think I've made an entire mess of it?" The priest wiped scone crumbs off his dark trousers and looked at her in anticipation.

Marjan smiled. "Not at all. I only caught the last of your program yesterday, but I think it's a wonderful idea." She paused. "I wouldn't call myself an artist, though."

"Oh, but you are, my dear. Masterpieces, those bits of heaven you call chickpea cookies. You saw how many I gobbled up during the Bonfire."

Marjan smiled again, remembering how she had caught the priest slipping a handful of the clover-shaped cookies into his jacket pockets after his eloquent speech. Glancing around, she took in the radio equipment wedged into one corner of the vestry stockroom, which, besides a mixing deck and microphone, boasted a shiny, top-of-the-line turntable. "You're able to transmit from here? That's amazing."

"All you need is a satellite," the priest explained. "Modern technology has its advantages, though they are few and far in between." He flicked on the transceiver. "This miraculous box, along with the antenna I've got out back, pins down a frequency, one that is not already taken by nearby stations—akin, you might say, to divining water with a mere rod."

"Is that when someone points a stick at the ground?"

"That and the same. But this stick goes up into the cosmos, sending my voice out on waves. *Radio* waves." He paused, his face alight with excitement. "But you've not come here to talk about my next monologue. What can I do for you, my dear?"

Marjan wasn't really sure what the priest could do for her. She knew she could trust him to keep the girl's secret, but confiding in him would still be putting both Dr. Parshaw's and Estelle's reputations in jeopardy, not something she was willing to do in order to unburden her own worries. But then, what was she doing here, in a church, in the middle of the day?

"It's about someone I know. Someone who has been going through a hard time lately," Marjan began.

Father Mahoney nodded encouragingly.

Marjan continued, feeling out her words as well as the reason behind them. "I'm worried about this person. I don't know what I can do to help her—them."

"And has this person come to you for help? What I mean is, does this person want your help?"

"Maybe. I'm not sure. She's been in a lot of pain, that I know. But I don't think she's ready to talk about it." She paused. "I think her situation has reminded me of things I had hoped would stay in the past."

"I often find it interesting how we mirror each other's concerns without knowing it. Have you talked to this person at all about the matter? Maybe if they, er, she, knew you were worried about her, she would be happy to open up and let you into her world."

"That's the problem, Father. She won't talk. She can't talk, it seems. And it has the two of us very worried."

The priest mulled over the information. "And you are sure this person is in pain? Currently?"

Marjan nodded.

"But it was my understanding that the migraines had long gone."

"Migraines?"

"Er, the pain. The pain was gone."

"No, I mean, I don't think the pain is gone." Marjan thought of the antibiotics Dr. Parshaw had prescribed. "Well, maybe the physical pain. Most of that might be healing, but not the real pain. Not the real reason behind her actions."

"And you've tried expressing your concern, in a gentle manner? The soft touch after all . . ."

Marjan nodded. "I tried. I think I made things worse, though. I wish there wasn't so much sadness in her—it seems to be everywhere I turn lately."

Father Mahoney gave her a sympathetic nod. "It's your sensitive nature talking. You're open, that's all, absorbing your loved ones' feelings. You are like the transmitter here, taking in the waves, scrambling them, and trying to make the most of all the information."

He paused, forming his fingers into a studied steeple. "My

best advice to you, Marjan, is this: her search is not over yet. Her road is a long one, so give her some time. She'll come around to talking about it soon enough."

"That's the thing about time, Father. I'm not sure if it does help at all. With the past, I mean," Marjan said quietly, staring down at her teacup. "Every time I think we are all getting better, stronger, something comes along to shatter that idea."

She paused again, unsure of where she was going. She was about to end the conversation when suddenly it came pouring out of her: "All my life I've been struggling, trying to build a home for us, trying to make something beautiful we could all be proud of, but it doesn't seem to be enough. It's my responsibility, I'm the eldest. I am supposed to protect us. But I was the one who went away, I'm the one who hurt them."

She stopped, realizing what she had just said. Her face reddened. "I am being silly, I am being silly. I don't know what's come over me. I don't know why I'm talking like this."

She burst into tears. Bending her face onto her hands, she let the tears run into her palms.

What was happening to her? One minute she was here to talk about the girl and her unwanted baby, maybe ask Father Mahoney what he thought she could do to help her, the next moment she was thinking of Ali and Hossein, and Gohid, those terrible three days she had spent in the detention center.

How had it all turned to that time again?

"Thank you." Marjan sniffed, accepting Father Mahoney's handkerchief. She blew her nose and hiccuped. "I'm sorry. I don't know what came over me," she said, wiping her face.

"Nothing at all to it. All natural, my dear. You're just a sensitive soul, that's it. I said you were an artist. I can spot them a mile away."

He smiled and poured her another cup of tea. "Though if the tears are a result of my disc-jockeying, then I'll have to reconsider my extracurricular activities. Belly dancing perhaps. Or water polo. I could definitely get into water polo."

Marjan gave him a small smile. "I'm just worried, that's all. It's hard being the eldest. Having to take care of everyone."

"Of course it is. And I know I shouldn't be saying this, but take heart: your sister just needs some time. After all, it's not every day a person finds her path to the Almighty. That's once in a lifetime, if we're lucky. Just give her time, and she'll come around with it herself. Just give her time."

He stopped, a beatific smile on his pink face. "She might surprise you, after all."

❄

"WHAT DO YOU MEAN you're going to be a Catholic? How can you just decide something like that?" Layla exclaimed loudly from her post at the refrigerator.

"I didn't just decide it," Bahar replied with an indignant air. "And really, it's not any of your business."

She looked very uncomfortable, cornered as she was at the kitchen table, with her back to the pantry door. She desperately wanted to reach into her apron pocket for her laminated card, the watercolor rendition of the prayer to Our

Lady of Knock, but she resisted, not wanting to have to explain that as well.

"But how long have you known?" asked Marjan.

Unlike Layla, Marjan had had a few hours to mull over what Father Mahoney had let slip.

"Look, I came in here to tell the both of you the truth, because Father Mahoney thought I should, because *I* think I should. But if you're going to act as if I'm guilty of some crime, then I'm just going to get up and leave," Bahar said, pushing herself away from the kitchen table. "If you want crime, you know where to look."

She pointed at Marjan accusingly. "What were you doing seeing Father Mahoney, anyway? Making a confession? Can't do that if you're not a believer, you know."

"What is that supposed to mean?"

"I think it's pretty obvious. We've never had any kind of faith, nothing to rely on growing up. Doesn't that just strike you as a little strange?" Bahar crossed her arms with a pointed air.

It took Marjan a few seconds to answer. "Of course we had faith. Maybe we weren't religious as such, but we were taught what was right and wrong."

Bahar snorted. "You and I have completely different memories, Marjan. All I remember is asking Baba what God was and getting the craziest answer ever."

"He told you the same thing he told me," Marjan replied softly.

"What did he say?" Layla looked eagerly to her older sisters.

Bahar smirked. "Go on, Marjan. What *did* he say?"

"He said . . . he said that God was all around us," Marjan replied, feeling defensive all of a sudden. "He said that there was no sense in looking to religion for the divine, that all we had to do was take a breath, see the beauty in our ability to do something as simple and complex as taking in a breath."

"Simple and complex." Bahar sniffed. "How can something be two opposite things at once? You make it sound so romantic." She turned to Layla. "Do you want to know what Baba told us? What jewels of wisdom I have to pass on to you?"

Layla stared at Bahar, not entirely sure she wanted her to continue.

Continue she did. "He told us we come from monkeys—no, wait, bacteria—we all, every single human being on earth, came from bacteria that lived in the sea. And that, when we die, we have nothing to hold on to. No soul, no memories, nothing."

She turned to Marjan accusingly. "Do you think that's what happened to Maman? She just disappeared? No heaven, nothing to go up to?"

Marjan sighed. "Bahar, it's more complicated than that. Both Baba and Maman believed the same thing. They were humanists. They believed humans have a key to their own fate." She had forgotten about the issue of fate. "They were different from most people, you know that."

"They were hippies, that's what they were. Had no sense of practical things. Do you think we would have ended up without a penny after Baba died if they'd had any sense?"

"Now you're taking it too far."

"Really? Well, tell me this, you think that girl—the one who is or isn't Estelle's niece, depending on what day it is—do you think she knew what she was doing? She chose her destiny?"

Marjan did not respond.

Bahar sniffed. "I don't think so."

Layla propped her elbows on the island, resting her chin in her hands. "So what do you think made her do it?"

"Something evil. That's what made her try to kill her baby. There's no doubt in my mind. Evil, to even *think* about killing your unborn child."

"Oh, what a good Christian you are," Layla remarked, throwing Bahar a nasty glare.

"Look," said Marjan gently, "we're getting off the subject. I was just trying to understand, Bahar. This is big news, you becoming Catholic."

"Big news! This is crazy news!" Layla said, standing up. A look of uncharacteristic fear had come across her face.

"No crazier than what you get up to when no one's looking," retorted Bahar. She stood up too.

Layla narrowed her eyes. "What do you mean?"

Bahar snorted. "Don't act the innocent. I know what you and Malachy have been doing. It's not only necking you're after, is it, little sis?"

Layla blanched. "What do you mean by that?"

Bahar smiled triumphantly. "Don't forget, this is a small town. I only have to go to the butcher shop to hear all about your love life."

"At least I have a love life. What are you going to do now, become a nun?"

Bahar stared at her sisters. "Maybe."

Layla and Marjan looked shocked.

"Are you serious about that, Bahar?" Marjan moved away from the counter.

"Yes, maybe. I don't know. All I know is that I have found God, and you two have no business telling me otherwise." She came from around the table, her hand in her apron pocket.

"You're right, we don't have any business telling you what to believe. But are you sure, Bahar? This is a big step."

"I know it's a big step. I've been working toward it for over a year. Ever since that first time up on Croagh Patrick." Bahar paused. "Look, doesn't it mean something that I haven't had a headache for nearly the same time? Don't you understand that I've found some peace finally?"

Neither Marjan nor Layla said a word. It was true; Bahar had not reached for her jar of migraine medicine—a tribal mixture of cardamom, cloves, and nutmeg—for a very long time.

Bahar moved to the stairs up to the flat. She placed her free hand on the banister and turned around. "If either of you is interested, I'll be attending full Mass for the first time on All Saints' Day. That's the first of November. You are both invited, if you care to come along." She stepped resolutely up the stairs and slammed the flat door.

Marjan spoke first. "She's happy. And we have to be happy for her. Even if we don't understand all her reasons. We can't worry about things we don't know about."

Layla rattled the silver carousel on the island, plucking at an old order. "Last time she decided to go all religious on us we ended up having to run away. Aren't you worried about that?"

The carousel spun noisily, throwing shards of light into Marjan's eyes. She watched the pieces of paper fly by, their edges smudged with food stains and curling back like delicate fabric swaths. Suddenly, they seemed to resemble the curtains of chadors, the black cloths rushing by her as she stepped into the apartment that day so long ago.

She could see them again, those women, the ones who had taken her sister under their darkened wings. Like stark ravens, swooping in while Marjan was held against her will in Gohid. Marjan had lost everything she held dear in the space of a few days, her thoughts whittled down to a cycle of regrets. In the end, it was Khanoum Zanganeh who had brought her out of her stupor.

Her cellmate, a working girl of some experience, had been feeding Marjan bits of survival technique, as well as stale bread and water, during her time at the detention center.

"Make sure you cover your whole face with your hands. Like this," Khanoum Zanganeh had advised her, flapping her fingers over her heavily made-up face like shadow puppets.

"You'll be blindfolded again, so you won't know where you are landing. Just be sure to hold up your hands—they'll unshackle you a second before they throw you out. Make sure your beautiful face won't get marked. You hear me?" Khanoum Zanganeh wriggled her brown fingers again. "Just like this, Khanoum Aminpour. Just like the dove of peace."

Part of Marjan wanted to believe the old prostitute, to imagine that she was really going to be released. It was the same part of her that had thought Ali's precautions overly dramatic, his warnings of what might happen if they got arrested highly unlikely. She remembered clearly, as though he were sitting before her once again.

"They'll use wires. On the bottoms of your feet. Listen to me, Marjan, are you listening? If they beat you, I want you to tell them a lie. Tell them anything but the truth. Then let yourself faint. Don't be brave."

His green eyes had flickered in the low light of *The Voice*'s basement offices, the steam from their bowls of food rising between them. Their late-night meals of soothing noodle soup or cheese and bread were a ritual, something they shared when everyone else had crept back home to their families.

Their talks turned often to what they would do if either of them were ever arrested. Everyone who worked with the movement, the uprising, had to be prepared for interrogation. It would have been naïve to think otherwise.

Neither of them had ever contemplated the end result— what would happen once she was released. And when the time had come, when they had been arrested that night in the offices of *The Voice*, Marjan knew why. Ali did not expect to be released. He knew he would never get out of the Revolution alive.

"Aren't you worried?" Layla had said. Yes, she was worried, thought Marjan. She worried about it, them, everything, all the time. Despite her best efforts to do otherwise.

❋

THERE WAS NOTHING LIKE a good bike ride to bring joy to a lonely spinster's life. The sheer sensation of the ride was right up there with flannel bedclothes and hot bubble baths, a red hot-water bottle pressed against old and tired thighs.

Marie Brennan grinned inwardly at the thought as she pumped the ten-speed bicycle up the nettle-lined hillside. The clank of chain and pedal was even more harmonious than she remembered. It had been a long time since she had last heard that simple noise.

A proud owner of a Schwinn since she was a girl of fourteen, Marie had not ridden the blue bicycle of her youth in over ten years, not since her sister, Dervla, had come to live with her. Dervla did not approve of bicycles for women. She believed that there was something entirely unseemly about the motions, straddling and siphoning and all, so Marie had obliged as she always did when it came to her older sibling's commands: she had kept the bike stored in the shed they shared with Antonia Nolan's relics shop and run all her errands on foot, bar the few necessary trips a year to Castlebar or Dublin.

Marie had kept the bike hidden away, but she had never forgotten about it—some of her fondest girlhood memories involved that blue Schwinn—so when Dervla had insisted she unearth it to visit Estelle Delmonico's cottage, she had not needed to be asked twice.

Marie guided the bicycle past a burbling freshwater stream. The bouncing water flowed directly from a gully that found its estuary deep on the other side of the Reek, not far from where she'd started her journey. It would eventually end in the basin of Clew Bay, which announced itself as she turned the side of the hill. She glanced out at the Bay, breathing in deeply. The sky over the water was overcast as usual, the depths of blue shrouded for their mystery. Those waters contained a thousand stories, Marie told herself, moved to tears by the beauty. The Bay always brought out her emotions, its divine essence something she did not enjoy or appreciate enough, at least not in her everyday existence.

With her days spent in routine—squeezing Dervla into her girdle and stockings was an hour's work at the very least—she rarely left the environs of the musty little flat, let alone Main Mall. Sure, a walk to the mini-mart or the Butcher's Block did help break up the monotony of her sister's carps, as did the highlight of her day, the only lining in her ever-constant cumulus: noontime Mass inside Saint Barnabas's alabaster hush.

Father Mahoney was always at hand when she had a moment's confession. She wondered what he would think now, to see her rounding the hilly corner. Wouldn't think too highly of her, that's what. Would no doubt dispense thirty Hail Marys next time she faced the confessional's latticed window. He might even expose her on his new radio program as an example, tell the whole world what a mean spirit she was really.

Marie's face flared with shame as goose bumps rose along her soft neck. She had had a speech prepared for when she saw the

Italian woman, but the words seemed to be slipping from her mind the closer she got to the cottage. She had never been steady under any kind of stress.

Trying her best to ignore her jitters, the spinster turned down a brambly lane and slowed her pedaling. Her sister's voice, unfortunately, was harder to ignore: "Even that witch can't be dumb to the proper manners of tea. She'll invite you in a jiffy, I'd say. Then you can see what kind of heathen she's been hiding away."

Marie frowned. She did not understand Dervla's drive to know every single thing that went on in town and out of it. Hadn't Padraig Carey said that there was nothing to fear? That Anne-Marie O'Connell had no clue what she was talking about? Why couldn't Dervla be happy to leave it at that?

Marie sighed and took another look at the ocean. She could see all the way to the islands, the drumlins that rose westward in cliffs and melted eastward into soft, dandelion coastlines. The last she had heard there were over three hundred of those drumlins along the Bay.

If only she could get herself a drumlin all of her own, Marie Brennan told herself. She could be quite happy there, alone with her beloved Schwinn.

❁

LEANING HER BICYCLE AGAINST an alder trunk, Marie turned away from the water and quickly crossed over a small stone bridge. A trio of mallards, their green, iridescent feathers gleaming, turned to stare at her as she hurried across the humpy moat and water. Just above it stood the Delmonico homestead.

The tidy, whitewashed cottage was indeed neat and beautiful, thought Marie. Green shutters and a flagstone path bordered its front, a Dutch door opened into what she supposed would be the front parlor. She had never been to Estelle's cottage before; although the Italian widow had been living in town for over forty years, ever since Marie had attended Saint Joseph's herself, not three sentences had passed between them.

Marie climbed the gravelly path to the front door, taking in the sweet smell of the rosebush to her left. Tightening the knot on her head scarf and clutching her purse to her chest, she took a deep breath. She lifted her hand to knock just as she heard Estelle. Her voice was coming from around the house, where a thicket of willows created a natural gate blocking most of the view.

Creeping slowly along the front of the cottage, Marie came to the willow gate. There, between two entwined branches, she saw the Italian woman.

She was talking to someone sitting near the back door. Marie's heart began pumping in her chest. It was the girl, the one from the hospital.

Yes, a redhead. She was sitting in a low wheelchair, a tartan blanket over her legs. Her tangle of dark red-brown hair masked her face, but Marie was sure it was the same girl Anne-Marie O'Connell said she had tended. Could Dervla be right in her suspicions? Was Estelle really harboring a baby-killing heathen?

The spinster knelt closer and squinted, holding her breath. Estelle seemed to be busy at something on the lawn before her.

". . . so when my Luigi said he was going to build me a door to his heart, I think he talk about maybe a new kitchen here in the house. Something with a good sofa so I could sit and look when he try his new recipes, yes? By this time my feet were bad too, so I can only stand in the shop and kitchen for small times, no more than one hour before I have to take a chair or something. This is okay for my Luigi, because he was the *artiste*, the creator. I only support his dreams, his vision for new cannoli or *pavlova a la fresca*.

"So I was thinking he wanted me close to him while he is a-baking here. And I wait and wait, but no sofa comes. Instead, my Luigi is out here every day after work in the shop, putting plants here and there, doing this or that with the ground, but never letting me see, yes? Big surprise again. But this time it was not a Vespa. This time it was something that would make me travel even longer way, without ever leaving my back garden. This time it was the walk to my inside. To my heart and to his heart."

Estelle paused and placed her hands on her soft hips. From where Marie crouched, she could clearly see through the willow to the Italian woman's feet: planted there was a sea of lavender bordering a flagstone path.

Estelle leaned down slowly and patted the plants. "Here is the lavanda. And over there is the rosemary. Lavender and rosemary, over and over again. But it was not the plants but this stone that is the important thing. Here, look at this."

Estelle stamped on the flagstone with her sandaled feet. "One," she said, smiling. "One, and then . . . two." She stepped forward onto another flagstone. "One, two, and then three."

She stepped again, following the flagstone path in a clockwise manner: "Slowly, I understand what he mean by heart. This stone I walk, slowly in a circle, around and around. You see?"

Estelle nodded to the quiet girl as she kept walking. "I walk around and around, step by a step, every moment coming closer and closer to myself. Every step closer to my Luigi, my home. To God. I walk slow, and then I reach the center, like this."

Estelle stopped in the middle of the flagstone path, turning to face the girl in the wheelchair. "This is the center of everything. Here I find peace. That is what Luigi had built for me. A circle garden I can come to when I have problems, anytime, yes? I walk this when I can't walk too far because of the weather or my feet, and I walk this circle when I have too many pains in my thoughts too.

"Step by step, to the middle. And then I turn, like this"—Estelle swiveled and followed the path out—"until I reach the beginning again. And this makes my mind and heart sing, rest. It is like the circle of life, then death, then life, *la vita*. Again and again, one cannot be without the other, yes? Again and again, *el raffinatezza*—how do you say? Refinement? El refinement of yourself. Every time you walk you can solve any problem, any sadness, if you ask God to help you as you do it. The answer is at the center. At your center. Yes?"

Estelle paused and turned to the girl once again. She took a moment before extending her chubby hand. "You come now, yes? You come and walk, and we will find your answer. You will see that you can be okay."

Marie held her breath, a large gulp forming in her throat as she waited to see what the girl would do. She felt as though she was dizzy from the anticipation but also needed to have a good weep, a great big yell.

She felt utterly unlike herself.

The redheaded girl took a long time to respond. Just when Marie thought she was going to sit in the wheelchair forever, she lifted her head and turned to Estelle. Her left foot came off its footrest, then her right, the blanket pushed aside. She stood up, her tall and thin frame enveloped in the billowy folds of the pajamas and the chunky Aran sweater she was wearing. Slowly, she stepped forward, meeting the Italian widow's invitation. At the beginning of the path, she held up her right hand, touching it to Estelle's.

The widow smiled and nodded. Behind them, Marie's eyes widened: she had no better response to the sight of those unmistakable fingers, the marks of an otherworldly creature, fanning open again.

Chapter 10

Lady of the House

MARJAN WAVED AT CONOR JENNINGS as he turned his Guinness truck off Main Mall, making for the back of Paddy McGuire's. With her cup of tea in hand, she turned once again toward the statue of Saint Patrick and the presently deserted town square. She could hear Father Mahoney's voice streaming out from the dining room, his morning radio program a pleasant change to her usual quiet breakfast. Upstairs in the flat, Bahar and Layla were still asleep, giving her some time to think without interruption.

She needed this time. Needed it desperately. Her conversation with Father Mahoney the other day had made her all too aware of that. Although she hadn't expected to be so candid about her fears, she was glad she had opened up to the kind priest. Had she gone into the church with the intention of confessing, she probably would not have been so honest about her anxieties.

Maybe there were some things you couldn't tell even yourself, thought Marjan. For what was the self but a mystery?

And yet, what she had told the priest had been true; she was the eldest; it was still her responsibility to take care of her sisters. She had made a promise to herself a while ago, not long after they had moved to this tiny western village, that she would try to let Bahar and Layla find their own paths without her constant help. But she also knew that without her vigilance, keeping a sense of security, a sense of home, her sisters could easily come to some harm again, as they had those three days she had spent at the detention center. If it hadn't been for her being involved with Ali and his revolutionary cause, if she hadn't been in the offices of *The Voice* instead of at home with them that day, she could have prevented what had happened to Bahar.

She could have saved her from the baton and Hossein.

To this day, Marjan did not know the exact details of what had happened to her sister during those four months of marriage. Even after their move to London, years after their dash across the desert, they had never broached the subject.

There was a tacit understanding between them, a silent agreement that neither of them would mention why Bahar had left Hossein, showing up at their apartment in the middle of the night with only her chador on her back. From the bruises and marks scattered across her body, it wasn't hard to guess the reason.

For her part, Marjan had tried to avoid upsetting Bahar, so she didn't ask too much of her sister. Bahar was so susceptible to migraines and their living situation was so stressed that she didn't want to make things worse with questions.

Even here in Ireland, this last year of security, the topic had been taboo. Whenever Marjan tried to bring it up, her sister would find a way of changing the subject. But to look at her lately, thought Marjan, it didn't seem as though she needed any help.

"I know it's a big step. I've been working toward it for over a year. Ever since that first time up Croagh Patrick," Bahar had said.

It was as though she had discovered a secret herb on that mountaintop and was keeping its tonic close to her heart. And if her sister found her peace in religion, then Marjan was not going to object.

A shiny black car eased up to the sidewalk. Julian Winthrop Muir leaned out the open window, his arm over the side. "Wouldn't think someone like you would be saddened by such beautiful surrounds."

Marjan tilted her head. "Hi there," she said with a smile. God, he looked great. "New car?"

"Renting it for the moment. Can't decide whether it's a BMW or a Benz I'm after."

"Ah. The dilemma."

"If I didn't know better, I'd say you were taking the Mick out of me," said Julian.

"Just a friendly jab," Marjan replied. She pointed to the dawning sky. "You're up early."

"Got to get down to the site before the lads. Show a little slack and you're done for."

"So the work's well under way, then?"

"You could say that. Found a crack in the dining room the size of the San Andreas yesterday. Those are original frescoes, mind you." He gave her a speculative look. "But you look like you've had some trouble yourself."

Marjan ran her fingers through her hair, realizing she hadn't put it up yet in her customary ponytail. "Just tired, that's all. I could use a week of sleep, pure, sweet quiet."

Julian cut the car's engine. "Or a meander through Raven's Coppice." He stepped out onto the sidewalk, shutting the car door.

"Raven's?"

"Coppice. Raven's Coppice. It's the road leading into Muir Hall. There's nothing like it for the senses." He pointed to the car. "Come on. Play truant for an hour. You won't regret it."

Marjan looked back into the empty dining room. Bahar would be getting up soon for breakfast prep. "I don't know . . ." she started.

"No rain checks this time, Miss Aminpour. Come along, your chariot awaits." Julian rounded the gleaming vehicle and opened the passenger door.

Marjan could see Dervla Quigley across the street, squinting between her curtains for a better look-see. Perhaps it was the old woman's contemptuous expression that made Marjan take out her keys and lock the red door quickly. Or maybe it was the sheer joy of escape, her need to feel like a young girl once again, that had her slipping into the luxurious leather seat next to Julian.

❊

THEY PARKED BEFORE a vast opening off the Westport Road, in a side lane cleared of swooping elm trees. Fieldstone walls wound their way around the firs to the right and left, purplish ferns and whitewash from Cromwellian times still embedded within their stony layers.

A path, wide enough for two cars, led from inside an opened gate made of rusted wrought iron. Beyond it lay a forest of moss and fairy tales, columns upon columns of firs receding into the dark.

Marjan stared into the green abyss. The ground, littered with dead pine needles, seemed to disappear in the hush of coppiced greenery, the squawk of a raven's cry breaking the silence only momentarily.

"It's a bit of a walk, I must warn you."

Marjan looked at the man next to her, then glanced again at the green tunnel. "Does it get any brighter? It seems so dark in there."

"Once you see the house, it'll feel like you'll never see the darkness again." Julian offered her his arm. "My lady?"

Marjan smiled and stepped closer to him. Linking her arm in his, she let him lead the way.

❈

HALFWAY DOWN THE PATH, with the song of ancient ferns at their backs, the smell hit Marjan. "Is that smoke?" She stopped and looked around.

Julian stopped as well. He smelled the air before him. "Debris. The men must have started the fire already. You can't imagine the amount of rubbish discarded around the woods by the locals. There was even the shell of a DeLorean racing car. Who knows how that came to be parked here."

"When was the last time anyone lived here?"

"Eighteen eighty-nine. Burnt down partially. The southern wing."

"And no one ever rebuilt it?"

"Left to rot. I have only been here twice before. When I was much younger," he said, looking at her.

"That's a pity," said Marjan. What was it about this man that made her feel so shy?

Julian smiled. "Well, I'm here now." He stared ahead again. "And so are we, it seems."

Marjan had been so engrossed in Julian's voice that she had not even noticed that the woods had finished their haunting. She followed his gaze. Perfection, in the form of ivy-covered walls and buttery hydrangeas, cloaked a magnificent Georgian house. Four columns took a regal stance on a landing before the Byzantine doorway, discreet valets in a queen's boudoir. Running on either side of the arched entryway, beyond an extensive system of scaffolds that held the workmen, were the three stories and windows that encompassed the pearl of a mansion.

Nearly all twelve windows still had their original glass, gleaming from a mellow break in the clouds.

Marjan took in a quick breath. Not since the ruins at Persepolis had she seen a structure so simple and fine.

"Welcome to Muir Hall," said Julian, taking her hand.

❊

"IT'S THE MARK OF THE DEVIL, that's what I say. No decent person goes around with those kinds of fingers," remarked Dervla Quigley, tucking her legs under her straight-backed chair. Joan Donnelly nodded from beside a shelf of New Testaments and dunked her biscuit in her teacup again. "I always knew there was something fishy about that Estelle Delmonico. Never thought she'd be consorting with the dark forces, mind you."

Dervla sniffed. "She's Italian, isn't she? Wasn't it the Romans that had a hand to play in our Lord's fate?"

The women of the Bible study group nodded, musing soberly.

"If you ask me, that girl's no niece of hers. Not with the ginger hair on her. Marie saw it clearly, ginger as Benny Corcoran's. And his kin go as far back as any to this place."

"And Padraig Carey not doing a tit about any of it, then? Not even taking it up with the hospital people?"

"Useless man." Dervla sneered. "Best thing he did was marry that Margaret—not that you'd know it now; she's gotten too big for her britches with all the running around she's doing. From one pub to the next as though she's living it up in Dublin."

"Sure, her kiddies are all up at her mam's now after school," said Antonia Nolan. "No time for her motherly duties, that's what I hear."

"Terrible," spat Dervla. "Shocking all round, I say."

"But what of the girleen? What was it you saw after she got up from her chair? Sure, they started chanting in tongues, did they, Marie? Something to the Lord of Darkness?" Assumpta Corcoran's eyes were filled with terror.

From her corner, near the bargain bin of chastity key chains, Marie Brennan gave a meek shake of her head. She was about to replay what she had heard Estelle say when Dervla interrupted.

"Can't you see she's in shock from the whole thing? As it stands, we'll be saying novenas till Easter before she'll be right again."

Antonia puckered her lips. "It's the work of the fairies, that's what I say. Potions and all. Goes all the way back to olden days—sure we've had our share of witches as well."

June took up her mother's prompt: "Biddy Early, isn't that so, Mam?"

"The one and the same," Antonia replied, recalling the famed witch doctor from County Clare. Like the greatest Druidesses before her, Biddy Early worked her magic through the all-seeing eye of a blue egg, a crystal ball that held the answers to maladies of villagers across the West. Fame and fortune had been hers in a time when famine took hold of every stomach in Ireland. "That Estelle Delmonico's probably thinking of reaping her benefits from this girl here. Now that there's no bakery for her to run and no husband as well."

Assumpta nodded. "I'd say she'd got Father Mahoney onboard already. What with flaunting his dirty mind on that radio like he is."

Antonia's eyes widened. "I nearly keeled over when I heard the show. Didn't I now, June?"

June nodded. "Keeled over nearly she did. Who does he think he is, talking about Frank Sinatra's mistresses? And what of the virtues of volleyball? I've never heard of such filth!" June paused. "What's this volleyball, anyhow?"

Dervla placed her teacup firmly on the counter and shook her curly gray head. "It won't do, I tell you. It just won't do," she said. "Something has to be done about all this—before it's too late."

June moaned. "But what can we say of it, Dervla? What's there to be done about the whole mess?"

The Bible group awaited their leader's decision.

Dervla Quigley thumbed her rosary, smacked her lips decisively. "You just leave that to me. There's only one way of sorting this hole of decrepitude we've fallen in."

She paused, squinting at the women seated before her. "Judgment Day could be upon us and we'd have no mind of it. It's time to put an end to all this shame."

✳

SHE COULD NOT BELIEVE the beauty of the place, the grand mansion surrounded by the deep forest.

As Julian took her through its many rooms, most of them filled with scaffolds and covered in sheets, Marjan felt herself transported back to a time when dances were held in its velvet-walled ballroom and horse-drawn carriages, complete with plumed footmen, took their water breaks at an adjoining ivy-covered cottage. There were parlors after parlors, each grander than the next, and an entire ground floor for what would eventually be the restored kitchen.

They had taken a detour around the burnt-out southern wing and made their way to the dining room, a generous room with a vaulted ceiling. The fresco on one large wall was indeed the marvel Julian had promised. It was a Pre-Raphaelite portrayal of the Children of Lir, those four siblings cursed to remain swans for nine hundred years. Despite a ragged crack that was making its way down the plaster, the fresco was as pulsing with life as though one was actually looking out on a placid freshwater lake.

When Marjan turned away from the painted wall, she saw its real-life inspiration outside the window. There, through floor-length panes, stood a pond complete with a flock of those gracious birds, the white-necked swans. There was even a maze on the property, the kind shaped like a Rubik's Cube of greenery. They had only stopped at its opening, for, as Julian had pointed out, people had been known to get lost in its fifteen-foot hedges for days.

It was then that he had leaned in for a kiss.

Running his hands down her arms, he gently skimmed his lips over hers, so taking her by surprise that she didn't have the time to turn away. It was only his lips, but to Marjan it felt as though she was crossing a great divide, traversing boundaries she had not realized existed deep within her.

She closed her eyes, taking in that gloriously manly scent of his, of leather and the pinecones crushed beneath their feet. She was sure he could hear her heart pounding, bursting against her jacket, wanting release, wanting to feel his. She allowed herself that moment, ignoring even the scar on her shoulder, which pulsed in counterpoint to her myriad, kaleidoscope-like emotions. And then it ended, just as simply as it had begun. He pulled back, taking a step away.

"You need to say yes to me." He looked at her intently, those green eyes taking on the color of the forest.

"Yes?" She felt so dizzy. For a moment it seemed as though they had been walking the maze for days.

"Yes to dinner. This Friday night. Yes to seeing me again. And again."

Yes, she said. Yes.

Chapter 11

Labor of Love

THE ARBOR OF ROWAN TREES curtsied along the curve, masking the inlet from view. It shimmied demurely as Marjan steered the van onto a leafy road, following Estelle Delmonico's directions toward Clew Bay.

"You think you are lost," Estelle had said on Tuesday, "but suddenly you turn and there is the tree and you are found again."

And just as her dear friend had described, the next gullied corner led straight into the dome of a majestic valonia oak. Like the arms of an aged and grand doyenne, its silvered limbs reached up and over the hillock, casting berry patterns that Layla's boyfriend, Malachy, would have likened to far-reaching constellations. As Marjan maneuvered the van around the tufted crest, an Atlantic breeze coaxed a handful of its mistletoe onto the lime green roof. The next instant brought into view the shimmering waters of Clew Bay.

Estelle's voice rang in her ear once more: "We have to help her, Marjan. Nobody is alone in this world. Someone knows this girl. Someone cares very much for her. We have to find this someone."

The widow had been sitting on her linen couch when she said this, cradling the cup of warm milk Marjan had made for her. The young woman was asleep in the bedroom, away from their hushed voices.

"Tomorrow," Marjan promised. "I will go to that beach tomorrow. I'll see what I can find there." She paused, turned to the widow. "I still think you need someone else here to help you with things full-time. You can't take care of yourself and her as well," Marjan pointed out. "Do you remember what Dr. Parshaw said?"

Estelle shook her head. "What is there to do anyway? A little sewing, a little talking, some eating—I do this for myself all the time. No, we will be okay."

Despite her exhaustion, Marjan could tell that the widow was happy to have the new responsibility. Still, she felt it important to ask: "But what about your arthritis? What if you get a bad spell again? Are you sure sleeping on the sofa won't be bad for your back?"

"Pfft! That is nothing. You should see the skinny hammocks we sleep in during the war in Napoli. We were lucky we didn't break our heads, we fell like melons in the night!" Estelle chirped, waving her hands around her head. "Don't worry so much, darling. The doctor is coming here every day. If I have any pains, I tell him." She hoisted herself up from the cushiony sofa, the empty mug in her hand. "Anyway, my hands, they are much better today. See?" Estelle wriggled her chubby fingers happily.

They did look less puffy, thought Marjan as she helped Estelle into a straighter stance. "Then you'll let me make all your meals," she conceded. "I've got the barberry rice for today. I'll bring you lunches and dinners for as long as you need them."

Estelle's face brightened even more. "Well, that I cannot say no to," she exclaimed. "Energy for all of us! Energy for living!"

SHE HADN'T BEEN ABLE to keep her promise to explore Clew Bay until Thursday morning. On Wednesday the café was packed with tricolored revelers making pit stops from the pub during what turned out to be a rousing success in the world of mullet haircuts, testosterone, and fancy footwork: football's coveted Cup. Football, as the inhabitants of Ballinacroagh were prone to say, was as true an Irish venture as the telling of tall tales and that black stuff called Guinness. For what other sport in history gone required such grace from grown men, every travel and kick taken from the reels and jigs of this craggy little island? Not as far a leap of the imagination as once scoffed, for on Wednesday, Ireland at long last managed to qualify for the Cup.

As a consequence, Marjan had not stopped rolling out *sangak* sandwich bread and turned off the stove until well after sunset. She would go to the Bay as early as possible the next morning, she told herself. Thursday was one of their slower breakfasts of the week anyway, giving her plenty of time to investigate.

At least she no longer needed to hide her reasons for taking the morning off. Both her sisters had seen her drive away from the back alley, Bahar with a sour and disapproving face, Layla with waves of encouragement.

Those two, thought Marjan. Sometimes, they just didn't see how hard it was to keep everything running so smoothly. Not just in the café but in every other area of their lives as well. Her sisters never had to worry about anything beyond their everyday duties. She was the one, for example, who had to take care of the bills, make sure their business licenses were in order, and sort through the mess that was the Irish tax system. She was the one who had applied for their residency, ensuring that they were all on their way to becoming citizens of this land of endless green acres.

Neither Bahar nor Layla had ever questioned her about any of these matters, taking it for granted that Marjan would fix everything. Part of it was her fault, Marjan admitted to herself. She knew she often strove to protect them, to shelter them from upset. She had been taking care of everything since she was seventeen and didn't know how to be any other way. Maybe she should start, thought Marjan, staring out the van window. Start a different way of being.

The sky was overcast, sifting pensive gray onto the surface of the inlet. There had been a pub on the road a half mile back, but there were no houses around this part of the Bay.

She drove up a narrow lane to the secluded spot, just off the main Beach road. She could clearly see the large dune Estelle had described: it resembled a small hill, covered with pebble trails and pin-tucked coves. It was a place that bore no witnesses, thought Marjan, no one to stop you from your determined mind. A determined mind, Baba Pirooz used to say, was a prerogative as well as a burden.

Most things in life were, thought Marjan.

Noticing a clearing up ahead, she turned in to it and parked the van. The communal parking spot was surrounded by clusters of more oaks, ancient specimens whose branches Druids once slept under. According to Danny Fadden, who in addition to owning the mini-mart on Main Mall was a connoisseur of Celtic lore, the oaks were not merely places for Druids to doze. In those moments of hibernation, known to last days or even weeks, the Irish seers would command the realms of the dead, commune with the forces beyond, and ask the questions posed by the High Kings of Connaught. Waking to a shower of mistletoe, they would relate the visions they had seen, messages from the underworld and beyond.

She could use a Druid's help, thought Marjan. Someone who could reveal some clues to the girl's origins.

She locked the van, more from habit than from necessity, as the back was empty of its usual load of precious spices, and walked to the edge of the dune. Crossing over patches of stinging nettle, she stepped onto the sand. Directly behind stood Croagh Patrick, a mile away but looming as large as ever.

Marjan had never been this far out on the Bay, so she would be relying entirely on Estelle's directions to guide her forward.

"She curl like a ball beside a bush of grass," Estelle had said. "I think to myself, my God, *una angela*, she is dead. But she was only fainted. Her breathing so small, almost like nothing."

Marjan stared up ahead. A choir of darkening sea grass shuddered in the breeze. The bushes jutted out from one side of the dune, which sloped right into the water. All along the dune, clusters of prickly saltwort were asleep to the ardor of carder bees. She glanced back at the clearing where the van sat snug on the gravel before stepping gingerly down the slope.

Chances favored some clues, she told herself; somewhere along this dune there could be a purse or some sort of personal belonging the girl left before stepping into the water. Maybe some keys, a ring, a wallet; less than two weeks had passed since Estelle had found the girl, lying nearly blue with a piece of dark fabric up around her throat; if anything had been left beyond the reach of the waves, it could still be there.

Their only clue to date—the piece of sodden fabric—had turned out to be a crepe dress, a simple shape with pearl clasp buttons and lilies printed on black in repeating patterns. Washed and dried, and hanging from a hanger in Estelle's living room, the dress gave no more hints than when wet. There were no tags inside to indicate a brand or place of purchase, and were it not for the tiny, regimental stitching along its bodice and hem, Marjan would have thought it handmade.

Marjan shivered, thinking of what Dr. Parshaw had said that first night in the hospital: "It was an act of desperation, that is my solemn opinion. The manner in which she tried to terminate indicates this, you understand."

When Marjan had asked him to explain, the doctor had looked at her with his sad, dark eyes. "It is my opinion that she used a thin, sharp, and very unsanitary instrument. Clothes hangers or similar metal objects have been used before for such actions. Desperation would have driven it, yes?"

Marjan sighed. A clothes hanger. It seemed a horrible choice to have to make.

She looked out on the Bay again, her arms folded. According to Avicenna, there were only two options in the matter of surprise pregnancies, both involving carefully chosen recipes. A woman could either consume ingredients that would strengthen the womb, giving the growing seed the right soil to bloom; or, digesting the philosophy of less being more, she could opt to burn the bud out from its very roots.

Marjan had scoured the *Canon* early that morning, before opening the café. With a cup of bergamot tea in hand, she had gone through the section titled "The Universal Pregnancy Diet." On the one hand, according to the Persian doctor, eating raisins, sweet quinces, pears, and pomegranates would keep the womb properly bolstered, feeding directly from the mother's intentions to the baby's growing limbs. On the other hand, a steady diet of fried chickpeas, green beans, and capers, as in a plate of green bean *narcissus*, was bound to induce a shedding of motherly responsibilities.

The *Canon*'s advice set in motion Marjan's own tumbling conscience.

She had been delivering fortifying stews to the hospital and then to Estelle's cottage every day for the last two weeks, with the idea that they would strengthen the girl and her growing baby. It was the right thing to do, helping the girl toward better health. Anyone would do the same in her position.

Yet, Marjan told herself after reading through the *Canon*, she had not considered the other side of the picture: what if the girl did not want to be fed fortifying stews? What if she did not want her baby and was being forced to eat for two anyway? Marjan hadn't really stopped to think about the hand she was playing in all of this; after all, she could be contributing to a decision that wasn't really hers to make. What would Avicenna say about this situation? she wondered. What choice did she really have in the end?

She reached the other side of the inlet. The water lapped at her shoes and sped away. The dune towered overhead, creating a little cave where the tide could not reach. This was the spot Estelle had described; this was where she had found the girl, lying facedown in the sand. Yet there was nothing unusual here, nothing left behind. Just water and more sand. Nothing to point to who the girl was, where she had come from. If only she would talk.

Marjan watched as the water foamed and frothed toward her. A girl had come here to kill a part of herself, she told herself. Alone, with no one to help her through her thoughts. Where would she and her sisters be today if there had been no one to help them along? No Gloria or Estelle, no Ballinacroagh to come home to? Would she even have the luxury of wondering? Or would she be too busy struggling to survive? Marjan thought with a sigh. She would definitely not have the privilege of thinking about her needs, her feelings, had they stayed in Tehran. She would be too busy trying to make ends meet, trying to keep them all alive.

She sighed again, this time louder. From above, the sea grass shook in solemn response. She never wanted to forget how truly lucky they all were, Marjan told herself. To have one another, to have people to love.

❋

THE PUB SAT DIRECTLY across a small dock, on a section of the Bay that was littered with large boulders. There was only one small blue boat tethered to the dock, bobbing in the splashing water. Marjan nosed the van beside the thatched pub and turned off the ignition. She stared at the sign swinging in the wind. The Aulde Shebeen, Inn Keeping with the Sea. It couldn't hurt to ask a few questions, she thought.

The bar seemed empty but for one customer, a man in rain gear conversing with the bartender, but as Marjan made her way up to the counter, she noticed a familiar face in a musty corner: Old Lady Lennon, coddling a large pint of gin and lemonade. A female equivalent to the Cat if ever there was one, the old woman had not been seen in Ballinacroagh since the summer season. Having fallen out with Margaret McGuire in June over the price of a packet of honey-roasted peanuts, she had been banned in all the town's pubs for an indefinite period of rehabilitation. So this was where she had been hiding out, thought Marjan, noticing that the old woman was wearing her customary navy peacoat and green skullcap, pulled tight over her ears and graying eyebrows.

Marjan approached the bar. The bartender was in the middle of an impassioned discourse, holding a remote control and pointing up to a television on a shelf above the liquor wall.

"Here's the thing, Horse, here's the magic," he said, turning up the volume on the screen. John Wayne had just pulled Maureen O'Hara kicking and screaming across their cottage yard by her long red hair. A classic scene from the movie *The Quiet Man*, also one of Marjan's favorites.

"Going soft, now, John? A bit of a romantic, eh?" the man at the bar said with a wry smile. "Sure, wouldn't catch you saying so in front of your Maureen, I'd bet."

The bartender reached up and smoothed his large gingery mustache. "Wouldn't I now? How do you think we spent our wedding night, eh, Horse? That"—he pointed to the television again—"that there is the surest way to get a filly into your bed. Number one aphrodisiac next to a hit up the backside. Mind you, it was my Maureen took a swing to me and not the other way around."

The other man laughed.

"Excuse me," Marjan said. Both men turned slowly to face her. The bartender smoothed his mustache once again. "Well, hello there, little lady. What's tickling your palate today?"

"I was wondering if you could help me. I'm looking for someone."

"Say it's John Neddy and you'd be making my day." A sound of clicking heels came from behind the bar. Marjan couldn't help but notice the bartender's barrel of a chest: hairy and spangled with several gold medallions, it was held in by a half-buttoned shirt and a tight leather vest.

"I'm looking for someone who may have been a customer. Maybe in the last few weeks?" Marjan described the girl to them.

The man on her right kept staring intently at her face, though Marjan only glanced at him once as she spoke.

The bartender shook his head. "Can't help you there. I don't recall any young lass like so coming in recently. Mostly locals that frequent mine. You're not from around here yourself, now?"

Marjan was about to say she was from Ballinacroagh when Neddy's face brightened with recognition.

"Now wait, aren't you that girl with that restaurant? Sure, sure, from the *Connaught*, eh?" He addressed the man drinking beside Marjan. "It's famous, she is!"

"You don't say," replied the man, his tone tinged with sarcasm.

The bartender grinned. "Got any steak in that place of yours? I like my steak done well."

"We have something similar. Kebabs."

"It's not steak."

Marjan smiled politely. "Are you sure you don't remember anyone coming in, maybe about two weeks ago? Friday, the ninth?"

Neddy caressed his mustache thoughtfully. "Not a drinking customer, that's certain. But if they'd be looking for a room, you'd have to talk to my Maureen about it. She'd be the one that does all the bookings."

"Is she around?" Marjan gave the barroom another look, ignoring the man sitting on the stool beside her on purpose. There was something in the way he was looking at her that made her feel strangely nervous, as though she were on show for a sale.

Neddy shook his head. "Not in at the moment. She's in Dublin at the Neil Diamond concert." He whipped out a napkin and placed it on the counter in front of her. "How about a wet now that you're here? A gal like yourself, now, I'd say would go for shandy on ice."

Marjan smiled politely. "Thank you, but I really have to keep going. Maybe I'll come back in a couple of days?"

"Anytime, darlin'. John Neddy's the name. Caterin' to the ladies is my game." Neddy winked at her and puffed out his golden chest once again.

BACK OUTSIDE, Marjan stood for a moment observing the wide expanse of the Bay. Maybe it was a long shot, looking for answers here, but at the moment it was the only lead she and Estelle had. She hoped the girl would start talking soon. Until then, she didn't know what else they could do to help her.

"Are you in any way looking for a cure?"

Marjan turned around. The man from the bar, the customer who had been talking to John Neddy, was standing next to her. She hadn't even heard him come out.

"A cure?"

"That's right. Cure: healing water, New Age crap. You're not an American, are you, now?" The man moved slowly around the van, looking at the peace signs with raised eyebrows.

Marjan stepped back. "No, I'm Iranian."

The man paused, as though unsure of what to make of the information.

"Oh, right," he said somewhat flippantly. He came back around the van and stood next to her again, his dark raincoat flapping in the wind. Before Marjan knew what was happening, he had raised his fingers to his mouth, giving out a piercing whistle. At the sound, a black-and-white head popped up from the deck of the blue boat below. As Marjan stared, a large sheepdog leapt onto the dock and trotted across the road toward them.

The man knelt down to pet the shaggy mutt. "Good boy, Escher, good boy." The dog rolled onto his back, his paws raised in surrender. His owner took his time rubbing his belly before looking up at Marjan once more. "So it's not enough you've got the *Connaught* calling you magic, now you want to take it from others as well?"

Marjan frowned. "Excuse me?"

"You heard me. If I were you, I would just let it go. I'm sure you can cook up something to take care of whatever's ailing you. Heartburn, indigestion, your local bout of salmonella." He stood up, pulling the cords of his raincoat tight. He started toward the dock, the dog trotting loyally after him.

"I'm sorry, but I don't know what you are talking about." Marjan was surprised to hear the anger in her voice.

"I'm sure you don't," he said. "Dogs are innocent, Miss Aminpour. Not men and women. *Especially* not women." And with one last scowl over his shoulder, he crossed over to the dock.

Chapter 12

Teenage Kicks

WITH A STRAW BASKET hooked on her left arm, Marjan set about clipping long stalks of cilantro in the backyard. A fat bunch would be just what she needed for the afternoon's special platter: New Year's *kuku*.

A concoction of fluffy eggs, sweet herbs, and clarified butter, the pancake was a springtime dish by the usual standards. Marjan had decided to add it to the café's autumn menu not on a whim but after careful consideration. It was the *kuku* that had finally given her the answer to the questions posed yesterday on the shores of Clew Bay.

As soon as she had woken up that morning, she had known what to cook for Estelle's dinner. She had not even needed to consult the *Canon* to check whether or not the *kuku* was part of the abortive diet. Neither did she look into the fat botanical guide she also read on a regular basis, double-checking to see whether the herbs would aid a healthy pregnancy.

She did not have the power to make those kinds of judgments, she had finally decided; at least not for someone else's life.

Of course, thought Marjan, there was no denying that her meals had certain persuasive elements, especially over the diner who sat down to them willingly. It was common knowledge that her food had the ability to move some tongues into song. She considered the potency of her dishes as a basic truth, not hinging on potions or magic but a direct result of her fresh, earthbound ingredients. But it was not her dishes alone that prompted customers to start acting on dreams last remembered in adolescent years. That, she decided, rested entirely on the diner, on his or her ability to recognize their inherent, individual power. All she could do was provide her food with an open heart and no expectations. *Kuku*, with equal mixtures of *garm* and *sard* ingredients, and its beaten center of beginnings—the egg with its yolk heart—was one of the best recipes for freedom, a gentle place from which the eater could choose her own outcome.

Marjan finished her clipping and stood up. The basket had just enough herbs for the *kuku*: fat bunches of parsley, dill, cilantro, and chives, glistening still with the morning dew. She crossed the backyard and ascended the stone steps, pushing the kitchen door open with her right elbow. She had made the mistake of using her left shoulder a few weeks back, completely forgetting about the healed wound in its juncture, a softly puckered inch of skin that was still sore to the touch.

Once, a long time ago, she had pulled a wooden stake from that very spot. Pulled it out and used it to ward off the devil himself.

It had been the first time she had not remembered about the cut, and she had decided to take the forgetfulness as a good sign. Maybe the past was truly behind them now, thought Marjan, stepping in just as another drizzle began its march across the western sky.

Wasn't that where the past belonged, after all?

❁

THE FIGURE IN THE CHAIR was enveloped in shadows and lethargy. Time seemed to have stopped still somewhere around the seat's wingtips, mummifying the man in its ugly patterned upholstery.

His face, once a puffy cross-stitch of capillaries and ragged eyebrows, was reduced to a series of flapping jowls, cemented by deep forks that ran along the sides of his unhappy mouth. A heart attack would have been enough to do it, thought Padraig Carey. But then there was an uneasy diet of disco music, bland dinners, and Cecilia McGuire's red-light rubdowns to contend with. That would be enough to throw any man over the edge.

As the councilman crept nervously into the room, which was still carpeted in that psychedelic brown and orange, he couldn't help but recall the summer's eve he had first entered that very house, as a young man come a-courting. That night he had come laden with chocolates filled with vanilla cream and a handful of pansies, feeling dapper and quite confident of his prospects, with the lusty looks of Margaret McGuire to prompt him. A quarter of an hour later he had left with the wilted flowers still clutched in his fist, and the first of many anxiety attacks seizing his small, hairy body.

Fourteen years hadn't changed things. He could still feel his flesh creep.

"How's it, Tom? Catching up on the reading?" Padraig's throat emitted something between a cough and a wheeze. He rocked back and forth on his heels, taking on the Ballinacroagh stance of manly camaraderie.

Thomas McGuire continued to stare at the LP record on his lap.

"Margaret's been telling me the good news, how the profits are up at the pubs. By twelve percent, last notice. Isn't that grand, now?"

Thomas's cracked knuckles whitened as he gripped the record cover. He had not said a word since Padraig entered the parlor.

Once a month the entire McGuire clan—or what was left of them—met at Thomas's for a rump roast and an afternoon of screaming kiddies and business concerns. And while this was a weeknight, the earlier side of the month, Padraig could not shake the sensation it was his hide being barbecued this meal.

Another minute passed before Thomas opened his mouth. "Everyone said Barry was the better bachelor, taking Studio 54 by its bollocks, but it wasn't true. It was Robin—he's the one with the teeth and glasses—that had the birds lining up two at a time to get into his pants. Wouldn't think to look at him, now, would you?" He pivoted the record cover toward Padraig. *The Best of the Bee Gees, Volume One.*

Thomas's brother-in-law shook his head, swallowing the lump in his throat. "No. No, you wouldn't, Thomas."

Thomas scrutinized the councilman. "Take yourself, now. A man might look at you and think he's chatting away to some imbecile, some little fart from the bog roads of Ballina, all the while not knowing what you're really about underneath that stinking suit and all."

"W-what do you m-mean, Thomas? What's the trouble?"

Thomas let out a low growl. "Listen to him, trying to hide his poxy ways from the Lord above. The truth can't be hidden from me, you should know that by now, Padraig."

"Why, Thomas, what are you saying? I'm as clear as water, you know that."

"Not when it comes to manning the post, you're not. Sitting with your thumb up your arse."

"Eh?"

"The girl, you feckin' eejit! The girl!"

Padraig began to sweat, finally understanding. "Oh, right."

"I'd get myself up to the witch's but for the stink. The smell of that place sends my liver up to a knot, so it does." Thomas punched his flaccid stomach, groaning at his enfeebled body.

"But I've done the rounds," Padraig replied. "There's nothing to the rumors, Thomas. You know how Dervla likes to talk."

"It's Dervla herself who saw it all, you feckin' gobshite! Or her sister—all the same, anyhow!" Thomas tossed the Bee Gees

LP off his lap. It landed on a nearby ottoman, the polyester trio grinning up at Padraig.

The councilman held up his hands. "Now, Tom, calm yourself. All this talk is not giving your heart a chance."

Thomas rounded on his brother-in-law. "Feck my heart!" he barked. "You think I plan to spend my days rotting away, listening to old records? It's Thomas McGuire you're talking to, now, boyo!"

Thomas pushed his large hands against the arms of the wing chair, swiveling his massive trunk toward Padraig. The heart attack might have restricted his day-to-day activities, but it certainly had not lessened the sheer terror the publican could summon when he put his mind to it. Thomas pointed a large, crooked finger at his brother-in-law. "And don't think I don't know what that Margaret is up to: must have really hit her well to think me caged up here like this. Thinks she's some feckin' queen with her hand in all the pots, does she? Taking in every bit of trash that comes off the streets, so Dervla tells me."

"Sure, I tell her to stop with the Cat and such. She won't listen to anything I say, Thomas. What can I do?" Padraig loosened his tie, lowered himself onto the edge of the ottoman in dejection.

"What can I do? What can I do?" Thomas mewled in imitation. "You can get yourself up to that witch's nest, that's what you can do." He spat, stamping his boots. Despite spending most of his days in that wing chair, he still wore the mud-encrusted boots he had favored in his working days.

"Take the guards with you when you do. And do something about that Paki doctor as well. If it's not a law you can take them on, then try on some accounts of foul play." He stopped, took a breath. "Dervla says she's not the old bat's relation after all."

Padraig nodded. "That Marjan Aminpour, she said it's some stranger she feeds like the rest of them. Taken into Mayo General on some sort of woman's business. Marjan said . . ." The councilman trailed off. Thomas was gritting his teeth so hard, the sides of his potato face were twitching uncontrollably.

Padraig gulped. "Er, right, right. All a load of bollocks." He cleared his throat. Where was Margaret when he needed her?

Thomas leaned in close to his face. So close that Padraig could smell the brussels sprouts he had consumed with his pork chop dinner. "You listen to me, you little hairy excuse for a fart," he growled. "When the time comes—and I won't say when, now, but it'll come—when the time comes, I'm going to get myself out of this feckin' chair, out of this feckin' room, out of Cecilia's feckin' clutches, and march straight down to the Mall. You hear me?" His eyes bulged with anger.

"I'm going to take back what's mine, twice over. But this time I'm going to do it right. This time I'll have the law on my side." He looked off in the distance. "Feckin' whores, the lot of them."

Padraig stared at his brother-in-law and swallowed back his own anger, that sizzling fear that came from such blatant and constant emasculation. What could have possessed him to come a-courting that long ago day? he wondered. Couldn't he just have kept the notion in his pants, where it belonged?

Thomas seemed to have read his regrets. "Just remember," he said, leaning in even further. "I gave you your life and I can take it back as well. Just like that." He snapped his fingers. "One word and you'll be right back on the bog with your old dad, turning up turd and turf with a donkey for a mate. Just one word from my lips, Padraig, to the man in Castlebar."

He cast a ruthless eye on the sweating councilman. "Didn't think I married the old mayor's daughter for her fat rump and mangy cooking, did you, now? Eh, Padraig?"

❊

MARJAN EASED THE VAN outside the Wilton Inn on Main Mall and turned off the ignition. She would rather have parked somewhere more discreet, but the square up ahead was no better for privacy. By the time she made it out of the van and past the Saint Patrick monument, the whole town would know she was on a date.

On a date! She could hardly believe it herself.

With hands trembling, Marjan tilted the rearview mirror and checked her lipstick once again. A nice subtle pink, it was the most makeup she had worn in years. Satisfied with the results, she turned away from the mirror. Her heart was bumping against her tight black turtleneck. The sweater nicely matched her long pencil skirt and boots, knee-high numbers purchased on her last shopping trip to Dublin. She had felt silly for spending so much on the boots but decided to treat herself all the same. This would be the first time she would be wearing them out—on a date!

A giddiness took hold of her; she felt frozen in her seat and couldn't seem to get herself to open the van door.

On the passenger seat next to her was the book Julian had given her, his novel. She had not had the chance to return to it since last week, when she had read its first few pages, but she intended to get down to it as soon as she had a moment's peace. She had brought the paperback with her tonight, hoping Julian would sign it. Perhaps write something special as well, for her eyes only.

Marjan felt her heart dancing again under her turtleneck; she didn't know what was happening to her; she had not felt this excited about a man since Ali, and the effect was entirely disconcerting. But also exhilarating.

Love is reckless; not reason, she told herself.

She grabbed the book and opened the van door.

❋

UNLIKE THE MOSSY NORMAN RUINS and quiet rectitude of its Georgian surrounds, the Wilton Inn took a rather more Wagnerian view of life. Looming three stories above the other businesses on Main Mall, it had been built to resemble a turn-of-the-century Bavarian lodge, with a gabled rooftop and light brown shingles overlapping like pieces of gingersnaps. Pine wainscoting traveled the length of the lobby and lounge, directing the bewildered guest straight to the Lucky Lederhosen, a velour-boothed watering hole with a daily buffet of boiled ham and carvery vegetables.

A local boy, Jerry Mulligan, was at a lectern serving as a check-in counter. Four clocks on the wall behind him gave the times in Ballinacroagh, New York, London, and Los Angeles.

"How's it goin' there, Marjan?" said Jerry. He thumbed his suspendered uniform and grinned broadly.

"Hi, Jerry. Another job?" Besides his latest concierge status, Jerry Mulligan worked at Healy's Hardware, delivered lunch orders for the Babylon Café's summer season, and on weekends manned the sole machine at the local Wellington boots factory.

Jerry clucked his tongue. "Paying the way somehow. Got a missus down in Galway now. You know how those city girls are—top of the range, all out. Fancy steak dinners and drives up to Donegal. No Blue Thunder burgers for her, no sir," quipped the young man. He flashed her a freckled smile. "You're looking mighty tonight, I might add."

Marjan smoothed her black skirt. "Thanks," she said and paused, biting her lower lip. "I'm actually here to meet someone. He's staying at the Inn."

"Julian Winthrop Muir? The Third?"

Marjan nodded, surprised. "How did you know?"

Jerry winked. "Talk of the town, you two. Personally, I'd thought you'd have nothing to do with a poncy two bit like him, but then I'm a bit prejudiced, you might say."

Marjan was glad she was wearing her turtleneck. She could feel her blush creeping up her neck. "Because he's English?"

Jerry snorted. "Is that what he's been tellin' ya?"

"Oh, I don't know . . . He's from here originally, isn't he?"

Jerry scratched his hairless chin and shrugged. "Sure, who am I to know?" He grinned. "Just say the word, Marjan, and that Galway piece can go." He snapped his suspenders again.

Marjan gave the young man a bemused smile. "I'll keep that in mind." She looked around. "Julian, is he around?"

Jerry stared at her uncomfortably for a moment. "That's the thing, Marjan. He's not."

"Oh. Did he step out?"

Jerry shook his head. "Checked out."

"I'm sorry?"

"Left this afternoon, it says here." Jerry pointed to the ledger opened on the lectern. "Thought you would have known yourself."

Marjan shook her head. "No," she said quietly. "I didn't know."

Jerry scowled. "Ah, that bastard. He didn't have the balls to tell you he was leaving?"

Marjan frowned. "Did he leave anything? Any note for me, maybe?"

"No, I just came on shift. Let me check out the back, so." Jerry disappeared through a side door.

Marjan let out her breath. She was feeling sick all of a sudden.

She gave her surroundings another glance. There were a few locals at the bar but no one she immediately recognized. They seemed to know her, though; one particularly mud-encrusted farmer flashed her a toothless smile and tipped his flannel cap.

Jerry came back shaking his head. "No. Nothing for you there. I'll find him for you, though. I'll do that. Get a few of my mates to show him what's what."

"I'm sure there's a reason. Just, um, if he comes back, will you let him know I stopped by?"

Marjan turned around as though in a daze. All the excitement she had felt since the morning came crashing down on her chest.

Was she being stood up? She had no idea how this dating thing worked, not really, but she was sure that when a man did not show up for a dinner date, he was making his feelings known clearly. Had she somehow taken Julian's advances for more than they were?

Marjan thought back on that moment earlier in the week, his surprising kiss near the maze's opening. His lips had been soft, softer than she had expected. Somehow he must have felt she wasn't ready for more, for he didn't press closer. He hadn't even pulled her into him, caressing her arms only, holding his space.

The hedges of holly had gathered around them, taking them in red-berried sleep, as did his mouth, taking in hers, gathering her breath.

The ache between her arm and left shoulder brought Marjan out of her daydream. She rubbed the spot thoughtfully. It hardly ever itched, only when she was especially filled with longing. She liked to think of the itch as a sign of things changing, of excitement and opportunity. Or was it a warning?

She drew in another quick breath, clearing her head. She was being silly, she told herself. There was no reason for her to jump to conclusions. There must be a good explanation for his leaving on such short notice. Hadn't Julian said there was a crew from Castlebar working on the plumbing today? He was nervous about handing such a large job to a local contractor, if she remembered correctly. That was probably it, she concluded. Something must have happened today at the Hall.

Whatever the reason for Julian's abrupt checkout, she wasn't going to make sense of it until she talked to him again.

Marjan walked out of the Inn into the dark, rain-swept main street. She stood on the wet sidewalk, staring at the green hippie van. The cast-iron streetlamp threw a spotlight on it, making it look unearthly. It suddenly looked so comforting, that clunky old thing. It was one of her first purchases in Ireland, a possession she was very proud of.

She had just made it around to the driver's side when she realized she had left the book, *Dominions of Clay*, on the lectern. Leaving the van door open, she hurried back inside.

She spotted the paperback immediately; it was balanced precariously on the stand, though Jerry had disappeared once again.

Grabbing the book, she turned and was about to walk out when, across the lobby, the elevator door slowly opened.

Marjan stood in stunned silence.

Out of the elevator stepped Layla and Malachy, the latter with his shirt buttoned up wrong, the former with her usually immaculate hair completely undone.

❋

"I CAN'T BELIEVE IT. What were you thinking?" Marjan turned to Layla in the passenger seat.

"But we didn't do anything! I swear!" Layla's voice was at its highest pitch. Her face was still burning a bright pink.

Marjan looked past her sister, out her van window. They couldn't see him from where they sat, outside the Wilton Inn, but Malachy McGuire was waiting out their talk in the Lucky

Lederhosen, a glass of Lucozade in his shaking hands. No doubt he was calling upon the stars he studied so diligently at university to beam him up and fast.

Layla turned to Marjan, her eyes narrowing. "What were you doing in the Inn anyway? Weren't you supposed to be up at Mrs. D's?"

"I'm sorry, Layla, but this is unacceptable!" Marjan pounded the steering wheel with her palm. She turned to face her youngest sister once again. "We are not talking about me. This is about how—"

Layla interjected. "She shouldn't be living up there all by herself. Something could happen to her, and none of us would know for days."

Marjan shook her head, keeping her voice stern. "Layla."

"But who could blame her? That cottage is so beautiful. You can even see Clare Island from the kitchen."

"Layla."

"Clare Island. Isn't that where that pirate queen used to live?"

Marjan couldn't help herself: "What pirate queen?"

"Grace, Grace a woman pirate. I've heard Danny Fadden talk about her a few times."

"Layla, we were talking about you and Malachy."

Layla winced. She glanced out the windshield. "Can we not? Please? It's really embarrassing."

"Joon-e man, I'm not trying to embarrass you. I just need you to understand how important this all is. The whole town will be talking about this little experiment of yours, you do know that, don't you?"

"Now you're sounding like Bahar!"

"Listen to me. You have to be careful, we have a business to keep going. And like it or not, this little town has its prejudices."

"That's what Malachy said. I don't know what's the big deal." Layla pouted. "This is 1987, not 1907."

"You and Malachy have just made a decision that will affect the rest of your lives. What were you thinking?"

"I told you, we were just fooling around. Jerry told Malachy about the empty room, and, well, we just wanted to see what, we just wanted to try—" Layla paused, squirming in her seat.

"What? Come on, Layla, what happened?"

Layla looked out the window and shrugged. "Nothing. It just— We're both kinda not, not . . ." Her voice trailed off, and her blush turned a deep crimson.

"What? What did you do?" Marjan grabbed her sister's arm. "Layla, did you and Malachy have sex?"

Layla grimaced again. Marjan loosened her grip, sat back in her seat. She took a deep breath. "Well?"

Layla gave another shrug. "Kind of. Not really."

"What do you mean, kind of? Were you even protected?" Oh, God, she thought. Why hadn't she written to Gloria?

"Malachy got some stuff from his roommate. He tried to get some from the chemist but chickened out at the last minute. Got foot powder instead." She scrunched up her nose. "Anyway, all the Trinity boys apparently come to Philip—that's his roommate. He's got a Norwegian girlfriend. She gets boxes sent over from her parents! Can you believe that?"

Marjan merely stared, unable to find the right words to say.

"Don't worry. We didn't do anything. Malachy got nervous, being in his family's place of business and all." Layla sighed. "It's not like his dad's going to walk in on us or anything. He doesn't even see him half the time he's down anyway."

Marjan propped her elbows on the steering wheel, laid her forehead on her fisted hands.

"Marjan . . ." Layla whispered.

"Yes?"

"I'm sorry. I should have told you, I know."

Marjan lifted her head. "I just don't want you to do something that you'll regret."

"You mean like the girl with the baby?" As always, Layla had a way of boiling things down to their most concentrated elements. "That's not something I would ever do."

"You never know until you are in that position," Marjan said.

"Malachy and I love each other. We're going to be together forever. And there's nothing to regret. I thought we had been over this when we first started going together. Remember, you told me about Ali?" Layla turned to her oldest sister with a pointed look.

Marjan stared at the quiet Mall ahead. Ali. Her last real relationship. She rubbed her forehead: what was happening to her? Who was she to give advice on love anyway? She let go of her breath. "Malachy is a good boy. I'm glad you are happy, I really am. Just promise me you'll be careful, okay?"

"I promise. Now can we change the subject?"

Marjan stayed quiet, staring out the van window. She felt so foolish all of a sudden.

Chapter 13

Turning Over the Leaf

"RIGHT, SO. MRS. BOYLAN has just handed me a notice from Guard Grogan . . . let me see now: Will the owner of one galvanized bull's harness, recently left in Saint Joseph's gymnasium, please pick it up at the Garda station. That's down in the square, for anyone new to the area. Next to Shaughnessy's Salmon Hut and the Town Hall . . .

"And here's a bit of exciting news: it seems that our own Margaret McGuire has been on to her brother Kieran—you might remember his exhilarating group of thespians from the Dance two years back: I'm still reeling from their Punch and Judy exhibit! Hah hah!

"Well, folks, it looks like we might be in for another treat of the McGuire Family Circus this time around. As I speak they're not a hundred miles from here, finishing their gig at the Galway

Oyster Fest. And coming up to us for the All Hallows' Eve ceili! How's that for interventions divine?

"So, on that note, and for your groovy pleasure, here's Lionel Richie, with a particular favorite of mine: 1986's 'Dancing on the Ceiling.'

"I'm Father Fergal Mahoney, and you're listening to Craic FM!"

✻

BAHAR AMINPOUR LOWERED the veil over her face. She turned to the tarnished mirror in the bedroom above the café, lifting her chin from right to left. In this dim light, and with her face covered as it was, her profile took on entirely new dimensions; she could be anybody, go anywhere. Under this veil she was sixteen again, young and full of adventure. Blinking, she stepped closer to the mirror. From behind the delicate French embroidery, her large brown eyes looked almost demure, kittenish.

Unlike Layla's bewitching gaze, Bahar was well aware that her own eyes sometimes gave too much of her fear away; panes to her world, they often reflected the sadness that came over her, sometimes without a moment's notice. But now, staring back at her from the latticelike fabric, her eyes gave off a mysterious and confident air. Suddenly she felt like Scheherazade, that Persian princess with the gift of tales, donning a servant's chador to sneak out of her nightmarish palace.

Like Scheherazade, Bahar had covered herself once. On that morning when she slipped out of the apartment she shared with her husband, Hossein, she had vowed never to wear another chador or veil, certainly not of her own free will.

Yet here she was, placing one on her own head, her own hands securing it behind her ears. Stranger things have happened, Bahar told herself.

Turning away from her reflection, she shuffled softly to the bedroom door, which she had locked as an extra precaution. Bending to peek through the keyhole, she could just make out the small living room across the way, a simple space that had served as a ramshackle office when the Delmonicos ran their little pastry place. The futon sofa was vacant, and the bathroom door was ajar, revealing its empty tiles.

She was alone, Bahar reassured herself, safe for at least another quarter of an hour. Layla was probably reading her little play somewhere, and Marjan was in the kitchen getting breakfast under way. No chance of anyone interrupting her preparations. She would have plenty of time to practice her walk as well.

Bahar made her way back to the middle of the room, but instead of returning to the mirror, she sidled up to the double bed. When they'd first moved in, they had only a mattress, but bit by bit they had acquired some furniture, pine units that were nice enough but nothing like what she'd always imagined for her own home. One day she would have her antiques and lace, Bahar promised herself. Until then, knotty pine would have to do.

Still, she would rather sleep on a rack of nails than share her dreams with Hossein Jaferi again. Even after all these years, she couldn't believe she had given herself to such a man—at the age of sixteen, no less. The signs had been there from the beginning, but she'd paid them no mind. The first time he had shown her his baton, she should have turned on her heels and run, but instead she had indulged him with a young girl's awed attention.

"See these grooves," Hossein had said, pointing at the lightning bolt lines carved deep in the stick. The baton was his number one weapon against opposing factions, the gangs that were vying for control of the Revolution. "These leave gashes that never heal. They reach deep into muscle and tear apart every strength. No one survives the Jaferi Jab, khanoum. No one." He had laughed heartily and with such pride then, as she had lowered her chador-framed face in humility. He was to be her husband, after all.

Nine years had passed since Bahar's marriage had ended so abruptly, and in a manner that still gave her nightmares. And over the years she had had a few momentary glimpses into the reason behind her acquiescence, why she had leapt into the fire that was the Jaferi way.

It wasn't exactly fear, not really; Bahar thought the word too mundane; it wasn't fear that had made her join the Women's Party and give her devotion to Hossein; it was something much more sinister. A dark void that was somehow connected to those migraines she used to get. That unnameable chasm had first made itself known to her during those nights when Marjan was away.

Her sister had been working at the Peacock, the Hilton Hotel's premier restaurant, for nearly two years, ever since they had moved out of their childhood home in northern Tehran. With no life insurance, their father, Javid, had left little that could have justified their living on such a large estate. The three of them barely had the means to keep themselves clothed and fed, without having to worry about running a property as well.

Oh, how desperately she had wanted to leave school and apply for a paid position somewhere, anywhere, just to help! Perhaps something at a seamstress's workshop or the local museum, a small building that boasted antiques from all over the world. She had always loved antiques, the weight of them, their certainty, their immutable essence. Working in a museum would have been paradise. But Marjan had forbidden her to drop her studies. She was to take care of little Layla while Marjan washed dishes at the restaurant and studied part-time at Tehran University.

Bahar shook her head. Those shifts when Marjan worked late were the most dreadful times for her. Though part of her knew that her older sister would be home by eleven, midnight at the latest, it did not stop the hole inside her from growing.

Perched at the apartment window, she would watch for hours as the sun sank behind the neighborhood mosque. Once the moon had ascended over the mosaic turrets, painting the tenements of their neighborhood with its indigo tears, Bahar would begin her own night's mourning.

In the darkness she would imagine an alternate ending, Marjan found dead or dying, lying on the side of a road somewhere, killed by marauding gangs or a roaring truck on her way home from the Peacock Restaurant.

The night would tell Bahar that she and Layla were alone now, alone to fend for themselves.

The moon would tell her to begin again, begin with a cleanse.

That was when she discovered the power of the copper scour. As the gory image of their dead sister flashed across her eyes, Bahar would begin to clean, taking a scrubbing coil and bleach to all the kitchen appliances, moving down to the linoleum floor, cheap like the rest of the apartment they were living in, rubbing, rubbing away at the hole forming in the pit of her stomach, her breast. She had to be self-sufficient, the hole would tell her; she was mistress of the house now, it was up to her to cleanse it of its terrible fate.

Clean it away, Bahar. Clean it away.

And she would, night after night. It was a method that worked well. By the time her sister came home, Bahar would be back to feeling calm and secure, ready for school the next morning. But she knew that things would change one day, one day when Marjan would finally leave.

Bahar lifted her face off the mattress. She hadn't realized she had laid her cheek on it. Giving the locked bedroom door another glance, she slipped her hand along the base, her fingers touching on a bit of lace. She sighed with relief: it was still there, in the place she had left it on Monday.

At first she had been angry for having to sacrifice her Sunday morning for Marjan's schedule change, but now she was glad of it; Monday's afternoon break had allowed her the time to go into Castlebar for her necessary errands. Otherwise she would have had to ask Mrs. Boylan to get the last items on her list, and the kind lady had done enough already, keeping her secret all these months.

Unlike the women who frequented the relics shop, Father Mahoney's housekeeper and the chairwoman of the Ladies of the Patrician Day Dance Committee was nothing if not a monument to discretion. Look how she had kept her employer's new radio show a secret—now that must have been a challenge!

Bahar recalled the priest's radio program with a smile. In all her time of taking initiation classes, where they had carefully gone over all manner of Scripture passages, Father Mahoney had not said a word about his new venture. Bahar didn't know what she would have said had he told her of his idea, but she liked to think she would have been as encouraging as the priest had been to her during the last year. His guiding voice had led her to many discoveries within her own soul; it wasn't much of a leap, Bahar mused, that he would turn it to a larger medium.

She gave a little giggle. And wasn't it just like Father Mahoney to come up with a send-off that went with the greatest of Scripture verses: "All is right with the world, dear listener." All is right with the world. Bahar hoped that was true; the events of the last few weeks had her seriously questioning the evil in the world. There was just too much wrongdoing going on, even in places where you least expected it. Even in your own household.

Sure, Marjan was being a Good Samaritan by feeding this stranger, this girl up at Estelle's, but what good did it do in the end? What good was it to help someone who was capable of such lunacy, to try to kill her own beautiful baby? Wouldn't it be better not to have such a person around at all, making room for someone who really wanted a child? Wasn't that what being a righteous believer was all about?

Bahar sighed. There seemed to be no good answers. Still, she had to admit Father Mahoney's closing message was comforting.

His new spiritual sound waves were further guidance, she thought, toward a smooth and clean conversion. *All is right with the world.* Every sign was pointing her in the right direction. Next stop was her first Mass, for which she had bought this outfit.

Bahar hoisted the mattress off its base. She pulled the lacy fabric from its resting place. Even in the darkened room the dress radiated cleanliness, pure and white as the Alborz snow. As white as the peak on that mountain up the street, Croagh Patrick, the Reek.

It was on that mountain that she had discovered her need for something greater than her own pain, a need to surrender to whatever it was God held in store for her. It was as though a prism had turned inside her during her climb, letting in light, letting in air, as she ascended.

She had felt happy, simply happy for standing on that peak, turning her gaze out to the Atlantic. She had needed no copper scour while up there; she was cleansed all the same.

Bahar held the dress up to her body and studied her reflection. Yes, she told herself, everything had changed once again; now she was happy to be alone, happy to wear a veil again.

TACHEEN IS A DOMED MEDLEY of baked saffron rice and chicken, forming the shape of a cathedral ceiling. On first glance, the dish looks curiously like *chelow*, plain steamed rice; it is only after slicing through its center that the layers of fortitude are exposed: first buttered rice and almonds, then fried chicken and sautéed spinach, the yogurt binding them into a brotherhood of delicious play. *Tacheen*.

Marjan estimated another ten minutes before she would need to turn the baked dinner from its casserole dish. She usually had much more patience when it came to making *tacheen*, especially that last step, which always verged on exhilaration, but the unease in her belly was making it impossible to stay still today. She had not been feeling entirely rooted since her disappointment yesterday. Just thinking about her uneventful date sent a flush of embarrassment across her chest. Dreaming up possible excuses for Julian did not ease the strange loneliness that was making its way into her stomach. Had she really been so ready to plunge again into an idea of romance, one that might never fully blossom?

Marjan sat down at the round kitchen table, her thoughts traveling back. She had never, not in all these years, blamed Ali for her having ended up in Gohid Detention Center. He hadn't forced her to help out at the offices of *The Voice*. She had come of her own free will, decided to contribute what she could without being asked.

She had even chosen to wear the *roosarie* scarf—motivated not from a spiritual yearning but from a need for solidarity: she had wanted to show her support for the Revolution that had begun to sweep through the university halls, she had wanted to bear witness in the form of a dark scarf.

That scarf had turned into a blindfold, quite literally, the day *The Voice*'s offices were taken down by the Shah's police. The day she said good-bye forever to Ali's sweet green eyes.

Marjan sighed. She had never told her sisters about that time; not being involved in the cause, not meeting up with Ali after their high school years, not even the reason she had disappeared for three days that spring of 1978, disappeared without even a phone call.

How could she? Where could she have started?

How could she have stood in front of those two—Layla not yet seven, Bahar only sixteen—and explained how she had placed them all in danger for the sake of a man's affection?

"*Tacheen* always reminds me of Christmas." Layla's voice startled Marjan.

"When did we have *tacheen* for Christmas?" she asked, rising from the table and making her way back to the casserole. She adjusted the platter over its hot rim, closing in the plume of steam that was escaping over the edges.

Layla shrugged, bounding down the stairs. "Never. But it kind of looks like a Christmas pudding, its shape and all. A savory Christmas pudding. It makes me think of cozy things, like blankets and fireplaces and Bing Crosby." She plopped down at the table with her copy of *Much Ado About Nothing*. "Though I hear old Bing wasn't that great of a guy offscreen. You wouldn't know it, to look at his twinkly blue eyes."

Marjan gave her youngest sister a fond smile. Layla would never stop surprising her. "Don't you have that memorized by now?" She pointed the spatula at the book.

Layla smiled. "Yeah, but I like to see the words on the page as well. It's awesome. Listen to this:

BENEDICK: *It is certain I am loved of all ladies, only you excepted: and I would I could find in my heart that I had not a hard heart: for, truly, I love none.*

BEATRICE: *A dear happiness to women; they would else have been troubled with a pernicious suitor. I thank God, and my cold blood, I am of your humor for that: I had rather hear my dog bark at a crow than a man swear he loves me.*

BENEDICK: *God keep your ladyship still in that mind! So some gentleman or other shall 'scape a predestinate scratched face."*

Layla sighed. "Now that's what I call sexual tension."

Marjan laughed.

Layla gave her a quizzical look. "What?"

Marjan shook her head. "You are so funny sometimes."

Layla shrugged. "Don't tell me you don't think of that English guy. What's his name? Julian?" She said the name in a singsong manner. "Have you read his book yet?"

Marjan remained silent as she slowly circled the spatula along the inside rim of the casserole dish. *Dominions of Clay* remained where she had left it yesterday, jammed under a road map of Mayo in the van's cavernous glove compartment. "Is Bahar asleep?" she asked, changing the subject.

Layla wet her thumb and flipped a page. "I don't know. She said she was taking a nap. I don't think it's a headache, though. No medicine near the bed," she said.

"I hope not."

"Maybe she's praying or something," Layla said, scrunching her nose. "I still can't believe she wants to be a Catholic."

"It is a bit unexpected," Marjan admitted. But then, it was Bahar.

"She'd have a fit if she knew about me and Malachy." The corners of Layla's mouth rose mischievously.

"If she doesn't know about it yet, she'll surely know all about it by tonight," Marjan replied, thinking of the Ballinacroagh grapevine. She turned to Layla. "You're going to keep your promise to me, aren't you?"

Layla sighed. "Yes."

"And what was that promise?"

"To tell you the next time me and Malachy think we are ready. To tell you so that we can talk about it and figure things out." She closed the play, tucked it under her chin. "How about you spring for a hotel room in Dublin? I'd pay you back."

"Oh, Layla, what am I going to do with you?" Marjan shook her head. It really wasn't up to her anymore. Her youngest sister was about to embark on her own, become the woman she was meant to be. It was time for Marjan to let go.

Turning back to the stove, Marjan secured the platter over the casserole. She could tell the *tacheen* was ready from the way the steam had gathered along the sides of the dish.

She turned to Layla. "Okay. Ready?"

Her youngest sister nodded, her eyes widening with anticipation.

Marjan held her breath and held tighter to the tea-toweled platter: "One, two . . . three!" She flipped the casserole upside down.

The structure that emerged a moment later was a cake of buttery rice ensconcing honeyed almonds and chicken, the lot.

Layla clapped her hands as Marjan took a bow. "It's perfect! Mrs. D's going to love it!"

Marjan smiled at her little sister, wondering how it was that Layla could sound so grown-up and so young in the space of a single second.

It was a mystery as deep as the treasures found in her sweet and savory *tacheen*.

Chapter 14

A Fairy and a Healer

IT WASN'T OFTEN that the moral scions of Ballinacroagh were correct in their conjectures, but in the case of Estelle Delmonico's new ward, they were not all that far off-course. A descendant of Biddy Early's may well have been channeling her powers inside the Delmonico homestead. But rather than calling forth the eventide of Judgment, her results were as glorious as the morning dawn.

Marjan noticed a marked change in Estelle right away. The widow was snuggled into her hearth chair in the blue and yellow kitchen, in her favorite lace and eyelet nightgown. With her hair held jauntily back by a lavender ribbon, and a healthy twinkle in her warm brown eyes, Estelle Delmonico looked like a sweet toddler waiting for her bedtime story. You wouldn't think she's nearly seventy, thought Marjan, placing the *tacheen* on the pine counter.

"You look so nice," Marjan said. "Like you've slept for ten years, refreshed."

Estelle smiled coquettishly. "Thank you, darling. You look so pretty too. Just like Sophia Loren." She pointed to the Lavazza coffee sign blinking sleepily over the periwinkle cabinet. The neon was one of the few mementos the widow had kept from Papa's Pastries, having it rewired so that it gave off a brilliant red hue.

The coffee sign illuminated a framed poster stationed beside it, a large photograph of that buxom actress Sophia Loren, a crush of her late husband's.

"Is that a new skirt? *Bellissima!*"

Marjan looked down, nodding. She spoke softly: "I wore it last night. On a date."

"A date! Oh my goodness! How wonderful!" Estelle clapped her hands like a schoolgirl.

"It would have been," Marjan replied. She explained Julian's disappearance. "I guess I just feel foolish, really. I got so excited over nothing."

"But why shouldn't you get excited?" Estelle said. "It is only natural that you want to feel joy and love, especially when you are young. I tell you, men are very difficult to understand. Even my Luigi, who was almost perfect, he had problems also, my goodness."

Estelle paused for a moment. "Maybe this Englishman, maybe something happened like an emergency? Yes? You must first wait and see before thinking the worst. And if no, then there are many Irishmen waiting for you. You are famous, in newspapers, and you own the best café in Ireland."

"Maybe you're right," said Marjan, believing the kind widow's words as she uttered them. "We'll just have to wait and see. Now, how about some *tacheen*?"

She lifted the cheesecloth off the casserole. The scent of saffron and almonds wafted around them.

"It's still warm, but I could heat it up for you again. Is she awake?" Marjan nodded toward the hallway, where Estelle's bedroom door remained closed.

"No, so tired. Sleeping already." Estelle lifted her eyebrows and grinned. "We walk around my garden today."

Marjan looked surprised. "Your meditation garden?"

"Yes. For three hours today! Yesterday also! Can you believe it!" Estelle turned to her guest with eyes shining. The Lavazza sign blinked, lighting up a series of pearly droplets above her upper lip.

Marjan gasped. "Are you sweating again?" She peered into Estelle's face.

"Sweat?" The old lady drew the pad of her thumb along the soft slope above her lip, wiping off a band of glistening water. "Look at this!" she said, showing Marjan her thumb. "And it is still cold outside!"

She popped the end of her thumb into her mouth and sucked on the water, a concentration better known in baking circles as sugarcane extract. "Did I ever tell you how I met my Luigi? No? It is all because of this sweat. Remind me, I will tell you the story one day."

Marjan was astounded. "But if you're sweating, that means your arthritis is much better."

Estelle nodded and grinned, as though she had a wonderful secret. "Yes, much better."

"But how is that possible?"

Estelle winked. "Magic, Marjan. Magic."

IT HAD STARTED AFTER DINNER on Monday night, said Estelle. Though if they were to get technical, it really began the night they brought the girl back from Mayo General, when Estelle had dropped the spoonful of plum stew from pain. The widow had not known what to expect when the girl reached over and grabbed her long-suffering hands, but the last thing was a cessation of her arthritis.

The young woman had held her gnarled knuckles for only a few seconds, but it had been enough: a heat, simultaneously silvery and as intense as hot mercury, had rushed up her arms and shoulders, instantly soothing her. It was as though a dam had broken, releasing something from the young woman's palms, sending medicine through her fanlike hands. And then, just as quickly as she'd taken them, the girl let go of Estelle's hands, falling back to her pillow with exhaustion. Before Estelle could question what had occurred, the girl had closed her eyes and surrendered to sleep.

That night, Estelle had also slept—without interruption, without one single needle of joint pain anywhere in her body. She couldn't remember the last time she had felt so free.

Whatever the girl had done to clear Estelle's hands had also drained her of all energy, for the girl slept all night and the following day. Feeling guilty for causing her any weakness, Estelle had not dared wake her for dinner. Nor had she brought up the subject once her new ward had woken in her hospital bed. Although her arthritic pain had come back over the weekend, it had been more manageable than she remembered in a long time. Estelle considered the moment of healing as a gift sent from above, something best left unexplored, especially considering that the girl was still not talking. But the mystery had deepened without her inducement, becoming even stranger on Monday evening.

Having polished off Marjan's cherry rice, Estelle was clearing away the last of the dishes and getting ready to wet a fresh pot of tea. Although she was sleeping on the linen couch in the living room to make space for her new guest, Estelle still ate her dinner on the mattress. She was accustomed to eating in bed, insisted upon it, actually.

Not only was the four-poster—a lofty structure that would have put princesses and peas to shame—a place of rest and relaxation but it was, and had been for quite some time now, a portal for her magic carpet escapades. It was there that Estelle first began to practice what Marjan had called "eating at the edge of a ready *sofreh*."

Estelle always followed the same routine when assembling her dinner *sofreh* on her bed. First, she would spread the paisley blanket Marjan had given her, tucking the fringed ends in tight around the sides of her mattress. Then, having already wetted a pot of jasmine tea, she would dig a trivet into the blanket's left corner and place the piping pot on top of it.

Following the Persian etiquette of placing the main dishes at the center of the *sofreh*, Estelle would position the plate of saffron *chelow* (with crunchy *tadig*), the bowl of stew or soup that was the day's special, and the *lavash* or *barbari* bread accordingly. She would frame the main dishes with a small plate of *torshi*, pickled carrots and cucumbers, as well as a yogurt dip and some feta cheese with her favorite herb: balmy lemon mint.

Taking off her pink pom-pom house slippers, Estelle would then hoist herself onto her high bed and begin her ecstatic epicurean adventure. She savored every morsel of her nightly meal, breathing in the tingle of sumac powder and nutmeg while speaking to a framed photograph of Luigi she propped up on its own trivet next to the tea.

Dinner was usually Persian, but her dessert was always Italian: a peppermint cannoli or marzipan cherry, after which she would turn on the radio, always set to the *Mid-West Ceili Hour*, and dream of the time when a young Luigi made her do things impossible, like when he convinced her to enter the Maharaja sideshow and stand on the tallest elephant's trunk during carnival season in her seaside Neapolitan town.

Estelle had recalled the carnival as she picked up the last platter. "Time for dessert, yes?" She turned to the girl sitting in the wheelchair. Although the widow had insisted she try to sit up in bed, the young woman had preferred to stay in her borrowed seat for her meals. "Some orange tea and black-and-white biscuits. Lovely!"

Estelle's smile was returned with a solemn look. The young woman shook her head, a sign that she wanted Estelle to wait. Wheeling her chair closer to the bed, where the remnants of their supper still stood, the mermaid girl placed a hand on the patchwork duvet.

At once, Estelle understood what the motion meant.

Without another sound, she took off her aforementioned razzmatazz slippers and climbed up on the mattress. Her veiny, swollen feet looked funny to her from this distance; they flopped open like trunks themselves, withered and white with age. Her palms were also open, resting on either side of her round hips, just as the girl was showing her.

"Like this?" Estelle asked, holding her arms out.

The girl turned sideways in her wheelchair and nodded slowly. In the lamplight, her spread fingers looked more than ever like organza pastry, the veils of skin between them taking on an apricot tinge. Although Estelle had seen those fingers up close a dozen times, she was still amazed at their magical appearance.

The girl reached over slowly, but instead of grabbing the widow's fingers, she clasped her own hands, raising them over Estelle as though in prayer. Estelle watched in fascination as the young woman began to rub her palms quickly, as though she were kindling a fire between them.

She rubbed her hands for what seemed like thirty seconds, then slowly she pulled them away from each other, easing them out.

When her hands were about three feet apart, she took a deep breath, swung her elbows out, and swept her fingers in again.

Estelle gasped. From the center of her belly, where the girl's hands had stopped, a powerful surge was taking over. It was as though she was being lifted from the very core of her being, a pulling sensation arching her back off the mattress.

Then: heat, a warm rush of pooling blood similar to the sensation she had felt in her hands that other day.

Before Estelle had a chance to say anything, the girl's hands began to move again.

As though pulling invisible threads, her fingers plucked, plucked, plucked, pulling heat from Estelle's navel.

On and on the girl kept unspooling, as the widow watched her in pure awe, no longer frightened by the heat emanating from her body. There was an intense concentration in the girl's gray eyes as she plucked the threads that were visible only to her. Still a teenager, somehow she also looked older than time itself.

Estelle had intended to shut her eyes and welcome a soothing darkness, as she had done when the girl had treated her hands before. But this time she decided to leave her eyes wide open, and what she saw were the dreams of a little princess.

"SO YOU SAW A PICTURE, like an image, when she touched you?" Marjan asked in puzzlement.

"No, no, you mistake: not a picture but a film. Like an old film, with some color. And she did not even touch me this time."

Estelle waved her hands in the air, showing their limber state. "I think when she put her hands over me, I see her memories. I see her thinking. Like energy too."

Marjan sat back in her seat, sifting through what the widow had just told her. "And it's happened twice now? I don't understand—two times you've seen a film?"

Estelle nodded, licking her upper lip. "Two times, yes. Monday and last night. Tonight she is very tired from all the walking."

The older woman paused and looked at Marjan. "I know this is amazing to hear, darling, but it happened. I have my eyes open, but I still see this film. It was a film of a little girl. She was wearing a beautiful white dress and turning, turning in the same spot. Like trying to make herself dizzy. That is all I saw and then the film was finished. And my hands, my feet, even my hips—no pain. Nothing for three days. Like magic. Strange, yes?"

The Italian widow was too busy licking her sugared sweat to see Marjan shake her head; nothing was strange anymore, she told herself.

Baraka, *the blessing of Allah, is given only to a select few in a lifetime. These chosen people are able to fully transmit the* dam, *or breath of life, onto the sick and needy. It is the* dam, *the rhythm of the breath accompanied by prayer, which heals most ailments. The chosen healer with the power of* baraka *is called the* hakim . . .

Marjan turned the page, her eyes scanning the small print; the *Canon of Medicine* was certainly living up to its name in length. The edition that Filomina Fanning had procured for her from the university library in Dublin was a condensed version of the five-volume masterpiece written by the physician over a thousand years ago, but it was still proving too vast for a quick skim.

She had spent the last hour scouring the book, and although thoroughly captivated by the techniques of breathing to heal ailments, she hadn't found anything on the peculiarities of healing hands. As much as she hoped to locate some clues within its pages, she was growing somewhat discouraged. She squinted at the fine print. No, nothing about hands transferring memories. Massage and oils, yes. Sandalwood oil, for example, when dropped onto the ledge of the ear, cures the body of all egotism. A perfect ablution before prayer. Here it was again, the universal pregnancy diet, all those foods she had been so anxious about serving.

Still, nothing like what Estelle had experienced.

Marjan frowned. Estelle had said that she felt a warmth course almost immediately through her body when the girl drew her hands above her, followed by a freezing sensation when the girl began pulling the air. Then she saw the picture of a young girl, in what looked like a white dress, twirling on the tips of her toes.

A young girl with red hair.

It was as though the girl was transferring her emotions or desires, maybe even past experiences, to Estelle while she tried to soothe her arthritis. A whirling little girl. Marjan's eyes followed the stairs in the kitchen. She thought she had heard a noise on the landing above her. It was only dawn, too early for either Bahar or Layla to be awake, she reminded herself. She wouldn't know where to even begin explaining her latest finding to her sisters. She brought her eyes to her hands, resting them in the hollows of her palms.

Healing hands. Transference of memories. A whirling little girl. What was she not understanding about all of this? She looked up again.

Whirling. It was a practice done in many circles. Among the Sufis, those followers of a mystical strain of Islam, it was a treasured practice, as sacred as the prayers to Mecca. Sufis believed that whirling brings you closer to the center of God. It was a method similar to Estelle's meditation garden, where she traveled in a circular pattern while praying or thinking of her problems. By whirling, you align your core to the earth's core. Legend had it that the dance started with Rumi, who wrote poems to the Beloved nearly three hundred years after Avicenna wrote his *Canon*.

How was it that the image Estelle had seen was that of a girl whirling?

The knock was soft, hesitant. It came twice, then paused before sounding once more. Marjan reached behind her and opened the kitchen door. A familiar face stared back at her. "Hello," she said, looking up at the old woman on the stoop.

The woman brought her hand to the knot on her head scarf. "I'm Marie Brennan. I live across the street." Her voice and hand were both shaky.

Marjan smiled politely. "Of course." She closed the *Canon* and turned to greet the woman fully. "How are you?"

Marie blinked and looked down at her orthopedic shoes. "Thank you. Good. Thank you." She continued to stare at her shoes.

Marjan tilted her head. Dervla's sister had never been to the café before. "Do you want to come in?" she asked, pushing the door open.

Marie looked around uncomfortably. The alleyway was quiet but for a soft cloud of flour billowing out of the bakery next door.

"I came as early as I could, I can't stay longer than a minute the most."

"Is there something wrong? Are you all right?"

Marie tightened her lips, looking as though she might burst into tears right there on the spot.

Marjan opened the back door wide. "Please, come in."

❊

FADDEN'S MINI-MART had changed very little since Marjan had bought her first bag of groceries there. The same rows of raggedy turnips, rhubarb, and parsnips piled in deep wooden bins; fishing tackle interspersed with ladies' stockings and cans of Batchelors baked beans; jams and biscuits galore, lined in neat pyramids along the back wall. The same leprechaun haunting its midnight aisles. "Hello, Danny. How are you doing?" Marjan said, stepping into the shop.

Behind the Formica counter, Danny Fadden jumped in surprise. "Oh! Hello there, Marjan! Grand, grand. On a bit of a creative zephyr, to be exact."

Danny pushed his large glasses up his red nose and smiled. As Marjan approached the counter, she noticed the shopkeeper's hands: they were covered by Rorschach splotches of indigo ink, which had also found its way onto his chin and wrinkly brow.

"What are you up to now?" She glanced at the large bound notebook opened on the countertop.

"Back on the C's. I've the first draft finished, you see, so now it's the meticulous act of correspondence, check entries against entries, making dead certain I've not missed any cross-references."

Danny pushed his glasses up his nose again. "You see, Marjan, every fairy creature out there has a like, a relative or twin, in every language and culture there is. Take the cluricaune, for example. A happy cousin of the leprechaun but for his preference for red *vino* instead of the Kilkelly stout. Now, the cluricaune meets his mirror in the English boggart— not to be mistaken for that lovely scoundrel of the silver screen, mind you—which in turn is almost identical in temperament to the croissant-mad *rongeur d'os* of the Normandy coast. Who, in a roundabout stroke of fairy paterfamiliarity, is similar to the bullbeggar of Somerset, and the spirit—which, to be perfectly frank, has a bit in every pot of every land." Danny took a deep breath, his eyes burning with inspired light.

Marjan shook her head. "My goodness. And how's your Finnegan doing?" she asked, following local protocol. It was customary practice to ask after the shopkeeper's fairy before tending to the more prosaic business of groceries and the like.

"Mighty. Had his summer holidays in Cabo San Lucas. That's Mexico country. Got back and left me this just on the Monday." Danny disappeared under the counter and emerged a few seconds later with a large piñata bull.

"Tucked in behind the case of Beamish, so he was. Wouldn't have a clue what it was doing there but for his IOU." The grocer cleared his throat and read from a piece of green felt he held in his hand:

"Had me a sweet señorita in the land of tequila
A couple of mariachis for the afternoon archies
Nevertheless, missed my Beamish the best
Promise my pesos *at the end of my rest.*
Andale Andale Andale!!!

IOU El Finnegan*"*

A stranger to Ballinacroagh would have been quick to flee the mini-mart right around then, but like the rest of the patrons who frequented the shop, Marjan knew that Finnegan was a leprechaun who visited the mart on Sunday nights for a rig or two of his favorite stout. The wily shoemaker would always leave an IOU note promising the shopkeeper payment in full someday soon, but payment never came. Payment enough, most patrons agreed, was the smile of camaraderie brightening Danny Fadden's usually lonely face.

In fact, Marjan was one of few in town who knew of the leprechaun's true origins: according to Fiona Athey, who had in turn heard it from Evie Watson, whose information came straight from the horse's mouth, her on-again off-again boyfriend Peter Donnelly, Finnegan was a high school prank gone out of hand. Although graduated and on their way to larger debaucheries, the Donnelly twins still kept up their ruse of a leprechaun stealing stout, for they knew how important it was to Danny Fadden's creative life.

Marjan trailed her hands slowly along a display of Cadbury's chocolate fingers. The biscuits were among Layla's favorites. She grabbed a box and approached the counter again.

"Danny, what do you know about healers? People who have special powers?"

The grocer sat up on his stool. "Well now, that is one of our greatest legacies. Going back to the times of the Druids themselves. Sure, those bearded fellows had their work cut out for them, planning out fates and fortunes for all those kings and minions."

"Could any of them bring out sickness, heal with their hands maybe?"

"Let's see now . . . What I know of healers is limited, not as standard as I'd like to be on the matter, that's for sure. Spent too much time on this *Encyclopedia of the Folk*, you know . . . Healing with hands, you say?"

Marjan nodded. "Special hands. Not like ordinary fingers. Sort of like webs."

Danny's bulbous eyes blinked rapidly behind his glasses. "Webs," he whispered and tore through his notebook, flipping pages until he reached the middle. "Webs . . . only one bit about webs here. But nothing to do with healing. That's it, here we go: the merrow."

Marjan waited for the grocer to read from his encyclopedia.

Danny cleared his throat once more. "The merrow: siren of the sea, Irish to the core. Cousin to the mermaid, who finds her home in Atlantis, or as the Celts call it, Hy Brasil.

"Merrows have legs like the rest of human folk but carry fingers with webbed skin. From time to time they make their way to the land, escaping the chains of domesticity below. It seems the poor creatures are mated to rather ugly mermen, squat little toads. They much prefer the company of men onshore."

Danny looked up from the book and grinned. "Sure, why wouldn't they?" he said mischievously, pushing his glasses up his round nose.

The mermaid again.

That fairy tale wasn't going to help solve this problem, Marjan told herself. She thought of what Marie Brennan had warned her about that morning.

"They've written to the bishop in Tuam. It'll take a month to reach him; he's off on his holidays at the moment. But there'll be a mighty price to pay when he gets the letter. Oh, a mighty price."

Despite Marjan's offer of tea, Marie had chosen to remain standing just inside the kitchen door.

Marjan had leaned forward in her seat. "What do you mean? What price?"

"The price—the price we all have to pay!" Marie's voice quivered; she clutched her black purse fervently to her chest.

Marjan thought that the older lady might faint. She certainly did not look well.

Marie lowered her voice. "Dervla is going to tell the bishop that Estelle Delmonico's practicing devil worship. And that she's got some sort of witch up there with her. And that Father Mahoney is in on it, channeling the source from his radio station! There's no way to stop it! It's done already!"

Marjan shook her head at such a preposterous accusation. Imagine Father Mahoney channeling spirits. What would Dervla Quigley think of next?

"Will I ring this up?" Danny pointed to the products on the counter.

"Thanks, Danny. I'll have a bottle of buttermilk as well." She pointed to the large glassed-in refrigerator in the corner.

Danny tapped his fountain pen against his broad forehead. "Now that's what was picking at my mind just then! You'd think I was off with the fairies!" He rushed out from behind the counter and made his way to a refrigerator filled with soda and milk cartons. "I knew there was something I was meaning to give you as soon as you walked in. I just wasn't able to pin the thought, for my Finnegan." He swiveled around, a bouquet of luscious red roses in his hand. "This came for you late last night. From Buds of Mayo in Castlebar. Café was closed, so they dropped it off here. Had to keep it refrigerated, so." He handed Marjan the flowers. "There's a card in there."

Marjan opened the envelope. It was from Julian.

A thousand heartfelt apologies. Had to get myself to Galway for new contractors ASAP. A nightmare of pipes bursting, servants' quarters knee-deep in lake water. Half a mind to pack it all up, really. Be back day after. Dinner then? Please?

> *Your slightest look easily will unclose me,*
> *Though I have closed myself as fingers,*
> *You open always petal by petal myself as spring opens*
> *(Touching skillfully, mysteriously) her first rose*
>
> *—Julian*

Chapter 15

Manning Your Fort

MARJAN HAD PLACED the roses in a ceramic vase next to the samovar in the dining room. The red petals gave the tea boiler's golden belly a healthy blush, reflecting with a satisfied glow. As she always did in the mornings, she lifted the top half of the samovar and filled it with water before placing the top back on and plugging the whole thing into the wall. She flipped the power switch, listening for the hum of the samovar's inner coil as it started to heat up.

The samovar had come with them from London, along with most of their knickknacks and crockery, the delicate fluted teacups with their filigreed handles and the multicolored pots that lined the mahogany service counter.

Everything had been packed and shipped over within days, their plane ticket to Ireland bought with the last of their savings. The money they had borrowed from Gloria to start the business, along with Estelle's generosity, had seen them through those frightening first months of business.

In Marjan's estimation, Estelle Delmonico had a heart bigger than the whole of Ireland. It seemed almost preordained that she should be the one to have found the mermaid girl, that it was Estelle who had taken her in and not someone who might have gone straight to the authorities.

Bubbles began to surface inside the samovar. With a spoon in her hand, Marjan leaned down and tapped its center, testing the sound. The lower the *ting*, the closer the water was to tea quality. The sober sound reverberating back told her she needed to wait a few more minutes for that perfect cup of bergamot. Nothing like a good cup of tea, especially on a cold morning like this.

"Where did you get those?" Bahar asked, coming in with a tray of baklava. She slid them into the glass cabinet and walked to the mahogany counter. "Very expensive," she commented, gingerly touching one of the rose blossoms.

"I suppose they are," replied Marjan nonchalantly, turning away from the vase.

"So?"

"So?"

"So, where did you get them?"

Marjan picked up a purple teapot, took off its lid. "They were delivered from a florist. Julian sent them."

"Huh." Bahar crossed her arms over her thin chest. "Keen, isn't he?"

When Marjan did not respond, Bahar turned to her with a penetrating stare. "What's going on?"

"What do you mean?"

"This Julian. Are you in love with him or something?"

"Now why would you say that?"

"Siobhan said you were all made up and walking into the Wilton Inn the other night," Bahar replied. "Said he never showed up."

Marjan scooped up two spoonfuls of loose bergamot leaves, added them into the teapot. She had wondered when Bahar would mention her non-date with Julian. She had been prepared for a grilling about it for the last two days.

"My whole life is an open book, I see. When did you get this bit of news?"

Bahar shrugged. "Just yesterday, when I was at the Fish Hut getting the whiting." She paused. "She asked about you-know-who as well."

Marjan whipped around, the tea leaves sprinkling across the countertop. Bahar pretended not to notice the small mess. She took a teapot of her own, relishing her hold on a bit of information.

"What did she want to know?"

"Who?"

"Siobhan," Marjan said, impatience tightening her voice. She put down the jar of tea leaves, her hands on her hips. "What did she want to know?"

"She asked if I had heard about Estelle's kin. Was it true that she had a relative up at the cottage, and who was she—that kind of thing."

Marjan frowned. "And? Did she ask anything else?"

"No. But I knew she was itching to."

Marjan stared at the counter in thought. Word was traveling faster than she had expected. She looked up. "You didn't say anything?"

"What do you think I am?" Bahar huffed, grabbing the jar of bergamot tea. "Even if I don't think it's right, I wouldn't go behind Estelle's back," she said, holding the jar with one hand, rattling its contents. "It's *haram*, Marjan. I'm sticking to it. Even Father Mahoney thinks so."

"You didn't tell him, did you?"

"No. But the Church doesn't believe in that, and you know it. I'm learning a lot about how to live my life. You could do with a bit of instruction as well." Bahar walked over to the Victrola and turned on the radio below it. The dining room walls were instantly warmed by Father Mahoney's chirpy morning message.

"Oh, I forgot to tell you. I need an hour off this morning. Father Mahoney wants to take me through Mass procedures. For next week," Bahar said before pushing through the kitchen doors.

Biting her lip, Marjan turned back to the samovar. It was too early for another argument, she told herself. She just didn't have it in her. The matter about Siobhan was disturbing, though. It was bad enough that Dervla and her circle were gabbing away to the council and whoever had an ear, but when even Bahar was being questioned by neighbors, the rumor mill was clearly heating up. Sparks of gossip and wicked curiosity were surely heading straight for Estelle.

Marjan pressed the lever down, letting the hot water fill the teapot. *Haram* or not, a law had still been broken. Padraig

Carey had made it perfectly clear during his visit. She had better call Estelle and warn her. They might have to think of an alternative, a safe house where they could take the girl if the guards did come questioning. Stirring the bergamot leaves with the silver spoon, she replaced the lid on the pot and put it on a silver platter.

The doorbell tinkled behind her, a rush of air entering the warm dining room. Glancing over her shoulder, she saw him. Julian was standing at the threshold, his fists deep in the pockets of his corduroy jacket. His sandy, windblown hair, wet from the rain, sat against his broad shoulders, giving him the rugged look she had come to find so attractive.

"I wouldn't consider it out of place if you never wanted to see me again," he said, hunching into his jacket. "I acted the fool, that's certain."

Marjan hadn't really decided what she would say to him when she saw him again. She stared at him for a moment. "I didn't know what had happened to you," she replied, keeping her tone steady. "I wish you had told me before you left."

"You're right," he admitted. "Horrid manners on my part. Lost my head with the mess."

Marjan set a tea glass on a saucer, placed it on a platter. "Is everything all right? With the house?"

Pulling out a chair, he sank into it, shaking the wet from his hair. "Lunacy, that's what it is. Should have known not to hire a local plumber. Said he had tapped into a well on the grounds: 'Get the waters flowing, so I can.'" Julian winced. "Flooded the entire servants' quarters, the kitchen, the whole lower floor."

"That's terrible!" Marjan brought the platter and teapot over, placed it in the center of the table.

"It's going to take a month to get it all sorted. I have to leave for Dublin tomorrow. Paperwork, legalities, you know how it goes," he said, nodding appreciatively as Marjan poured him a glass of tea. "I was hoping to catch you before then."

"I know. I read your note." She gestured toward the mahogany counter.

Julian followed her gaze to the vase of roses. He smiled. "So I'm forgiven, then?"

Marjan shrugged, her lips curving despite herself. "Maybe."

He leaned over and touched her hand. "Let me take you out to dinner. Tonight. I want you to see one of the most smashing spots. I know you'll appreciate it."

Marjan watched his fingers linger on hers before moving her eyes up to meet his gaze. Of course she would go out with him, she told herself. How could she say no to those deep green eyes?

The kitchen doors swung open. "I'll be right back. Father Mahoney wants me to read through some psalms for—" Bahar stopped in her tracks, her tweed coat halfway across her back. She stared at Julian, then Marjan, then Julian again.

Julian left his seat, stepped forward with his hand held out. "We haven't formally met. Julian Winthrop Muir, how do you do?"

"Hello." Bahar shook his hand limply. She looked at Marjan with raised eyebrows.

"I hear you're the strength behind this operation," said Julian, flashing her a smile.

"Oh . . ." She lifted a shoulder. "I don't know."

He chuckled. "Modesty runs in the family, I see. Your sister told me how you take care of all the base work. She couldn't whip up all those lovely concoctions without you by her side, I'd say."

Bahar slipped her right arm into her coat sleeve. "It's just chopping and shopping," she said coolly, buttoning up her collar. Though she was pleased by the compliment, Marjan noted.

"She's lucky to have you, that's what."

Bahar tilted her head, giving Julian another assessing look. "And you're lucky to have her."

Marjan glanced at her sister, her own face flaring up. "Bahar."

"Oh, I wouldn't say I have her," Julian replied. "Though she certainly has my affections, if she wants them."

Bahar set her jaw. "So those are your only intentions—just your affections?"

"Not at all."

"Because you know, where we come from, a man doesn't just give out affections without a deeper meaning behind them. A *spiritual* meaning."

"Couldn't agree with you more," replied Julian, his lips twitching amusedly. He turned to Marjan with a meaningful look.

Bahar was on a roll. "A woman isn't something to be used for as long as she has flavor, then tossed aside when your taste for her is gone. There's got to be some promise, some agreement that you'll be around."

Marjan's embarrassment had reached combustible levels. "Isn't Father Mahoney waiting for you?" She threw her sister an icy glance. "Don't want to be late for your lesson."

Julian did not seem at all perturbed by Bahar's interrogation. In fact, he seemed to be rather enjoying it. "I couldn't agree with you more. 'The Beloved is all, the Lover just a veil.' "

Bahar shook her head. "It'll take a lot more than poetry to impress me. Every schoolkid knows his Rumi."

"Ah, but 'whatever is in the heart will come up to the tongue.' Isn't that what the old Persians used to say?"

Bahar fell silent, taken aback by Julian's knowledge of ancient proverbs. She tilted her head to the other side, her face scrunched up. Then, just as suddenly, her scowl turned into a relaxed smile. "Are you hungry?" she asked. "Would you like a breakfast plate? Cheese and *barbari*?"

Julian bowed his head. "I am at your whim, dear lady."

Tossing her purse aside, Bahar hurried toward the cluster of teapots on the counter. Choosing a large green pot, she began to plop spoonfuls of lemon oolong into its belly.

Marjan made her way to the counter, a puzzled look on her face. "I've already made a pot," she said.

Bahar ignored her, pouring the samovar's hot water into the lemony leaves.

Marjan stood looking at her for a moment. "Bahar."

Her sister looked over her shoulder, then moved closer to Marjan. "Go sit next to him," she whispered.

"What?"

"Shhhh . . . you heard me. Go keep him company. I'll get the platter." She handed Marjan another glass and saucer.

When her older sister did not move, Bahar turned to her with eyes wide. "A man like that doesn't come along every day, Marjan."

Placing the lid back on the pot, she hurried to the kitchen doors, pausing only long enough to throw her sister a goofy, approving wink.

❄

MARJAN CHOSE A CREAM DRESS with a nice scooped collar, one that revealed her slender collarbones and neck. Instead of the high boots of the earlier evening, she slipped on a pair of tan leather pumps over her stocking-clad feet. With her hair tied back and her mother's ruby earrings, she felt just about ready. She took her best coat from the rack and opened the kitchen door.

Julian looked at her hungrily as she stepped out of the back gate. "Breathless," he said, shaking his head. "That's what you do to me, Miss Aminpour. Leave me breathless."

Marjan grinned and slipped into the soft car seat, feeling purely happy all of a sudden.

He had told her he was taking her somewhere special, but she had not expected it to be a castle.

"Ashford Castle," Julian explained as the BMW wound its way through a grand gravelly entrance, studded by yews and guarded by a gatekeeper's house made up of eaves and window boxes. "Something else, isn't it?"

It surely was.

Arthurian parapets came into view, soaring high into the deepening sky. Mounted with jewel-colored flags and anchored by ivy-covered towers, they were the ideal stages for trumpeting heralds.

The castle's wings, encompassing centuries of architecture, appeared to spread out forever. Everywhere Marjan looked there were soft green mounds rolling away from a paved walkway of polished granite. It was her turn to be breathless.

Julian glanced over at her, grinning. "Thought you might like it."

"I didn't even know this place existed."

"Been here since the thirteenth century, actually. You can trace the line of Mayo's history in the stones, each conquering tribe adding their bit."

They had driven over a drawbridge on the way in, but it wasn't until the car pulled up to the entrance steps that Marjan realized the grounds were surrounded on three sides by ribbons of deep, sapphire water.

"It's the Corrib. A lake. Runs all the way to Galway." Julian handed the car keys to a tuxedoed valet.

"Gorgeous," said Marjan, turning a full circle to take in her surroundings. The sun had already set over the water, but it was still light enough to see the outlines of a Franciscan fort holding steady at its edge.

She took Julian's arm, as she had done that day in Raven's Coppice, and followed him into the plush, gilded lobby.

"Tonight we are dining like royalty," he informed her. "I know you will appreciate the menu."

A red carpet led them through parlors done in palettes of lilac, gold, and cream, the oak panels tastefully simple. Pausing beneath a plaque that read "The Connaught Room," they waited only a few moments before being seated by a waiter in full serving regalia.

A sunburst chandelier, hung with droplets of topaz, was suspended in the center of the intimate space. Every table was swathed in what appeared to be endless reams of silk, so glorious it might have been spun by Rumpelstiltskin himself. Marjan gingerly traced her fingers over the soft tablecloth as another tuxedo-clad waiter handed her an embossed menu. Julian watched with amusement while she studied it.

Tart of wild mushrooms, with truffle mousse sauce. Chilled champagne soup, accompanied by a scoop of limoncello sorbet. Stuffed venison with currant reduction. Her head began to spin.

"I don't know where to start," she said, her eyes drinking it all in. There were two other couples dining in the room, both equally entranced by the sumptuous setting and each other.

"How about some champagne to start?" Julian gestured to the waiter.

"That would be lovely." She ran her fingers down the menu. "I can't believe I have never heard of this place," she repeated.

"It's one of Mayo's most renowned landmarks. Ever see the film *The Quiet Man*?"

"Of course," Marjan replied.

"Well, its opening shots were done here. And many of the actors stayed in these rooms while filming," said Julian. "This place has hosted the crème of the crème. Presidents, sheikhs, film stars, you name it. It's a great example of what can be done with a bit of lateral thinking."

"Is this what you are thinking of doing with the Hall?"

"See, I knew you had a business mind about you. That's it exactly, Marjan," said Julian, adding, "if I get things in order."

"Must cost quite a lot to get it going."

"I was lucky enough to be set with some spending money. Plus, there are a few investors interested in bringing some glory back to the old place. That's another reason I've got to get myself to Dublin."

"Sounds like a great idea. I'm sure you could make it happen."

"I'll be needing your input as well."

"Mine?"

"Who do you think I'll be looking to when it comes to the Muir Hall dining experience?"

"You mean Irish cuisine?"

"Fusion. That's the new word in London. Somewhere in between."

Marjan's mind raced ahead. Fusion. Middle Eastern and Irish. Just think of what she could do with that combination. She smiled coyly. "So is that why you're trying to seduce me, Mr. Muir? An ulterior motive all along, eh?"

Julian grinned. "You've found me out. That's it all right."

"Hmm, I was wondering how you knew all about me. Read about me in the *Connaught* and all." She was enjoying her turn at flirtation. "Have you even been to Iran? Or was that another ploy to get me going?"

"What do you think?"

Marjan laid her menu on the table. "I'm not sure. You just appear, out of thin air, quoting Rumi . . . I don't know. It seems all too perfect."

"It is you who are perfect, Marjan Aminpour."

"Thank you."

"I meant every word of it."

Marjan looked down at the menu again. "You always know exactly what to say. I don't know if that's a good thing or not." She looked up again, staring intently into his eyes. She could take the compliment and leave it at that, but the small voice in her gut told her to be fearless. She wasn't going to let him get away with standing her up without a bit of a jab.

Julian looked back at her, his gaze unwavering. "It's true, I hide behind words. Or rather, they are my conduit. Without them I'd be helpless." He paused, reaching over to touch Marjan's cheek. "I am helpless."

There was nothing she could say to that, thought Marjan. Whatever upset was left over from the night at the Wilton Inn evaporated in the time it took for Julian to caress her face with his fingertips. Now she was helpless as well.

The waiter arrived with their champagne. He poured them two flutes.

Julian smiled. "So, fancy the notion? Irish and Persian?"

"It's a challenge," Marjan admitted, grinning back.

Julian raised his glass. "Here's to the challenge. To the future, then."

To the future, thought Marjan, her insides tingling with anticipation.

❋

AFTER DESSERT, a beautiful chocolate fondant and pineapple compote, Julian helped her into her long woolen coat.

"I want to show you something," he blurted, signing the bill the waiter had handed him. Placing his hand on the small of her back, he guided her out a side door, through a pavilion lit by wall-mounted torches. A walkway led past a fountain gushing with arching streams and finally to a ring fort on the lake's shore. Steps rose into the half-circle structure, where a diamond-shaped window opened onto the darkened Corrib.

Julian led her to the ledge. "Towers were built all around the lakefront. For protection," he explained. "To be a lookout."

He raised his hand to brush aside a strand of hair that had fallen in her face. "Thought you might like a warning before I do this." He reached down, grabbed her waist, drew her hips to his.

His mouth opened on hers, his tongue gently skimming her parting lips. She felt herself melt into his chest as his golden hair touched her glowing cheeks. Her head fell back as she surrendered to the sweeping wave, no longer thinking of the past, no longer worried about anything.

As the lake water lapped insistently outside the stone altar, his mouth found its course along her neck, skimming down her collarbone and to her beating breast. Her insides tugged at her in matching rhythms, wanting more, needing him.

She let herself go, flying free, clinging only to his arms, her skin humming with pure joy.

❋

MARJAN WAS STILL FEELING the heat of his hands on her when she stepped into the Babylon's dining room. Locking the front door behind her, she made her way across the carpeted floor, pushing through the kitchen doors. The lights were on in the kitchen, but all was quiet upstairs. It was nearly midnight, after all.

And then she saw the car. The lights flickered once. Opening the back door, she crossed through the garden to the wooden gate. As she unbolted it, Estelle Delmonico cut the engine on her yellow Honda and opened her car door.

Chapter 16

Fifi O'Shea Saves the Day

BAHAR STAYED GLUED to the sofa. She had not moved from it during the entire exchange. With her mouth set in a stern line, she had watched as Marjan and Layla helped the girl onto the landing, then into the bedroom, where she was now lying on Marjan's bed. Following them up the stairs had been a rumpled Estelle, her face a clear portrait of panic.

All of them, including that person who had attempted such an unspeakable crime, were now clustered in the bedroom. Maybe that was why she couldn't talk, thought Bahar. She had been rendered mute by the horror of it all.

Imagine, trying to kill your own flesh and blood with your own two hands, piercing that part of you without a thought to the evil you were inviting inside. How could she have done such a thing? How could that girl have deliberately cut her insides like that?

Marjan hadn't said how the girl had tried to do the deed, but it didn't take much for Bahar to speculate on the implement of choice. Anything sharp, easy to hold, would do the job. But how could she have actually hurt herself? Bahar asked herself again. Only men did that sort of thing. Men and their batons. Bahar shuddered at the thought. She ran her hands up and down her lap, trying to smooth down the goose bumps rising on her thighs. She'd had only her nightgown on when she heard the commotion in the kitchen, Estelle and Marjan rushing about as that girl had sat silently, perched on a chair at the round table.

She didn't look as Bahar had imagined, much more fragile and innocent than her actions. You just never know who crosses the line, Bahar reminded herself. She didn't have her prayer card with her, but she uttered the prayer silently to herself all the same:

Help me to remember that we are all pilgrims on the road to heaven. Fill me with love and concern for my brothers and sisters in Christ, especially those who live with me.

Easier said than done, she thought. Father Mahoney was right: faith was a continual challenge to the system. As was courage. Courage and faith. Two virtues this girl, this runaway from Lord knows where, lacked.

What would the priest say to what was happening in the café tonight? she wondered. Was what they were doing even within the law? Not likely, not by a long shot.

"This is Marjan's sister. Layla. Yes? She and Bahar over there are going to stay with you, okay?" Estelle's voice carried out to the sitting room. There was silence. "I will see you tomorrow. Tomorrow you come back and we walk the garden, okay?"

After a few more moments of silence, the Italian widow and Marjan reappeared at the bedroom door.

Bahar looked up. "Where's Layla?"

"She's going to keep her company until I get back," Marjan whispered, closing the bedroom door.

"Where are you going?" Bahar stood up from the sofa and came to them.

"I'm going to make sure Estelle gets back home all right."

"Oh, darling, I will be okay." The older woman wrapped her crocheted shawl around her shoulders. "You stay."

"What if the guards come here now?"

"Not likely at this time of night. Besides, they don't know anything yet."

Marjan looked around, trying to locate the keys to the van. She spotted them on the television.

"Marjan, they already ask questions to all the hospital people," Estelle pointed out. "They already know. And now my Dr. Parshaw is in trouble too."

"Are you sure, Estelle? Is that what Dr. Parshaw said?"

"I don't know. He would not say to me. All he said is 'Mrs. Delmonico, you be careful. Those guards are coming to see you too.'" Estelle paused, shaking her head. "But I can tell he is in trouble with his job. They can send him back to Pakistan. Suspended license. Terrible, absolutely terrible." Estelle tugged at the embroidered handkerchief in her sleeve, wiping her eyes with it.

"But he didn't do anything wrong," said Marjan.

"He must not lie, and lie he did. It's my fault."

"Of course it isn't. It's no one's fault."

"Yes, but maybe I could take care of her in my house. No need for a hospital."

Bahar stayed silent, though secretly she agreed with Estelle. A lie was a lie no matter how you looked at it.

"There was definitely a need for the hospital," Marjan assured the older woman. "She may have some special abilities to help you with your pain, but the antibiotics the doctor gave her helped her with hers. There was no other way."

Estelle nodded, sniffed.

Marjan patted her arm. "I have an idea," she said, stepping onto the landing. "Don't worry."

She looked back at Estelle and Bahar. "I'll drive you home in your car, Estelle. But I have to do something right now. Just give me a few minutes and I'll be back."

"Where are you going?" Bahar asked anxiously, following her down the stairs. "What are you going to do?"

Marjan stopped and looked over her shoulder. "I'm going to give all those gossips what they want. What they deserve."

"What's that?" Bahar's eyes widened.

Marjan smiled, tossed her scarf over her back. "A confession. A big old burning at the stake."

"RIGHT, YOU BOTH KNOW what to do. Leave the old woman to me. Leave the talking to me as well while we're at it."

"No need to tell us how to do our job, Padraig," Sean Grogan grumbled. "I've not held the post of sergeant for these past twenty-nine years on my looks alone, you know."

The guard tugged on his bobby stick as he followed the councilman up the gravelly walk. His officer, Kevin Slattery, trailed reluctantly behind, doing his best to keep from sliding down the steep incline.

The sergeant cast his deputy a pitying look before turning back to Padraig Carey. "Best thing is to have us have a look around while you keep the chat going," said Sean. "It's a mighty charge to bring on anyone, and I'm not one for placing blame where there's no cause."

Padraig raised a finger in warning. "We're talking of a law broken, Sean. The Offenses Against Persons Act comes with a sentence, you know that."

Sean grunted with discomfort. "You're not expecting me to take in an expecting mother and put her in a cell, are you now? I thought we had it down pat—just a chat, a house call, and we'd leave it at that."

"Who's in charge here, eh?" Padraig said, feeling his gathered gumption trickling away at the sergeant's bulloxing. "It's the grand Republic we're looking after, don't forget. Its mores and ways. Its bloody virtue!" He gave two abrupt knocks at the cottage door. "Just keep your wits about you. The both of you."

"*Si?*" Estelle Delmonico stood in the doorway, a frilly cream apron spanning her broad chest.

Padraig cleared his throat. "Hello there, Mrs. Delmonico. Padraig Carey, your local council officer here."

"Yes, hello." Estelle stepped aside, letting the smell of bay leaves waft out from behind her.

Padraig paused briefly, taking in the deliciously fragrant air. He blinked, his pose shifting. Thomas had warned him this might happen. The smells of the place were enough to send a man reeling into the Bay, he had said.

The councilman coughed and mentally pulled himself up by the britches. "I was hoping to have a wee chat, if that's all right now, Mrs. Delmonico," he continued, nodding curtly.

Estelle opened the door further. "Of course. Please, come in," she said, smiling at the three men.

The guards followed Padraig into the bright parlor. They stood for a moment staring at the quaint furnishings adorned with white and yellow linens, feeling utterly ridiculous in this feminine arena.

Estelle smiled again, patted a nearby cushion. "Please, sit down. I must go to kitchen again," she told them. "I am cooking minestrone. That is a soup from my country. My mama's country." Estelle paused, adding, "But Ireland is my country now."

Padraig nodded uncomfortably. "You've been here for a long time now."

"Forty-three years, yes. Such a long time since my Luigi buy the shop. We love it from the moment we put our foot on that Main Mall."

"Yes, well." Padraig cleared his throat. This was not going the way he had planned. "I've come on a serious matter today. A very important matter."

"Yes," Estelle said.

"You're aware now of the happenings in the hospital, I believe."

"The hospital?"

"Mayo General. On the Westport Road." He paused. "I'm here about your friend who was admitted a fortnight ago. Or should I say relation?" He smirked, giving the guards a self-satisfied nod. How was that for a proper turn of interrogation?

Estelle clapped her hands with delight. "Congratulations!" Leaning over, she planted smacking kisses on the councilman's cheeks.

Shocked, Padraig could only step back, bringing his hand to his face, which began to burn red. Behind him both guards let out low chuckles, amused to bits at his embarrassment. "Eh?"

"What is your congratulations? Something wonderful, yes? You must have a party for it." Estelle clapped her hands again, reached over to grab the bowl of fruity bonbons. She shoved it into Kevin Slattery's hands, nodding reassuringly. "Pass, pass," she said, as a look of delight dawned over the young guard.

Padraig shook his head in exasperation. "No, no. Not congratulations." He wrestled the bowl of sweets from the deputy, giving it back to Estelle. "I said relations. Re-lations," he enunciated. "Your niece."

"Gloria?"

"Not Gloria," he said, feeling very clever. "The other niece. I'm here about a Bella Rosa."

Estelle extended both arms and shrugged. "Ah. You want a beautiful rose. Bella Rosa. Yes, yes. You see." She pointed out the window to the gravelly walkway. "My pride and joy, those roses. You can take one each when you go."

"Now, Mrs. Delmonico." Padraig shook his head in admonishment. "It wasn't my intention to draw this out. Fact is, this here Bella Rosa, Rosa Bella—what have you—has breached a mighty law of the land. And for it she has to face some questions."

Estelle stared at him, not appearing to have followed.

"But roses don't speak English, Mr. Padraig. They are only flowers," she said slowly, looking at him with sympathetic eyes.

The councilman huffed with exasperation. "Mrs. Delmonico. That's enough, now. You have to abide by the law. This is your country, as you say."

"Okay, maybe if you want, you can go out and talk to the roses. I talk to them too, but it is only because Luigi is sleeping under them."

"I'll ask you one more time," Padraig said, his voice rising. "Did you visit a young lady by the name of Bella Rosa in the hospital this last week? Has she been staying here with you since then?"

"No."

"No?"

"*Si*, no."

Padraig opened his briefcase, took out a pad of paper from which he quoted. "Mrs. Delmonico, I have witnesses to the fact that you, along with Marjan Aminpour, had been frequenting the convalescent unit from the twelfth of October to the nineteenth. A whole staff of witnesses, actually. Not to mention

Dr. Hewey Parshaw's confession. We know what she tried to do to her unborn child. That is a breach of the law."

He stopped. Estelle was silent. "Well, if that's all you have to say on the matter, then I hope you don't mind, but the guards here have to do a search of the house. We have it on good authority that you are keeping a criminal, and if you are not willing to work with us, then we have to go it alone."

Estelle waved her hand around the room. "Please, go ahead," she said with a gracious smile before turning toward the kitchen. "Would you boys like some soup? You will need energy to look so hard."

Kevin looked longingly at the pot of minestrone steaming away on the stove. Sean shook his head. "Thank you. All the same."

He pointed to the bedroom door. "Sorry, this has to be done," he said, pushing down on the brass handle. The door opened to a dark and empty room.

Estelle sighed, nodding. "My Luigi used to share it with me, but no one now," she said, shoving her hands into a pair of sorbet-colored oven mitts. She returned to the stove as the guards roamed from the modest living room to the bedroom and back, ending their grand search in less than two minutes. Estelle stirred the pot of soup, seemingly oblivious to their presence.

"We have a witness to you and this Rosa spending time outdoors. In your garden." Padraig slapped the notebook against his palm.

"*Si*, I spend a lot of time in my garden. Many people know this."

The councilman pointed to the back hall. "Is this the way through, then?" He flicked his hand to the guards, who grudgingly made their way to the back door.

He turned to Estelle, his eyebrows raised. "Now, if I find anything out here, you will be coming with me as well, Mrs. Delmonico. I can't have this go unanswered, you understand."

"Of course," said Estelle.

Padraig opened the door and peered out. There, along the stone path leading out from the door, he saw the hospital wheelchair. And the redheaded woman coddled in the folds of a plaid blanket. Just as Dervla had said.

"Mrs. Delmonico." Padraig tuned back to Estelle with a knowing smirk.

"*Sì?*"

"I believe this is Rosa." He stepped out to the stony terrace, trailed by the guards and Estelle.

They all looked at the woman in the wheelchair, whose back was to them. "Would you like to change your answer now, or after we get to the station?"

Sean stepped forward, his thumbs hooked on his belt. "Now, see here, Padraig—"

The councilman stopped him in his tracks with a snap of his briefcase. "This is a state matter now, Grogan."

Estelle broke out in laughter. "Oh, Mr. Carey. I am an old woman, and have some problems, but my eyes are very good to see. How can you be so much younger and so much more blind?" She stepped onto the path, pointing a mitted finger at the girl in the wheelchair.

Padraig colored at the comment. "Right, I've had enough of this. Sean, take Miss Bella Rosa in," he ordered.

Sean Grogan's nostrils flared as he huffed to the end of the terrace, stopping a foot short of the woman in the chair. He stared at the lass, sitting all timid with her red hair flying in the Atlantic wind.

What did Padraig expect him to do, just wheel some poor girl out without a thought to her?

The sergeant frowned. "Now, Padraig. Wouldn't it be better to ask the questions here first?"

"Oh, for—" Padraig marched over to the wheelchair. "Miss Bella Rosa. I said, Miss Bella Rosa. I'm here on a very important matter."

The young woman did not respond.

"We're here on charges of your harming your unborn child. This is under the abortion act of the land. You are aware of the law, now?"

Still silence.

"You are forcing me to take you in to the station with these guards. It's not something I want to do, but if it comes down to it, I will."

A herd of cows mooed in the field below.

"Well, you give me no choice. Sean, take hold of the bars here." He pointed to the wheelchair's handlebars. Sean did not move. "For feck's sakes." Padraig snorted. "I'll do it myself, then." The councilman stepped forward, lunging for the chair.

He swiveled the seat to face the guards and Estelle. It took him a moment to register the movement at his feet.

"What the—"

"Holy mother of God," Kevin squeaked, falling back against the cottage wall.

Sean crossed himself and cursed.

The head rolling down the side of the hill did not stop for any of their words. It bounced along the ridge, butting against nettle and stone before finally coming to rest in a gully of freezing springwater.

Poor Fifi O'Shea. The once glamorous mannequin had gone from gracing the window of Athey's Shear Delight to losing her head among slumbering bovines, all in a working day. She would need a makeover when this was over, that was certain.

MARJAN STOLE A LOOK at the girl sitting next to her in the van. She was wearing a sweater and jeans, and a pair of Doc Martens borrowed from Layla. Her younger sister had spent the previous night compiling outfits for their guest.

Bahar, by contrast, had taken to clearing the refrigerator and sponging down the crevices and shelves in silent anger. She had woken up before all of them, even before Marjan, leaving a note to say that she would be spending the morning in Saint Barnabas, "praying against their eternal damnation."

"Layla said you liked the play she read to you last night." Marjan looked at the young woman. "She said you enjoyed the bit about the two police officers."

The girl stared at the road. The nettle-lined lane grew wider as they approached a fork. Marjan took a left, shifting gears to traverse the hill ahead. "I'm surprised Layla doesn't have that play memorized by now. She's really involved with theater in her school." She looked back at the girl. "She goes to Saint Joseph's. That's just off the Beach Road. Do you know it?"

She slowed down at a train junction. The red light was on, and the clang of an incoming engine, the morning train from Dublin, made any conversation, one-sided or otherwise, impossible.

Once the train had passed, Marjan got out and opened the gate over the tracks, then got back into the van and geared ahead. The breakfast she had prepared that morning—a platter of cheeses, bread, and herbs, and a bowl of Irish porridge she had bought at the mini-mart—had worked wonders on the girl. Or perhaps it was Layla's carefree good cheer that had made such a positive impact. Whatever the cause, her cheeks were fuller and glowing, her eyes more attentive than Marjan had ever seen them.

Layla had entertained their guest even more that morning, regaling her with stories of the last school trip her class had taken, to the Burren, a limestone landscape of shifting pillars south of Ballinacroagh. Marjan had been surprised at Layla's generosity, her ability to hold her tongue in check when it came to sensitive questions. Her little sister was growing up, she thought.

Marjan stole another sidelong glance at the girl. Her long red hair was tied back, showing her features, delicate and distinctly Irish.

"I know keeping things inside seems like the right way to go. I tend to do the same thing. Sometimes, when I'm tempted to just open my mouth and let it all out, my fear, my confusion, the fact that most of the time I don't know what I'm doing, even if it seems like I do, well, those times, I usually don't say a word. It sometimes seems easier, the best way to get through things." She paused. "But, well, sometimes it's not the easiest way. Do you know what I mean?"

She steered past a grove of alder. Up ahead she could see the little stone bridge that led to Estelle's cottage. "Sometimes, it's best to speak out."

Marjan looked at the girl again. She hadn't expected to see the glimmer of something akin to hope in her large gray eyes.

Marjan nodded softly. "It's all right," she whispered.

The girl nodded back. She placed her right hand on the dashboard, turned to Marjan, and then her face froze in alarm.

The crash came from Marjan's side, knocking the van into a skid across the damp lane. Slamming on the brakes, Marjan twisted the steering wheel in time to stop the back wheels from scudding into a ditch. The van spluttered as she switched the engine off. The young woman next to her had turned a deathly shade of pale. "Are you all right? Are you hurt?"

The girl shook her head.

Marjan looked out the windshield. A battered truck, the kind used to lug construction gear, stood at an angle, kissing the front fender of the van.

She opened the door and stepped out, her body jittery from the shock. Her anxiety was considerably heightened when she saw the dark raincoat disembark from his side. The coat's hood was pulled up around the bearded face, but she recognized it all the same.

He sneered when he saw her. "Salmonella not enough? Finding other ways to kill off all the locals?" He slammed the truck door and rounded the collision.

Shock gave way to anger, Marjan's temper flaring up almost instantly. "I had the right-of-way, if you haven't noticed," she replied, her eyes snapping.

"No such thing on these roads," he said, grimacing at the bent fender. He pointed to the peace signs. "That's false advertising, that. Better to have the skull and bones, if you ask me."

"No one did ask you," Marjan remarked. From the truck's passenger seat, the black-and-white sheepdog gave a short bark.

"That dog there saved your skin. His barking had me stopping in time. You'd be on your way to New York if not for him." Beyond the ditch, the hill split straight to the western shores of Clew Bay. As he flicked his head to the back, the man caught sight of the passenger in the van. A strange expression came over his face, and Marjan knew immediately that he recognized the girl. She whipped around. The young woman was staring back, her mouth a perfect O of horror.

Marjan stepped closer to the cantankerous driver. "Do you recognize this girl?" She pointed to the young woman in her van. "Do you know who she is?"

He didn't give her a chance to ask any more questions. Rounding his own truck, he hastened to open the door. He had started the engine and reversed the truck before Marjan could find the right question. "Wait."

She rushed in front of the truck, waving her hands over her head. "Wait a minute!" The crunch of wheels on the gravel drowned out her voice. "Wait! Stop!" Escher barked sharply, twice.

The truck gunned along the stony path and disappeared down the hill Marjan had just come up. A moment later all that was left was a hazy pillow of powdered gravel, rising to meet the misty air.

Marjan sighed, letting her arms fall to her sides. She gazed through the van's dusty windshield to the girl in the passenger seat. "Did you know that man?" Marjan asked. But the girl held her silence. Her delicate face, moments ago ready to open, was now veiled with fresh pain. Her eyes were a muddled marble, staring at the cliffs and glimmering ocean, far away from there.

Chapter 17

The Quiet Man

MARJAN STARED OUT of the van, slowing down as the wind battered the side panels. To her right were the fog-encrusted waters of Clew Bay, a patina of phosphorescent greens and grays reflecting the recent shower. She couldn't make much of what lay beyond the wall of dense air, just the large stone dock fading into the haze. She could barely make out an antiquated trawler bouncing against the wooden stumps, fighting to free itself from its tether. The westerly had picked up since she'd left the café, leaving a still sullen Bahar to take care of the breakfast plates.

Marjan parked the van in front of the pub as she had done the week before, and grabbing Layla's knapsack from the passenger seat, she walked across the road. The stone dock was studded with prehistoric moss and white shell, providing perfect traction against the constant rain. As she reached the edge of the dock, the black-and-white dog inside the cabin of a small boat bolted from his sleeping position. He gave a short bark, alerting his owner.

"Escher, you stay now. Good boy. Stay."

The man came out from the cabin, wiping his oily hands on a towel. He was wearing his usual dark rain jacket, but its hood was down now, showing his scruffy, windblown hair and a face darkened by a beard.

He didn't seem too surprised to see her.

"Before you try to pin me for a bastard, you should know it's my job to keep tourists at bay. Not everyone with a sickness deserves help."

"Is that what she does? She cures people?" Marjan asked, keeping her gaze on his dark eyes.

"Weren't you the one with her? Shouldn't you know that answer?" He climbed onto the dock and began to uncoil the anchorage from its stump, his back turned to her.

"I don't understand. Why did you drive off so quickly?"

The man threw the coil of rope onto the deck and turned around. "Whatever the two of you were doing was no business of mine. If she wants to take on the likes of your food poisoning or what have you, that's her bad luck."

Marjan took a breath, pushing her hair back from her face. She'd have to be more diplomatic if she wanted answers.

"This isn't about me or my café. Look, I really would appreciate your help." She had already decided to tell him the story, knowing it was the only way he would help her. "I took a chance coming here. Please, just give me a moment."

✳

WHEN SHE FINISHED, both man and dog were staring at her in silence.

"So, can you help me?"

He looked at the sea for a minute. Escher perked up his ears, his head tilted.

"Inishrose," he said, finally.

"I'm sorry?"

"Inishrose. The girl you were asking after. She comes from Inishrose. Her name's Teresa McNully."

Marjan moved toward the duo. "How do you know her?"

"I know her family well enough, I suppose. They live on one of the drumlins, a place called Inishrose." He nodded toward the foggy water.

Marjan nodded, feeling a sudden surge of determination.

"How can I get to Inishrose? Is there a ferry or something? From Louisburgh?"

He threw the rope onto the deck. "Next ferry out from the Pier won't be until the morning, and even then you'll be hard-pressed to convince them to make a detour. At least not for the likes of the McNullys."

He stepped back onto the slippery deck, then turned to Marjan again. "Only one way out and one way in. It's up to you to take it, so."

✳

THE MIST LIFTED as the blue trawler churned across the water. All at once Marjan could see the small islands, the dollops of green on the slowly brightening Bay. Some were as small as Fadden's Field, others larger than the whole of Ballinacroagh. What most had in common was a sense of departure from ordinary landmasses, as though they had been dropped from another universe already formed.

Marjan looked at the man by her side. He had introduced himself as Dara O'Cleirigh, and among a number of occupations he had remained fairly vague on, he ran the postal system for the inhabitants of the various islands that dotted the Bay.

Marjan steadied herself against a chipped stool in one corner of the cabin. Her stomach gave a turn, knocking against her sides; the wind had picked up bitterly as the trawler traversed the choppy waters, and the small boat was beginning to sway on the swells. Her eyes scanned the cabin as Dara shifted the trawler's gears beside her. It hadn't occurred to her that what she was doing could be dangerous. Bahar was manning the café, but she certainly didn't expect her older sister to be out all day.

"Do you have a telephone on the boat?" Marjan asked, swallowing back her fear.

Dara notched down the gear and turned the helm south-southwest. "No, but I have a radio transmitter." He focused his dark eyes on her. "You're not getting the willies now, are you?"

"No. Not at all," Marjan quickly replied. "Do I look frightened?"

"A little bit." He gave a self-satisfied smile and returned his gaze to the heaving water.

Marjan frowned. "I'm not scared. I just want to know how long I'll be out."

"Not long. We're almost there, now," Dara replied, gesturing ahead.

Marjan peered through the gray air; a green mass was coming into view, then a wooden pier. Behind it were a sandy cove and a large dune, from which jutted out wooden steps and a boardwalk that curved as it rose.

Above the boardwalk, on a plateau showered with dandelions, sat a circular structure made entirely of fieldstones. It grew from its circumference like a medieval monks' fort, not unlike the one on the grounds of Ashford Castle.

Dara steered the boat to the pier. As soon as the bow hit the end of the wooden stilts, the black-and-white sheepdog took a running dive and leapt onto the pier with four paws steady.

"Someone lives up there?" Marjan pointed to the round structure.

"Just the McNullys. Teresa and her father. No one else on the land."

Dara turned off the boat's ignition and stepped out of the modest cabin. As he tied the boat to one of the posts, Marjan lifted the knapsack onto her right shoulder and joined him on the pier.

The water lapping against the landing was considerably less angered, and her fear eased as she felt the ground steady beneath her. It was hard to tell how big the island was from where she stood, but she suspected it was one of the smaller ones.

On the western end, the cliff rose like a giant limestone wave, under whose shadow were burrowed nests of jolly black-and-white birds.

"Those aren't penguins, are they?" Marjan pointed to the chubby creatures.

"Puffins. Though it's out of season, them being here. They usually leave the drumlins by Samhain."

"So these islands, they're called drumlins?"

"That's it all right. Take a good look, they won't be here forever," said Dara.

With Escher leading the way, Marjan and Dara climbed the long boardwalk steps, the wind lashing them from all sides. Sea spray seemed to reach them even at the plateau point, and prompted by the puffins' exuberant squawks, Marjan felt as though she were rising from the depths of the ocean itself.

The hulking figure at the cliff top intensified the sensation that she was surfacing; his ice blue eyes pierced through her, causing Marjan to gasp inwardly. He had a Saint Brigid's cross in his hand and held the boomerang of woven rush with defiance. He lowered the talisman when he saw Dara O'Cleirigh.

"How's it going, Sean? Don't mind us dropping in on you like this, no notice and all." Dara shook the man's hand.

"Nearly had you for one of those Yanks. Was going to give them the Saint Brigid's blessing and be done with them." He pointed to Dara's face. "What's that now, a beard you've gone and got yourself?"

Dara reached up and touched his chin. He smiled sheepishly. "When in Rome," he replied. "Or in my case Patagonia. Why, don't you like it?"

Sean McNully stared at the facial hair for a moment. "It's grand, so. Suits ya." He waved his hand. "Well, come on in then. You're here now, so there's nothing to be done about it."

He started walking toward the round house, peppery Escher at his side. Marjan followed close behind, unsure of her welcome. The man had made no acknowledgment of her presence during his chat with Dara O'Cleirigh.

She remembered what the postman had said about the islanders as they set off from the stone pier: "Some of the islands have only a single person living on them. Take Seamus Harvey of Biggle's Rock. That's past Clare, just west. I've been running the post for five years now, and not once in that time have I known old Seamus to leave its shores, not for provisions even. I get a list of wants from him every month, and he's happy with that.

"He's eighty-three, been on that rock since birth, saw both parents live and be buried, and still he stays. You'll find a lot of characters just off the Bay, that's for sure. I'm only warning you now, for Sean McNully might not even want to speak to us."

But if they'd come about his daughter he would, thought Marjan, as she hoisted herself up the wooden steps.

The boardwalk led right to the short fieldstone wall surrounding the house. Similar walls ran circles throughout the patchy plateau, though it did not look like there were any animals to take advantage of what grass there was for the feeding.

Marjan turned back to the house. Round windows sat on either side of the door, a studded circle of alder wood. On the roof grew a patch of thick grass dotted with more dandelions to match the front yard. With the ivy and wisteria traveling along its façade, the grass roof was an ideal insulation, nature providing all the comforts of home.

A second circular structure, made entirely of glass, peeked out from one side. It was filled with greenery, what looked like a system of hydroponics suspended from the ceiling.

It was a greenhouse, Marjan realized. From the stonework, it appeared to have been built in recent years, though it seemed to blend perfectly with the older round house.

Sean McNully opened the circular door, and they followed him in. After stoking the fire that roared in a large stone place, the old man settled into a wooden armchair near the hearth. Escher snuggled next to his boots and sighed contentedly.

Sean turned his icy blue stare on them. "Now what can I do for the two of you? You're not poorly yourself, Dara, haven't picked up something from the natives on your trip, did you?" he asked gruffly. "I might not have a vial of anything to treat that."

Dara laughed. "Argentina was grand. No complaints or disease to report. Haven't come for a cure now. This lady here was asking about you at the Shebeen, that's all." He introduced Marjan. Sean nodded cordially her way. "She was looking for Teresa, Sean." Dara looked around. "Is she at the greenhouse?"

Sean's face turned stony. He looked at the fire for a few moments before speaking again. "Teresa doesn't live here anymore. Hasn't for a while now."

Marjan remained quiet as she watched the older man. There was something very familiar about him; perhaps it was his sadness, something in him that reminded her of the girl Estelle had taken in. "What's happened, Sean?" Dara leaned forward in his chair.

The old man's blazing eyes looked away again. "I can't tell you."

Marjan bit her lip, knowing it was her turn to offer her trust. She unbuckled the knapsack, unfurled its contents onto her lap.

"I wonder if this might look familiar," she said, leaning forward with the fabric in her hand.

Sean's face crumpled at the sight of the dress. He choked back a cry, his knuckles gripping the arms of his hearth chair. "It belongs to Teresa. Where did you get that? What's happened to her?" He began to rise, anger sweeping over his wrinkled face.

"Now, Sean. Hold on there, now," Dara interjected, also standing up. "Marjan here has been taking care of Teresa. She's all right, she's all right."

Marjan stepped forward, handed the dress to Sean. "It's the truth. She was sick for a while, but now she's much better. I'm sorry, I didn't realize bringing this would upset you," she said, stepping back.

"Why don't you say what happened, Sean? It'll do you the world of good," said Dara gently.

Sean McNully stared at the black dress with its landscape of lilies, his bright blue eyes deep with regret. A minute passed before he looked up, his face no longer hard as stone. "Better put the tea on, so, if I'm going to tell you."

❋

"YOU KNOW YOURSELF, Dara, how it's like to live here. Peace and the freedom to do as you please, no land eyes on you, none at all. It's a grand way of existence, the kind of life my Mary and I had envisioned for ourselves when we married. She came from Clare Island, like yourself, so it wasn't much of a trip one way or another to come to my family's plot. As long as we had our bit of land, our spot now, we were quite happy to stay by our own. With me and the greenhouse going and Mary doing her bit with her hands, it was too hard to stay on the mainland. We figured if they were wanting enough, if the healing was needed, then the people would find us out here. Not even when Teresa came along did we feel the urge to leave. Now I think to myself that it might not have been the best laid of plans. Maybe if Teresa had been amongst her own age, kiddies around since the beginning, she might not have done what she did.

"She was a wily child, our Teresa, always getting into scrapes up and down the shore. She had the gift, of course, but we let her do as she pleased for the first few years, knowing there'd be plenty of time for the serious work. Like her mother every way and bit. Same look to her, same coloring, same hands in the end. She was going the way of the hands, leaving myself alone to deal with the plantings.

"Now, Mary was delighted to have someone to pass the teachings on to. Her own mother had not been touched, but her grandfather had the gift, and it was from himself that she learned to heal the sicknesses. There was some talk of sending Teresa out to the Island for schooling, but as the seas get choppy on the best of days, there really was no point to it, we saw. Besides, all the teaching she needed was going to come from us.

"I began her on the course of weedings, all the way to the wrapping of poultices. Mary waited to begin her lessons, but the little one was able to look in on her sessions with the locals and the odd Yank that managed to find us. It was from these sessions that we made our living, and later, as you know yourself, Dara, the vials came in handy. Sure the sale of one bottle of my *agnus castus* could tide us over for two months! So you see, there just wasn't any push for us to send our baby out to the wide world.

"It wasn't until thirteen years of age that Teresa picked up the rays. All of a sudden she was a woman overnight, growing tall and strong. And her hands, her hands were the hands of her grandfather. Stronger than Mary's any given day.

"Soon it was Mary who stood by at the sessions as Teresa took to giving the healings. I've seen her mend bones and the pink eye in minutes flat, that's how strong her gift was. We were proud as proud could be, but a bit fearful as well, knowing that we couldn't hold the world back any longer. The world can eat you up for a meal if it knows you hold such a talent. It'll spit you out just the same, to be sure. Human beings, we're a strange lot. We want so much to believe in the greater forces, that some of us are touched by the mighty beyond. But once such a person is found, the population gets a mighty fright. It hurts them all too much to see how true talent is meted, that not all of us are worthy of its glory, its pain. So we destroy that kindling, take it out before it takes us. Fear, no cure for it, Dara. No healing hands to mend its ways. All too human, that is.

"Fear came on our little world the year last. In all her days of curing others' ailments, it seems Mary had not taken her own hands to herself. Hadn't paid any mind to the hump of matter growing right on her breast. That bit killed her before the year was out. And there was no planting, no bark of wood I could give her to stop it.

"As much as I tried explaining so to Teresa, that she had no means for mending her mother's cancer, she wouldn't hear of it. Sure, there are times when the hands have taken out the strands of the disease, but those were the early stage kinds. Mary's was incurable, even to the both of us. But Teresa would not understand the logic of it, not at all.

"She took to sitting on that pier come storm or not, shivering to the bone and looking out to the sea like she wanted nothing of this world. I was out of my wits to get her to come in most days, but she wouldn't listen. And when there was any boats around she would scamper off to the greenhouse or to the other side of the island, where our Mary's laid, God rest her soul. Some of them tourists still came for the vials, and looking for the hands, but Teresa stopped her sessions. Stopped coming in to lessons.

"Then, nearly six months back or so, time of the Saint Brigid's Day itself, here comes a fancy boat. A millionaire's yacht. And who steps off from it but the Minister of Health himself! The bollocks! That's right, Dara, that gobshite Willy Prendergast, that's who stepped off that yacht. I was thinking he's here for a feckin' cure, the bastard! Much good he's done for our health system, now he's devourin' our true talents as well.

"But no, he wasn't here for a cure, was here to see about a bit of business, he said. Would you believe it now, he wanted to buy the island right off from under our noses! Wanted Inishrose for himself, for a bit of a retreat from the buzz of Dublin, so he says. I put the feckin' buzz on him—nearly pushed him off the cliff, so I did. Told him to get off my island or I'd put the eye of hag on him. Off he took himself, coward that he is.

"Now, Teresa had come in during the time that man was here, right here onto the hearth, but she had slipped out just as quick so I never thought a thing about it until a month later. I wake up to find Teresa missing and the currach gone. No note at all to tell me whether she was thinking of leaving this life or not. Had to take a bit of eyebright just to see clearly, I was so distraught.

"I waited and waited, and sure, at sundown who comes walking in but herself. Would have none of my questioning. Locked herself in her room and wouldn't come out until the morning.

"Same occurrence every week, every Friday, and I not knowing what to make of it. Never thought of that politician, not one time. How can I have the touch of the plantings, how can I see things like this but not know my own daughter? How could I have been so blinded? You tell me now, Dara."

Sean paused, his blue eyes afire. He took the heavy poker and rustled through the turf blocks, reigniting them orange. He stared at the fire for a minute longer before continuing.

"Haven't seen her now for a fortnight. Finally got myself to look in her room. Found a stack of napkins and matchbooks from different hotels up and down the coastline. One for the

Aulde Shebeen even. Put two and two together and finally got my answer. The minister. The bastard. Now I've nothing. For not talking to her before, now I am alone for it. No Mary, no daughter, nothing but my plants, and what good are they to me now, Dara? What good are they? Nothing for this hole in the heart that won't go away."

Sean finished, and the three of them sat silent. The fire crackled and rose to the wind funneling down the chimney. Escher sighed and rolled onto his back.

Dara was the first to speak: "Why didn't you tell me about it sooner, Sean? On one of my days out? I could have looked out for her."

" 'Tis a family matter. Not for anyone but ourselves," replied the old man solemnly. "Truth is, I probably wouldn't have told you now, not to a stranger—no offense now, Miss—but for you bringing me her dress and all. And the weather. The brightening skies got me to thinking of my Mary. How I'd be glad to see her someday soon. Got me in a mood, so you did."

Marjan cleared her throat. She lifted her gaze into the man's hurting eyes.

"Everything's going to be all right," she said softly. "You have found your beloved. Everything's going to be all right now. I promise."

❀

THE MIST CLEARED as far as Clare Island as the three of them reached the pier. To Marjan it looked like the rising hull of Hy

Brasil, that ancient land known as Atlantis. With the wind at her back, she turned toward the mainland and was greeted by that king of mounds, Croagh Patrick. Standing there on that island, she felt as though she was coming out of her own fog, suddenly could see the land she had missed.

As an enlivening spray brought the sea to her senses, Marjan awoke to what she had to do as well; it was something she should have done from the very beginning, from that day she left Gohid.

Chapter 18

Rosewater and Soda Bread

TERESA STOOD AT THE START of the path, the circular garden bordered by powdery lavender. The kind Italian woman was inside, giving her room to be alone.

She felt alone all the time.

That was one of the questions she had decided to ask: why she felt so lonely, even now, with someone looking after her. The woman, Estelle, had told her that any question she asked while walking would be answered by the time she found the center. But she wasn't so sure this was true, especially as she could not find her own center. She had lost her compass last year, and now knew not where to begin.

She looked out onto the valley. The fields had taken a soaking in the past hour, but it had not deterred four Jersey cows from congregating in the next hollow, wet and luxurious in patches of dandelion.

A weed to many, the dandelion. Though she knew better than to disregard the bright yellow petals: roasted and grated, an infusion of the peppery plant strained all impurities from the blood—bar of course the one impurity she could find no potion for, the hurt she had already caused to those who loved her.

And to the baby below her navel.

The girl stopped at the path's center stone. One more step and she'd be in the middle of the meditative circle, where Estelle said she would know. Know what to do about all her sadness. The kind lady had not asked her any questions, even after their sessions in which Estelle had seen, despite all Teresa's efforts, one of her most beloved childhood memories: the day of her confirmation.

She had known she was transferring her memory of that day, that glorious morning when her mother had helped her change into her white dress and veil, her pearl rosary wrapped around her ten-year-old wrist; sometimes there was no way of stopping the memories. But the kind widow had needed her hands, needed some healing as soon as possible. It was the least she could do to thank Estelle for saving her, for taking her in from that sea, from the death of her baby.

She stayed still on the limestone square. She lifted her hand to her center. The pain there was no longer unbearable, and every day she felt stronger. She didn't deserve a second chance, but a second chance she was still getting. He had said he loved her in Irish. *Ta gra agam ort.* He had said he loved her but had left as soon as he heard about their baby. She pressed her hand against her belly. They could heal others, her fingers, but not her own soul.

She lowered her hand and stepped forward.

❋

THE RED LAVAZZA SIGN blinked with a sleepy, almost reverent glow as Sophia Loren blew them a kiss from her cupboard marquee.

Marjan looped her forefinger in the handle of a mug of hot tea and smiled. Across from her sat Estelle, grinning with a benevolent light; the older woman had not stopped smiling since Sean McNully had entered her cottage nearly an hour ago. So delighted was she with father and daughter reuniting that every few moments were punctuated by chuckles and snapshots of her married life.

"Today I am so happy it is almost like Luigi is alive again. You know, I think I could even climb a big elephant, I feel so young!" Estelle lifted her hands above her head and laughed. She licked her sugary lip. "I can hear them talking. Can you hear talking?"

Marjan cocked her ear toward the hallway; a gentle murmur of voices, two voices, emanated from the closed bedroom door. Sean had been in there for nearly the entire hour.

"I didn't know if she—Teresa I mean—would be happy. But it was important to bring her father here, wasn't it?" Marjan turned to Estelle.

The widow nodded. "Of course it was important, darling. He is her papa. And she was happy—I could see it in her eyes."

"And she did talk," Marjan said, relieved.

Teresa McNully's words had a silvery timbre to them and continued to ring in her ear. She had turned from her wheelchair when her father was shown in, her delicate features breaking into immediate tears: *"Ta bron orm. Ta bron orm."* There were only a handful of words Marjan recognized in Irish, and those weren't ones she knew. Still, it wasn't hard to surmise their meaning. Teresa's young face was filled with regret. Both Marjan and Estelle had broken into tears as well.

Estelle seemed to be recalling the same moment. "She was ready. After I saw her last memory, I knew she was ready to speak."

As Sean and his daughter continued their private conversation, Marjan filled the widow in on what had happened since she left for the Aulde Shebeen that morning, everything from the man who had helped her find Inishrose, Dara O'Cleirigh, to the puffins along the cove. She told her about the Minister of Health and his visit to that little paradise on earth.

Estelle was especially intrigued by her account of Sean's greenhouse; Marjan could tell she had a lot of questions to ask the man with the healing abilities.

The only part of the story she left out was her decision, the thought that had finally sorted itself out for her on that wooden pier. Marjan had never told Estelle what had really happened to her during those three days inside Gohid Detention Center, nor of the time right after it, when Bahar had married Hossein. The latter wasn't hers to tell, but the details of those three days and what led up to them Marjan did hope to confide in the kind lady sooner rather than later.

But first, she reminded herself, first she had to tell her sisters. First there had to be *sohbat*—there was no way around it.

Deeper than a tête-à-tête, more concentrated than everyday speech, *sohbat* was the word in Farsi for space: the area inhabited by two souls during deep and truthful conversation. *Sohbat* could take place anywhere, around a *sofreh* or within prayer: "The same whisper that made the rose open was hushed to me here inside my breast; the same advice given the cypress so that it grew with strength, touched the jasmine and its fluttering breath . . ." Those were Rumi's words, but they reflected her own emotions, Marjan told herself.

The poet was speaking of those midnight conversations when the moon spoons lovers and honesty is the only way to connect. He was talking of the trust one had to have in others, and in one's self. She had forgotten about *sohbat*, Marjan told herself. She had forgotten to be honest.

"You are all right, darling?" Estelle tapped her on the shoulder. "You look surprised all of a sudden."

Marjan smiled and shook her head. "I just realized something, that's all," she said.

Estelle raised her finger as though testing the air. "Ah. That is what my mama used to call 'the coin dropping.' Yes?" Estelle flashed her a grin and sipped her jasmine tea.

Marjan nodded. Yes, she thought. The coin dropping in her head. *Sohbat.* Conversation. That was what she would do when she got back to the café; she would tell her sisters the truth of Gohid, of why she had come to leave them for three long days.

❋

"AND THAT WAS 'The Monster Mash,' folks, right here on your local pirate station, Craic FM!

"Well, it's a proud priest I am for announcing that it's been two weeks today since we—my lovely assistant, Mrs. Boylan, and I—have been sending out happy rays to your hearth and home. We're a babe on the crawl for now, but I have great confidence in our bit of western craic.

"And don't think I don't appreciate a bit of criticism. Haven't heard too much from all of you out there, so don't be shy. Tell me what you really think of my latest foray. Two heads are greater than one, they say. And a village, well, with all your support we could carry this little ship to a whole new world!

"So, for letting go of all ego, here's a tongue in cheek if I ever heard it: Carly Simon's 'You're So Vain'!"

❋

MARJAN WAITED FOR Fiona and Evie to cross the street before lugging the two large pots from the window-side table. In honor of the All Hallows' Eve ceili, she had cooked up double batches of stew made with cinnamon, lamb, and apples, the fruit of the season.

Fiona took one of the pots and Marjan the other, while Evie held on to the book she had been reading.

Marjan had tried not to smile when she saw the young stylist in her latest outfit—fishing pants and Aran sweater to match her hardier employer's—and only nodded as Evie read to them from *The Female Eunuch*.

"I can't get her to put it down," Fiona explained as the trio marched up the cobblestoned Mall. "Makes me regret I gave it to her in the first place," she said with a smile.

Evie looked shocked. "But, Fiona, how could you say that? It's like my eyes have been opened. I can't believe what I've put up with from that gobshite Peter Donnelly all this time." She held the book out in front of her with both hands. "Germaine Greer is a goddess." She sighed reverentially.

Fiona winked at Marjan, who couldn't help but laugh.

"Let's go, goddesses. There's a ceili out there with our names on it."

❋

A FAMILIAR SIGHT GREETED the three of them as they approached the Town Hall. Parked in a semicircle around Saint Patrick's monument were four horse-drawn carriages heralded with lively pink and orange banners. The McGuire Family Circus had come back to town.

The youngest of the seven McGuires who controlled Ballinacroagh's drinking establishments, Kieran McGuire had been the only sibling with a taste for trails less beaten. The same strain that sent his nephew Tom Junior to seek the solace of a Californian ashram had driven Kieran to establish the troupe of actors and street performers setting up now in the square. Traveling the Continent, the McGuire Family Circus performed variations on Celtic themes and festivities and were in constant demand wherever they went.

On this All Hallows' Eve, they were going to enchant Ballinacroagh with a dance based on *The Faerie Queene*.

Fiona sniffed the air. "Can you smell the greasepaint? Makes me long for the stage again." She waved at Kieran, who was busy applying makeup to his face inside one of the canvas-topped caravans.

The Ladies of the Patrician Day Dance Committee had really performed miracles this time, thought Marjan. The Town Hall's Palladian exterior, crumbling as it was, looked for once as lavish as it must have when it was first built. Yards of twinkling lights swathed the pillars with their fluttering song, meeting wide steps illuminated by hurricane lamps that looked like their *Arabian Nights* counterparts.

After settling the pots on the refreshments table, Marjan, Fiona, and Evie joined the crowd walking into the main room, a large hall flanked by a wooden stage that was currently missing half its proscenium arch and at least thirty floorboards. Fiona surveyed the theater. Once completed, it would make a beautiful arena for Father Mahoney's many plays—under her astute directorial guidance, of course.

"You have a curtain already?" Marjan asked Fiona, pointing to the pearly screen of organdy stretched from one end of the stage to the other.

"That's just for tonight. Borrowed it from a pal at the Druid Theatre in Galway. It's for the fairies' sake," Fiona explained with a bemused look on her face.

"Finnegan?" Marjan said, moving to a side wall where bales of hay made for a scratchy yet convenient seating area.

The hairdresser laughed. "Finnegan, the Tuatha De Danaan, the Little People, the lot. It's meant to protect them from us. Or is it us from them?" Fiona shook her head. "I can never tell."

She shrugged. "Anyway, it's the veil that separates our world from theirs. Keeps all things in balance for this Day of the Dead. Do you have something like this back in Iran?"

Marjan smiled. "Something like this, yes." Veils were everywhere, she told herself. Even if you couldn't see them.

The ceili band—none other than the Covies—launched into a jigged-up version of Madonna's number one hit "Like a Virgin," prompting Godot to leap up onto his tipsy owner. The Cat made as though he couldn't be bothered, but a moment later saw him waltzing with his hairy companion.

Marjan giggled as she made her way to the left wall, where the All Hallows' Eve Games were stationed. There she found Layla and Malachy lined up to try their luck at a game called Apple Dookin.

Layla was busy trying to talk her school friend Regina Jackson into giving the game a go. "You have to put your whole head in if you want to catch one," she said, impatience in her voice. Regina was kneeling to the side of the large oak bin that held the Red Delicious apples.

"I just got this perm. I'm not about to ruin it for anything," Regina moaned, pointing to the red kinks springing every which way from her head. She stood up and shrugged. "I'd rather just give them a donation."

"You have to have an apple for the Mirror," Malachy said.

Marjan looked at the next game, for which many of the villagers had gathered: the Lady in the Mirror.

A large blackboard taken from the high school spelled out the rules. Once the apple had been procured from the Dookin Tub, it was duly handed to Maura Kinley, treasurer of the Ladies of the Patrician Day Dance Committee, who would slice it into nine even pieces. Eight were to be eaten, while the last one was to be held for the divination ritual of the Mirror.

Marjan craned her head to where a large gilt mirror hung on the wall. She couldn't read the rest of the rules over the crowd of heads. "What happens when you get to the Mirror?" she asked.

"You throw the last piece of your apple over your left shoulder and turn quickly to look at your reflection. Whatever picture you see in the mirror is supposed to be your future," Layla replied. She put her hand on her sister's arm, gave her a long, deep look. "Are you all right, Marjan?"

Marjan patted her hand. "Of course I am," she said. From across the room she could see Bahar looking at her as well.

Ever since she had told her sisters about Gohid and Ali, they had been treating her deferentially, nearly tiptoeing around her, really. She had even been ordered to take a holiday by Bahar, who had insisted on doing all the café's cooking herself for the rest of the week. They had a long and good cry about it, the three of them, especially when Marjan described her last glimpses of Ali before he was arrested. That was something she would never forget.

Marjan could see that Layla remained unconvinced. "I'm fine, *joon-e man*. Don't worry," she assured her.

Layla nodded, smiling with relief. "Is Mrs. D coming?" she asked, searching the crowd.

"She's resting tonight. But she'll be at the church tomorrow."

Marjan had not been up to the white cottage since yesterday, when she had brought Sean McNully to see his daughter, but the Italian widow had related the latest on the phone that morning.

"She is talking still! Yes! Not too much, but enough. Her papa was in there for three hours again today, they talk for three hours! Can you believe this? What a wonderful day! And she is staying here for more time. What happiness!" she exclaimed. "Tomorrow her papa and I are going to the hospital, to see Dr. Parshaw. He should not lose his job, he did nothing wrong. Nothing wrong at all."

Estelle was breathless with excitement. "And you want to know something else? You want to know what she said? Very quiet, only this morning? I bring her tea, just tea, and she says to me, 'Thank you, Estelle.' Just like this: 'Thank you, Estelle.' She knows my name, Marjan! Isn't that something wonderful?"

It *was* something wonderful, thought Marjan; there were so many blessings to be thankful for, so much beauty in their lives at the moment.

Malachy approached Marjan, a sheepish look on his handsome face. "About last week, Marjan. At the Inn. I just wanted to say that—"

"You don't have to say anything," Marjan said, holding up her hand. "That's between you and Layla." She winked at her youngest sister, who gave her a shy smile back.

"Thanks, Marjan," Malachy replied.

"Not a problem," she said, feeling suddenly very proud of Layla and Malachy. It was clear to her that they had a deep respect for each other. That was hard enough to sustain in any romance, let alone one in your teen years.

The young couple, with Regina in tow, moved to the Mirror line while a reel started in the open area in the center of the hall. Two rows of couples lined up for the traditional dance as the Covies jigged away to "The Boys of Belfast." Marjan thought of what Julian had said to her before dropping her off from their beautiful evening at Ashford Castle. "I'll be in Dublin during the ceili, but you save a dance for me all the same. There'll be plenty of dancing once I get back, I promise." She smiled at the memory. She couldn't wait.

Someone coughed behind her.

Marjan turned, knocking right into Dara O'Cleirigh.

Dara nodded cordially as he stepped back. "Hello again." He was without his usual rain jacket, though his dark hair was as windswept as it had been on the boat's deck.

Marjan couldn't hide her surprise. "What are you doing here?" She stopped. "I mean, hi. How are you?" The last time she had seen him was at the dock back in Clew Bay, before she and Sean had driven off to Estelle's.

"Grand now, if I get my workin' done." He lifted the large Canon camera hanging from his neck. "I do bits for the *Connaught* every now and again. Trips to Argentina have to pay for themselves some way."

Before Marjan had a chance to say anything else, Dara moved away, flicking his left hand from his head in an abrupt good-bye.

His faithful dog, Escher, had come with him and was currently sniffing away at a perturbed Godot.

Fiona sidled up to Marjan with a large candied apple. "Who was that?"

"Just someone I met the other day. He's very strange," said Marjan thoughtfully.

"He reminds me of my ex." Fiona sniffed, referring to her late German puppeteer of a husband. "Stay away from the artists, Marjan. They'll only give you heartache," she said, biting into her shiny treat.

"Oh, I'm not looking for an artist," Marjan replied. "At least not someone like him, that's certain."

Fiona clucked approvingly. "Good girl, yourself." She nudged Marjan. "Now why don't you get yourself a divination while you're at it?"

Marjan glanced at the line weaving its way to the gilt mirror. "Why not?" She turned back to Fiona. "Are you coming?"

The hairstylist narrowed her eyes in discontent. "Looks like my future's all set. I predict that devil of a goat's got his eye on the stage there. Better grab his billy before he tears down the veil." She marched purposefully toward Godot and his owner, both of whom were inching their way to the proscenium. Dara O'Cleirigh and his Canon were trailing the degenerate duo closely. The photographer had the same instincts as Fiona; his camera was shuttering away in anticipation of a grand old ruckus.

Marjan smiled as she watched Fiona brandish her candied apple at the Cat before turning to Maura Kinley.

"Got yours already sliced, Marjan," the treasurer said with a wide grin. "No one our age should be kneeling for her luck."

Marjan accepted the plate of apple slices. "Easy now, Maura. I'm not getting my pension yet," she said with a laugh.

"But you'll be looking for a husband soon enough, I'd say. That's the real purpose of the Mirror," Siobhan Kelly piped up next to her. The shoe shop owner pointed to the last rule on the big blackboard. "I'm not standing here for anything less."

Marjan leaned forward to read the small print.

Disclaimer: Maidens with marital aspirations beware: the Lady in the Mirror has a spiteful air. Freud has nothing on her, that's for sure. Keep away if you like your nights free from the desires of men.

Marjan smiled. Fiona's contribution, no doubt. Or Germaine Greer's. She turned to the growing line behind her. She had not noticed it before, but it seemed as though most of the village's unmarried women had taken their dripping turns at the tub of bobbing apples.

"Must have missed that last rule," Marjan said, feeling a little giggle rise in her throat.

"If you don't want to risk finding out, just take a bite out of your throw slice. That'll keep Cupid at bay for a while," Maura offered.

"Thanks. I think I might do that." Marjan picked up one glistening red slice. She took a healthy bite out of it, relishing the briskness of its red skin as it broke between her teeth. The fruit had a particular taste of earth and Atlantic showers that was nothing like the sweeter version she remembered from Iran. What autumn bounty, indeed, she thought.

With her mind on the coming season, Marjan faced her reflection in the Mirror.

"You have to turn away from the Lady, or she'll never tell you her secrets," Julian whispered in her ear. "Isn't that a woman for you?"

Marjan gave a little gasp as she felt his palm settle on the small of her back. She blinked at the reflection before her. It was him all right.

"Not a big fan of putting my life in her avaricious hands. At least not if I can help it," he said, inching closer.

Marjan smiled at the welcome face in the Mirror. "I think Lady Fate's disappeared for the moment." She tilted her head up at Julian. "What happened to going to Dublin?"

He smiled. "Had a change of heart halfway there. The local contractor can handle it, I told myself. It'll cost me an arm and a leg less. Not to mention get me into the good graces of this mercurial parish of ours." He leaned forward and winked toward the line of women behind Marjan. "Evening, ladies. Looking your usual gorgeous selves tonight, I see. Ah, if I could only stop the hands of time and have a dance with each of you—a happy man I'd surely be." There were blushes of delight all around, followed by a few faces looking rather hopeful at the thought. Marjan resisted a giggle.

"You'll have them eating out of your hands if you're not careful, Mr. Muir," she said, shaking her head.

"That's precisely where I want to keep them."

"Oh? And why is that?"

"Better to leave my lips free for you alone, that is, if you're willing." Then, right there, in front of the entire village gathered, with the swoon of the ceili band rising in four-step over them, his lips met hers in an apple-scented kiss.

The Lady in the Mirror could wait another year, thought Marjan. She had found her destiny.

❉

"IT'S A QUARTER TO MIDNIGHT, everyone, time to wrap things up before the fairy folk make their way across from their underworld!"

Father Mahoney stood at his post in one corner of the stage, his trusty Ari 3000 turned up to full hilt.

"Let's not forget, this All Hallows' Eve is a feast of the dead," he said. "As well it's a bit of a bash for all those who have yet to be born. There'll be a parade of souls, both fairy and otherwise, moving across the fields, and I for one am not taking my chances.

"Grab a loaf of Mrs. Boylan's currant soda bread on the way out. Leave it on your doorstep or on your kitchen table, with some whiskey if you can spare it. It'll keep the folk from knocking down your way.

"And be sure to tune in on Monday, when I'll recount the whole history of this sacred holiday. I'll be seeing you at Mass tomorrow, bright and sharp for All Souls' Day!" Father Mahoney waved at everyone.

The last of the ceili revelers filed out of the Town Hall, punch-drunk on merriment and cider. Most paused at the door, where a plank table was piled with cellophane-wrapped loaves of soda bread.

Marjan and Julian each took a loaf from Mrs. Boylan, while Danny Fadden waived his chances, not wanting to keep his Finnegan away.

✳

ALL SOULS' DAY broke like any given Sunday in the West of Ireland: cast in a downpour, a skull of rain hoisting the turf-infused air through the curving streets of hamlets. But for three sisters, standing in a warm kitchen, it was a morning like no other.

"It's my first full official Mass," Bahar said, standing on the landing of the stairs. "I've only ever sat for service a few minutes at a time," she explained with a timid smile. "Well, it won't be official-official until I'm baptized next year."

"You look beautiful," said Marjan. "Is that a new dress?"

Bahar grabbed the hem of the white wool and lace outfit, tugging it into an awkward but endearing curtsy. "Do you think it's too much?"

Marjan shook her head. "It's perfect."

"I'd rethink the hat, though," Layla said, smirking at her sister. A small pillbox, complete with speckled lace veil, sat at an angle on Bahar's dark head.

"I'm going to let that go this time. Are we ready?" Bahar said and grabbed her coat from the wooden stand.

Marjan and Layla slipped on their jackets and grabbed their umbrellas. Even though the church was only up the street, they would need to drive in order to miss a soaking.

Bahar had her hand on the doorknob when Marjan stopped her. "Wait." She hurried around the kitchen island and opened the cupboard.

"We're going to be late," warned Bahar.

"Hold on," Marjan said, reaching behind a tin of pistachio nougats. She found the bottle, unscrewing the cap as her back was turned to her sisters. She upended it, letting the rosewater, the priceless tears of that queen of blossoms, pool in her cupped hand.

She turned back to Bahar and smiled. "Better late than never," she said, showering her sister with a brand-new day.

marjan's recipe box

Now that the rose has faded
and the garden is ravaged,
Where shall we find the rose's essence?
In rosewater.

—Rumi

gormeh sabzi

¹/₂ cup olive oil	3 teaspoons turmeric
1 cup fresh fenugreek, chopped, or 3 tablespoons dried fenugreek	2¹/₂ pounds stewing lamb, cut into 1-inch cubes
¹/₂ cup fresh dill, chopped	3 tablespoons lemon juice
1¹/₂ cups fresh parsley, chopped	4 cups water
1 cup fresh cilantro, chopped	Salt
¹/₂ cup fresh chives, chopped	Pepper
2 cups fresh spinach, chopped	4 dried limes
3 medium onions, chopped	2 16-ounce cans red kidney beans, rinsed

Heat a deep pan with ¹/₄ cup olive oil. Add all herbs and spinach, stirring occasionally over medium heat for 15 minutes. Set aside.

In a large stockpot, heat remaining ¹/₄ cup olive oil, then add onions and turmeric. Stir until golden brown. Add lamb, cooking for approximately 6 to 7 minutes, or until brown. Add cooked herbs, lemon juice, water, salt, and pepper. Let boil, then cover and simmer over low heat for 1 hour.

Add dried limes. Cover and let simmer for 40 minutes. Add kidney beans, cooking for 20 minutes, covered. Using a fork, pierce the limes, releasing their juices into the stew. Remove from heat.

Serve with a side of *polow*, saffron rice.

colcannon

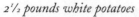

2½ pounds white potatoes
1½ pounds kale, chopped roughly
⅔ cup buttermilk
⅓ cup heavy cream
2 leeks, chopped finely

2 sticks butter, softened
½ cup chives, chopped finely
Salt
Black pepper

Boil potatoes in their skins, in salted water, for 30 minutes or until tender. Drain and set aside.

Blanch kale in boiling water for 4 minutes. Drain and set aside.

In a small saucepan, heat buttermilk and cream. Add leeks and simmer for 5 minutes, or until soft. Set aside.

Peel potatoes and mash well, adding softened butter. Add milk and leeks, kale, chives, and salt and pepper to taste, mixing well. Eat as much as your luck (and stomach) will hold.

chickpea cookies

³/₄ cup unsalted butter, melted, at room temperature	5 teaspoons ground cardamom
¹/₄ cup corn oil	4 cups chickpea flour, sifted
2¹/₃ cups confectioners' sugar	1 cup shelled pistachios

In a bowl, combine butter, oil, sugar, and cardamom. Slowly add flour, turning the mixture over until dough forms. Place on a clean surface and continue to knead until even.

Roll out dough to ¹/₄-inch thickness. Using a cloverleaf cookie cutter or similar size shape, cut out cookies, approximately 30. Place on a baking sheet lined with waxed paper and leave to set for 30 minutes. Add one pistachio to each cookie center.

Preheat oven to 300°F. Bake cookies for 10 minutes, or until slightly golden. Remove and leave to cool. Enjoy with a cup of sweet bergamot tea.

ajil

Salted pumpkin seeds

Salted sunflower seeds

Roasted cashews

Roasted peanuts, salty

Roasted hazelnuts

Roasted almonds, salty

Roasted pistachios, unshelled

Dried apricots, chopped roughly

Dried peaches, chopped roughly

Combine all ingredients in a large bowl. Toss to mix. Pass around to all guests and sundry in an act of true generosity.

rosetachio ice cream

| Vanilla ice cream | Pistachios, shelled and |
| 3 tablespoons rosewater | chopped |

Scoop three large balls of vanilla ice cream into a serving dish. Drizzle with rosewater and sprinkle with a handful of pistachios. Eat barefooted, sitting in a patch of clover leaves.

new year's kuku

7 eggs
1 teaspoon cardamom
1 teaspoon cumin
2 teaspoons salt
1 teaspoon pepper
2 tablespoons all-purpose flour
1 teaspoon baking powder
1/2 cup fresh chives, chopped
1 cup fresh cilantro, chopped
1 cup fresh parsley, chopped
1 cup fresh dill, chopped
1 stick unsalted butter

Whisk eggs in a bowl. Add cardamom, cumin, salt, pepper, flour, and baking powder. Whisk until well mixed. Add all herbs. Mix once more.

Heat butter in a medium-size, deep frying pan. Pour in egg and herb mixture, immediately lower heat, and cover. Cook for 20 minutes, or until *kuku* solidifies. Replace the lid with a large plate or platter, making sure it covers the pan completely. Flip the *kuku* over and slide it back into the pan. Cook the other side for 20 minutes on low heat. Eat with yogurt and cucumber dip, feeding the lover lying at your feet.

tacheen

8 cups water
4 cups uncooked basmati rice
4 tablespoons olive oil
3 pounds boneless chicken
  breasts, cut in strips
2 medium onions, chopped
  Saffron water (4 strands
  saffron dissolved in 8
  tablespoons hot water)

2 teaspoons turmeric
½ pound baby spinach
7 eggs
1½ cups thick, Greek-style
  yogurt
2 teaspoons salt
½ teaspoon black pepper
1 cup slivered almonds
1 cup honey

Bring water to boil in a large pot, add rice, and cover. Lower heat and simmer for 15 minutes, or until rice is tender. Drain any remaining water and set aside.

Heat olive oil in a large frying pan. Add chicken, onions, and half the saffron water. Sauté for 15 minutes on medium heat, stirring occasionally. Add turmeric and spinach and sauté for 5 minutes. Set aside.

In a nonmetallic bowl, whisk eggs and remaining saffron water. Add yogurt, salt, and pepper. Add chicken and spinach mixture. Mix well.

Preheat oven to 350°F. Grease a 9-by-13-inch casserole dish. Spoon in 2 cups of rice, patting it down evenly. Next, add half the chicken and spinach mixture. Layer again with 2 cups rice. Add remaining chicken mixture. Mix almonds and honey, layer over top. Cover with aluminum foil. Bake for 1½ hours. Remove from oven.

Let cool for 15 minutes. Remove foil and cover with a large plate or platter. Carefully but quickly, turn the casserole upside down. *Tacheen!*

mrs. boylan's currant soda bread

4 cups flour
1½ teaspoons baking soda
1 cup sweet dried currants
(raisins may be substituted)
2 tablespoons caraway seeds

1½ cups sour milk (add
1 teaspoon vinegar to
sour the milk)
⅓ cup sugar

Preheat oven to 350°F. In a large bowl, combine flour, baking soda, currants, and caraway seeds. Mix well before slowly adding sour milk. Knead into dough.

Shape dough into a round loaf and place on a greased cookie sheet. Make an X on the top with a knife. Sprinkle with sugar. Bake for 1 hour, or until golden. Test with a toothpick. It is done when the toothpick comes out clean from the center.

Serve hot or cold with butter, accompanied by rosewater jelly and your own personal Finnegan.

rosewater and soda bread

marsha mehran

a reader's guide
MARSHA MEHRAN CHATS WITH
MRS. ESTELLE DELMONICO

*Marsha Mehran spent a leisurely afternoon in
Estelle Delmonico's periwinkle- and daffodil-colored kitchen.
A grand fire snapped in the stone hearth while through
the window Croagh Patrick could be seen shrouded
in its usual misty, incandescent veil.
Over a pot of bergamot tea and bowls of minestrone
soup—sided by warm* barbari *bread and feta cheese with
mint—a lively chat ensued . . .*

Marsha Mehran: I have to say, Mrs. Delmonico, this is the best bowl of minestrone I have ever had. Is that dill powder you've got in there, or is it fennel? I can't decide.

Estelle Delmonico: Call me Estelle, darling. And thank you. I do think my minestrone is special, yes.

MM: And please, call me Marsha. So . . . Estelle. The powder, your secret ingredient? I don't think it's angelica. It's dill, isn't it?

ED: (*laughs*) Ah! That I cannot tell. Only one person in this world will get that knowledge.

MM: Marjan Aminpour.

ED: Yes, that is right. Marjan will get my minestrone recipe and all its special secrets. But that is only after I am lying beside my Luigi again.

MM: I can understand why you decided to give Marjan the recipe. She's very talented.

ED: Talented, beautiful, and so strong. My goodness. She doesn't even know how strong she is.

MM: Why do you say that?

ED: Well, because she is only beginning to see her strength, her power. All the hard times are for her in the past. Now that she is on good ground, *terra firma*, she is ready to blossom.

MM: Like your rosebush.

ED: (*smiles*) Yes, that is exactly right. Like my Luigi's rosebush.

MM: Estelle, I'd like to ask you about Teresa.

ED: Another young woman who is beginning to see her strength.

MM: I think some readers were surprised by your response. To her situation, I mean. Being Catholic, and all.

ED: I am sorry, darling. I don't understand what your question is. What does it mean "being Catholic"?

MM: Well . . . that is a good question. (*blushes*) I guess what I mean is that there are strict rules about what Teresa was trying to do. Rules that are there to protect the sanctity of life. Some might see your helping her as going against all that.

ED: But of course that is what I should do. To help. What is this life we have if we do not see the pain in others, that we do not walk with their pain and open the heart to help them? We must always open the heart to love, yes? That is the only way to the center. To everything that is good in this world.

MM: And to God.

ED: (*pats Marsha on the arm*) Exactly, sweetheart.

MM: It's been nearly two weeks since Teresa has left your house. Do you plan on visiting her anytime soon?

ED: Of course! Dara O'Cleirigh, he is the postal man. He is taking me to Inishrose in two days. That is when the showers stop again. I will have tea with Teresa and her papa. He is very special, too. Like his daughter.

MM: Yes, I hear you got along really well with Sean McNully.

ED: (*giggles*) Only friends, Marsha. Only friends. My heart belongs to one man only.

MM: Have you given any more thought to the healing you received from Teresa? Have you spoken to her about it at all?

ED: No. And maybe I will not. I think it is very good to have mystery for my life. Some things—who can say why some things happen, yes? There is so much magic in this world, so much wonderful signs. They show us that we are part of—how do you say—La Divina.

MM: The Divine.

ED: Exactly. We are all part of the Divine.

MM: And the Divine is part of us.

ED: Brava, Marsha!

MM: It was divine inspiration to have Fifi O'Shea sit in for Teresa. I would have loved to be there to see the faces on those guards. It would have been priceless.

ED: Ah, but you were there, Marsha. We all were.

MM: (*smiles*) I suppose you are right, Estelle.

ED: (*claps her hands*) Okay! Now I ask you something.

MM: Of course. Go right ahead.

ED: I know two, three things about you. I know you love to write, but also that you love to cook.

MM: Yes, that's right. Some of my earliest memories have to do with being in a kitchen, watching my parents prepare these intricate, beautifully perfumed dishes for the café they owned in Argentina. I think I associated love with food. From that early on.

ED: What good luck! What an education to get when so young. I am also filled with memories of my mama and my grandmama Luciàna in the kitchen, in Napoli. Always arguing but loving each other, sharing this recipe and that. I remember when they made *cacciucco*, always on my birthdays, but on Fridays also. Ah, *cacciucco*! Soft, buttery fish with mussels, chilies, and red wine. The smell of the ocean and the smell of the land, together in one pot.

MM: Stop, Estelle. I am about to faint, it sounds so fantastic.

ED: (*laughs*) I know what you mean, darling. But that is what cooking does, yes? Makes us love life. Makes us build a home.

MM: Well, that's exactly right. Wherever my parents went, whether it was Buenos Aires, Miami, or Australia, the one thing that really kept us afloat, that reminded them of the good days in Iran, was food. No matter where we were, if we could return to the *sofreh*, we were going to be okay. I think that is why I knew Marjan and the girls would be just fine here in this little Irish village. I wasn't worried about them at all.

ED: I am so glad you brought them here. This is their home now. I tell you something also, Marsha: even if I have this terrible arthritis, even if it rains every day for the rest of my life, I will never leave Ballinacroagh. You know why? Because this is where I let my love grow. Where Luigi and I became one. Where I became a woman.

MM: That is beautiful, Estelle.

ED: Thank you, darling. It is from my heart. (*sighs contentedly, then looks up suddenly with a spark in her eyes*) Okay! (*gets slowly up from the kitchen table*) It is time!

MM: What's happening?

ED: You see, over there at the mountain. Ten more minutes and another rain will come. Let's go! *Andiamo!*

MM: But where are we going?

ED: To the center, Marsha. To my garden, where you will see the peace I am saying to you. To the Divine. We will walk and walk until we feel it shine in us. Come!

MM: (*drains her tea and gets up, smiling*) Can't wait, Estelle. Thought you would never ask.

READING GROUP QUESTIONS AND TOPICS FOR DISCUSSION

1. Dervla and her circle have opinions on everyone and everything in the town. What purpose do they serve in the novel? Why do you think Mehran chooses to open the novel from their point of view?

2. *Rosewater and Soda Bread* is set in the late 1980s. Do you think anything would have been different if the story had taken place now?

3. Orphaned and isolated from their homeland, the Aminpour sisters are a family of three with no parents or older relatives to rely on. What role do you think each sister plays in this family? How might these be different if the Aminpours' parents were still alive?

4. Is Father Mahoney a typical Irish Catholic priest? Why do you think the radio station is so important to him? Is he an effective spiritual leader?

5. Marjan's cooking seems to have a lot of power in Ballinacroagh—uniting, alienating, and even healing people. What is so special about her food?

6. In thinking back on her relationship with Ali, Marjan wonders, "Was it only within boundaries that people were allowed the freedom to be themselves?" (36–37) What do you

think she means? Is this true of other relationships in the book? Has it been true of your own relationships?

7. In Marjan's box full of keepsakes from Iran, there is a rosewater wash that she had once planned to use to cleanse Bahar for her first marriage. What do you make of this memory? How is it significant to the Aminpours' lives in Ballinacroagh?

8. Why do you think Estelle is so taken with Teresa? What purpose does she have in Estelle's life?

9. Why does Marjan have such a difficult time trusting Julian? Do you think he is a good match for her?

10. When she is preparing for her first Mass, Bahar says that she had once vowed never again to wear a veil, but then, "Everything had changed once again; now she was happy to be alone, happy to wear a veil again" (219). What do you think the veil symbolizes for Bahar? Why do you think she is so drawn to Catholicism?

11. Why do you think Sean McNully didn't confront the minister about his daughter? What prevented him from trying to find her?

12. Mehran ends the novel with a short Rumi poem. What do you think is its significance to the story? What might the rose represent? The rosewater?